A _A Giant
in the House
& Other
Excesses

Also by Daniel Pearlman

A Giant in the House

in the House
& Other
Excesses

by Daniel Pearlman

The Merry Blacksmith Press

2011

A Giant in the House & Other Excesses

© 2011 Daniel Pearlman

"A Giant in the House" originally appeared in *Nemonymous 10: NULL IMMORTALIS* (Summer, 2010)
"The Death Club" originally appeared in *The MacGuffin* (Winter, 2011)
"Hannibal's Victory" originally appeared in *XX Eccentric: Stories About the Eccentricities of Women*, Main Street Rag Publishing Company (May, 2009)
"Facedowns" originally appeared in *Prole #2* (August, 2010)
"The Fetal Position" originally appeared in *After Dark: A Collection of Haunting Tales*, Diversion Press (2011)
"Lyonel Unbound" originally appeared in *Spectrum*, (May, 2010)
"Two-Time Losers" originally appeared in *The MacGuffin* (June, 2009)
"Double Occupancy" originally appeared in *TQR Stories* (posted online July 23, 2006)
"With Arms Outstretched" originally appeared in *Nemonymous #1* (November, 2001)
"Mariah My Soul-Mate" originally appeared in *Studies in the Fantastic #2* (Winter/Spring [June], 2009)
"Great White Hope" originally appeared in *Imaginings*, Pocket Books (Aug. 2003)

For information, address:

The Merry Blacksmith Press
70 Lenox Ave.
West Warwick, RI 02893

merryblacksmith.com

Published in the USA by The Merry Blacksmith Press

ISBN— 0-61554-713-3
978-0-61554-713-8

DEDICATION:

My love, as always,
to Sandy and Alison—

And my heartfelt thanks to the
keen-eyed members of my writing group
who first critiqued these offerings—

Janet, Seenat, Brian,
Theo, Kristi, and Gretchen

Table of Contents

INTRODUCTION
What I've Been Doing

As a writer, I've been asking myself that question lately—looking back at two novels and two previous collections of my short fiction. Clearly, I've not been attracted to typically realistic writing even though my characters and their settings tend to be real, recognizable, contemporary. LF, the Literary Fantastic, is the lens through which my world of fictional possibilities comes into focus.

Two varieties of inspiration drive my imagination. There is the impetus from the "bottom up," the instigation provided by a character I've encountered or event I've experienced; and there's the "top-down" type of story driven by an idea, an abstraction, perhaps a "what if" question— the idea generating the characters needed to embody it. In the present collection, "A Giant in the House" is an example of the "bottom-up"- inspired story, and "Mariah My Soul-Mate" a "top-down"-idea-inspired piece.

Apart from the question of their origins, my stories turn out to be of three general types (though the boundaries are not always sharp): science-fiction pieces, "fantastic" tales, and those stories that do not violate conventional reality but are best called "bizarre." This volume is monopolized by the fantastic and the bizarre.

– DANIEL PEARLMAN
ddpearlman.com

A Giant in the House

The earliest I remember is that my father was so tall, so tall was he, that when he drew upright after bending over my crib his head seemed to scrape the ceiling, cracking the paint that sometimes flaked down onto my coverlet. When I rode his shoulders out in the busy street I looked down on a stream of hats that parted to stay out of our path, and I could reach up and just about touch the BB-shattered globe at the end of a lamppost, or peek into the fire-escape window of our upstairs neighbor, or wet my pinky on the tail-end of a cloud. And I never grew dizzy when gripping the freckled neck of my battering-ram of a father as we charged through pedestrians and the traffic that would halt for us on our way through the Brooklyn streets to the grocery store for milk and, only sometimes, a penny's worth of chocolates for me.

Those rare chocolate treats I would suck on slowly, letting them melt into my fingers, hoping to prolong the sweetness of the silent hour before bedtime that I would spend curled up on the back-room floor observing my father humped over an uptilted desktop, lips always pursed, pen in hand, drawing something under the bright yellow light of a clip-on lamp, at work on something he never showed me, but which later—my mother it was must have told me—I found out was practice he had to do because my father was a Commercial Artist. How high off the floor was that desktop!—and higher still my father's intensely focused face, so near the dim bulb on the ceiling that I feared he'd smash it every time he leaned back to examine his progress without ever once noticing that I was still there, not even when my mother slipped in to whisk me off to bed.

So aroused was my curiosity, however, that one day I climbed up onto a tall stool next to the storage shelves that were fastened to the wall beside the desk. But before I could cop a clear view of those desktop hieroglyphics, down came much of the contents of a shelf, and a bottle of ink squirted black tears over the papers fanned out on the floor. The clatter brought my mother in. Moaning, she hauled me off the stool, warned me in a trembling voice never to mess with my father's things, ever ever again, and proceeded to clean up the wreckage I'd caused while I sat nearby, frightened by her unrelenting sobs and fearful of the unimaginable consequences betokened by those hiccup-like shudders.

Sobs that made sense to me when my father came home, found out what I had done, and vented his anger on her, not on me, using words I'd never heard before in an ear-splitting tone that made my now voiceless mother shrink to a height much farther below the lintel of the door than she had ever loomed before. And from that day I rarely rode his shoulders again, and when I did I could no longer reach high enough to touch any streetlamps. Instead, I could now reach low enough, if I wanted, to knock hats off people's heads. But I was not interested in kicking at hats, and the reduced elevation seemed to have killed all the fun, to the point where I no longer missed those sky-high jaunts and preferred trotting around on my own two capable legs.

I might have been five or six when my father brought home a full-page, full-color picture of Superman for me, my favorite hero in red, yellow and blue, soaring above skyscrapers and aiming for the clouds. I wanted to be like Superman, leaping tall buildings in a single bound, so I made myself a miniature city in a little cardboard box—a winter city blanketed in snow, lots of snow, which I procured by climbing up to the medicine cabinet in order to appropriate a box of serviceable cotton. I stuffed my little box abundantly with fistfuls of that soft white fluff, parting it in the middle for a street, and for houses and stores on either side I planted in the snowbanks some dice, matchbooks, gum-wrappers and a thimble, all of which together made a plausible-looking city if you happened to be flying over it.

How proud I was, so very proud, when my father came home and I could show him my painstakingly, artfully wrought winterscape! But just as I pointed to the Empire State Building—a wooden matchstick that I'd found on the kitchen stove—my father noticed the scavenged box of first-aid cotton that I'd discarded next to my sparkling diorama. His face turning red, in a booming voice he yelled at me for "wasting" all that cotton, and just as I began to be struck with remorse, and before I could express one syllable of apology, down came his giant foot to squash my beautiful city back into pads of cotton, matchbooks, and crinkled candy wrappers. Too shocked for tears, I stayed huddled on the floor, watching him storm off into another room, his head far short of the top of the doorframe and his shoulders not anywhere as wide as Superman's.

When the Nazis had been beaten, and I was ten, and my baby sister was already five, my father began to complain that our apartment was too tiny—as if finally he was listening to what my mother had been saying for years. He had spent part of the war checking for fire hazards in the Navy Yard, working overtime, and seeming hardly ever to be home. I contributed to the war effort by collecting tinfoil from cigarette packs and such and compressing hundreds of sheets of them into silver balls that would be used in making ammo to fight the enemy. My mother cooked cupcakes for me, read stories to me, and when she was alone, which was most of the time, except for me and my sister Sue, sang a lot to herself all through those happy years.

What she also did was to scrimp and save from whatever my father left for us out of his weekly pay envelopes so that she could eventually make a down payment on an actual house of our own. His own major interest during those years—and well after—was photography. He'd spend lots of time among the camera equipment at Willoughby's, where he'd buy whatever he liked, bring it home, but show it to no one. Then, after he'd use it for a couple of weeks, he'd pack it back up in its original wrappings, store it away out of sight on a shelf, and go out and buy something newer, with a faster shutter and a much more powerful lens. I don't recall seeing any picture he ever took except one with a self-timer taken of himself standing in the doorway between the living-room and the back room where he worked. This shot revealed him looking a full two feet shorter, I was much surprised to note, than the top of that very familiar doorframe. I did not think it was a trick of perspective.

Our family friend for as long as I can remember was the postman Jimmy who lived upstairs and never married and took care of his mother who had always been a great help to mine. Jimmy offered to lend my mother the difference between what she had saved and the actual cost of the down payment on a house out in uncrowded Canarsie that she had long set her heart upon, convincing my father that this would be the solution to our need for more space, if we could afford it. I happened to be present when my mother happily informed him of Jimmy's generous offer. How amazed I was then to see my father's upper body stiffen, his lips twisting back in a sneer as he accused her of depending too much on a "friend"! When my mother cried out that if not for her they would have no friend at all, my father swung out at her and knocked her against the wall. She crumpled to the floor, pressing her lips tight against the whimpering that nevertheless gushed out through her nose. I froze, ashamed to see my mother sunk so low as to make my shrinking father still seem giant-like standing over her.

Our little house in Canarsie had two floors, a basement, and a backyard, and except for a similar house next to it was surrounded by vacant lots, safe havens where I and other neighborhood kids liked to play. In a frenzied period of constructive zeal my father, following a stack of manuals purchased through some catalogue like Sears, built us a back porch and a shed in the rear of the yard. Over time the shed filled with piles of junk that he couldn't decide to get rid of and eventually the roof, built with bargain lumber, collapsed. During those first years in our new place my father couldn't get a job doing Commercial Art, and we lived hand to mouth on welfare checks, twenty-one dollars a month, but helped out by the occasional loan from Jimmy which my father knew nothing about—or perhaps wanted to know nothing about.

With time on his hands between fits of construction within and outside the house, my father gave me an occasional lesson in Art, teaching me the color wheel, perspective, and other technical matters that have stood me in good stead to this day. Once he set me the task of painting, in watercolors, a potato. I sat out in the sun on our back porch for hours going over and over a muddy wet patch that at last I had made to resemble the model potato in front of me. When he finally came out to check on my progress, he shook his head, tossed my effort aside, and in two minutes flat painted a potato that seemed more real than the one whose every shade and speckle had burned itself into my brain. He didn't tell me how to do it. He just did it, and I tore my own work to pieces and never again touched watercolors till Art class in high school.

On that same day he did what he would do every couple of weeks—measure my height against the kitchen doorframe. When I asked him, for the first time ever, how tall *he* was, he said five feet eleven. I thought that was preposterous. Perhaps he'd been that years ago, but I'd read that people shrink as they get older. Still standing against the doorjamb, I raised my hand about six inches over my head and told him he was no taller than that. Whereupon he burst out laughing, so I appealed to my mother, who was standing nearby. Unsmiling, she asked him to stand in the doorway, as I had done, and allow her to take his measure. Growling, he retreated to his basement hideaway, a darkroom he'd built for himself where he developed prints that no one remembers ever seeing. As soon as he disappeared, I looked at my mother and winked. I knew she had agreed with my assessment of his height.

My own interest in photography evolved over the next few years to the point where my father at last admitted me to the inner sanctum, his tomblike darkroom in the basement, where he taught me how to develop film, make prints, and even use the enlarger he'd bought a couple of years earlier, used very little himself, then stowed solemnly and respectfully away packed precisely as it had been when he had bought it. Although he ceased taking pictures himself, he had accumulated quite a stack of photography magazines. Thumbing through a few that he had shoved to the back of a shelf, I found them heavily devoted to images of female nudes. "This is Art," he said, when he caught me scanning one of those glossy publications. "You'll get to appreciate photography as an Art a lot more when you get older."

I started my photographic explorations with a box camera in front of whose cheap little meniscus lens I would ingeniously tape the lenses unscrewed from binoculars in order to take pictures of objects as small as a dead cricket, from only a few inches away, and wind up with surprisingly enlarged images of the original. Eventually I got as a gift, from Jimmy not from my father, a Zeiss-Ikon German bellows camera, somebody's war-booty maybe, and I thereby stepped up in technical sophistication to the point where I could manipulate lens openings and shutter speeds and achieve decent results even in indoor lighting conditions without the use of a flash, a luxury which I did not get to enjoy until my father allowed me to use his amazing Busch-Pressman press camera, unearthed from its original packaging several months after he had lost interest in using it himself.

I must have been about twelve when, one ordinary afternoon when Jimmy and my mother were having coffee in the kitchen, I took pictures of them and my sister Sue with my bellows camera, experimentally using half-second exposures to compensate for the low interior light. The bright idea occurred to me to ask my mother to sit on Jimmy's lap for a picture I thought would be comical. I didn't know why they both were so reluctant, but I wheedled and Sue pleaded and finally they caved in, laughing, to my request. When I got around to developing and printing that particular roll of film, I was so pleased by the results that when my father came home and found me in the darkroom I proudly showed him the whole series.

But he was interested only in the one of my mother sitting smiling on our friend Jimmy's lap. "Interested" in the sense that, his lips curling back into a wolfish snarl, he grabbed the print from my hands, rushed up the stairs into the kitchen—with me tremblingly clomping up after, and planted himself in front of my mother, who was puttering about near the stove. Shoving the picture under her widening eyes, giving her time to take it in, he tossed it at the ceiling and shouted, "You whore!" I had never heard him use such language. It grieved me to see my mother's pallid face as she stood in shock in front of the stove. Before stomping away upstairs, my father spun around and faced me. We stood there for a split second eyeball to eyeball. Literally. I mean I didn't have to look up. I realized, suddenly, that he wasn't any taller than I was. My mother meanwhile sank into a chair and remained oblivious to my choked, tearful apologies.

I remember my parents' happiness the day my father got accepted into the powerful lithographers' union. That mood did not last long, however. He found himself being sent around on jobs in Manhattan for several months at a time, and he would always bitch when finding himself reassigned. I didn't understand this apparent contradiction between the security of union membership and his bopping around from job to job until I reached fifteen. That summer he got me a messenger job at the latest place he was working at. I would deliver to various printing companies large, floppy zinc plates with advertising images etched into their emulsions by an array of blinding arc lights. The images were brought to light by means of acrid chemical baths whose eye-stinging fumes stank up the place and had to affect the lungs of everyone who worked there— including my father, who sat bent over an upslanted desk here too, just like at home, under a light fixed to his easel, meticulously "opaquing" out, with a fine paintbrush, unwanted areas on negatives that would then be clamped over the plates that were to be "burned." Luckily I spent more time outside the workplace than subject to that noxious atmosphere that no one there seemed to complain about. What I found out, in any case, was that this place, this and many others like it, was the glamorous center of the world of Commercial Art.

I found out also why my father kept moving from shop to shop. One day after work we happened to be walking toward the subway together with the shop's big blubbery owl-faced boss, my father in the middle, I on the outer edge of the sidewalk. They were engaged in shoptalk when the boss, who could care less whether I was present, told him, "Morris, we're in a crunch to meet deadlines this season. You do quality work, Morris, but you're slow. In fact, you're too damned slow." My father grunted something in reply, hunched his shoulders, turned beet red, and avoided looking at me. I cringed, feeling his searing humiliation, and when at last I turned to him, I could see the top of his down-turned head, which now unmistakably rose to just about the height of my shoulder.

A couple of years later, when my sister was about twelve, she developed a variety of uncontrollable nervous tics that the doctors, according to my mother, labeled St. Vitus Dance. My parents sent her away for the entire summer to a relative in upstate New York, a vacation I did not begrudge her if it was essential to her cure. My mother said that her condition was probably due to a shock she'd received from sticking her finger into a naked electric socket. I had no idea what bullshit all this was until one day, perhaps the day after Sue had been sent away, I overheard my mother and Jimmy talking alone, with considerable animation, in the kitchen. I had been in the darkroom and was about to come up the cellar stairs, but on hearing them converse in such urgent tones, I tiptoed up to the kitchen door and stood behind it listening. My mother bitterly spoke of wanting a divorce. My heart fluttered wildly and I was afraid my erratic breathing would give me away. Jimmy muttered in agreement, saying that any man who could do to his own daughter what my father did to Sue should live in a cage with animals and not among human beings. I tiptoed downstairs again and sat for a long time with my head in my hands in front of the empty developing trays in the darkroom. When I heard my father clomping down, I stood up to leave. When we passed each other by at the bottom of the stairs, I looked down at his shrunken head.

I shuddered as my elbow grazed his shoulder.

I was drafted into the army at age twenty-four. Fortunately I got out well before the call-up for Vietnam. During the two years I spent, mostly in an Intelligence unit at Fort Dix, I was comforted by a stream of letters from my mother and my sister. Finally, about a month before discharge, I received a letter from my father, written in a crabbed little back-leaning hand, and though I don't remember a single word of the perfunctory body of the letter, I recall that it opened with "To My Son," and I especially remember how it ended: signed "Your Father," with his full name, first and last, scribbled beneath, as if to prevent any mistake I might make regarding authorship. During the two years I was away, my mother had several times written telling me to expect a letter "shortly" from my father, and this is my only recollection of the missive she'd finally squeezed out of him.

After marrying and earning a Master's in Art History, I got a job teaching at some hick college in Montana. My career took me farther westward, through a Ph.D. at Berkeley and into a tenured position within California's burgeoning state-college system. As our two little girls grew up, I rarely made it back East but stayed in constant communication with my mother and little sister. Shortly after my older daughter turned thirteen, my mother wrote informing me that my father had been diagnosed with prostate cancer and was undergoing massive chemotherapy. She wondered if I could take off a few days and come home because he urgently wanted to see me. That letter I did not answer, but the following one, which arrived a month later, I did. In this new one she told me that the progression of the disease was extremely painful, that I would hardly recognize my own father now, and would I please tell my "boss" that I had a family emergency and needed to come home right away.

I had seen my father a year before, looking the same as ever, when I paid my parents a visit after flying in to New York to read a paper at an art-history conference. I had tried to dissuade them from coming in to Manhattan, but my mother dragged him in with her to sit in the audience and listen. As I read, I searched the auditorium and thought the seat beside her was vacant. It was just a trick of the light. The top of my father's head failed to rise above the back of his seat. I supposed that my droning had hammered him down into a doze.

Heeding my mother's call, I informed my "boss" of the situation and flew home. My bed-ridden, twisted, and shriveled father barely recognized his "son." The cancer had spread through his bones. I dared not shake his hand for fear of breaking his frail wrist. I told him not to give up, and that the therapy would soon show its effect. My mother told me that he had refused to enter a hospice, where the cost of care would have been zero and he would have been made to feel comfortable right until the end. But he was well aware that a hospice was antechamber to the grave. Since my mother could not personally provide the expert services he needed, he demanded private daily nursing care, and the upshot was the complete exhaustion of all their meager savings. On my leaving, he croaked out, barely audibly, "I love you." I gazed back at him and noted, without surprise, that from head to toe he was now reduced to a manikin about the length of a yardstick.

I mentioned this observation to my mother, but she objected. "No," she said. "Yesterday he measured exactly three and a half feet."

"That was yesterday," I replied.

I flew back again, of course, for the funeral, understandably a closed-casket affair. I hadn't seen some of my father's relatives for years and naturally had little to say to them. I wanted just to get it over with and get the hell back home. My sister and mother were there in solemn black. My mother fought constantly to hold back her tears and her face looked wrinkled and prematurely aged. Before the actual ceremony began, the funeral director called the immediate family aside—me, my mother and sister—and drew us off into the corner where the simple varnished casket lay, and asked us in pseudo-sympathetic tones whether the three of us wanted to "view" my father, right then, for the very last time. His downcast eyes and pinched lips suggested, without his saying so, that it would be a very bad idea. With a shudder, my mother and sister said no, just as he'd expected, but I was extremely curious.

I had heard a muffled little chirping sound coming, it seemed, from right under the lid. Was it a pocket radio belonging to a member of the staff? Without further discussion, I lifted the full-length top and cast a frantic, wide-eyed gaze inside.

The dark-walled interior was untenanted.

My mother looked in too, then blinked at me incredulously, then let out a shriek, and wound up fainting in my sister's arms. We both had seen the same vacancy, of that I felt sure. Much less surprised perhaps than she, I bent down closer and looked in again, searching for something, anything, to justify the need for this packing crate. Did it have a false bottom? I wondered. The fluffy cottony wadding was all laid out like the batting one might use to keep a piece of delicate equipment from incurring damage during shipment.

The parlor emcee was determined to snap the box shut, but I held it firmly open while I scanned the interior for whatever tiny creature might have caused the noise I'd heard. Finally I saw it, lying stealthy and still except for the quivering of its hind legs, a fairly noticeable black spot against the white, velvet expanse of the undented pillow. It was playing dead, but I plunged down thumb-first into the back of the deceiving little cricket. As I snuffed it out I felt it crack, and only then did I allow the Master of Cemeteries to have his way with the lid.

celebrated his eightieth birthday here surrounded by a dribble of friends and family, but mainly a troop of subordinates that dared not fail to show up. Propped up on a pillow with a tube stuck up his nose, the wizened bank president lay surrounded by flowers—yellow roses, tulips, birds of paradise—and boxes of gifts that still lay unopened on a linen-draped table next to his bed.

"Who are you?" sputtered the surprised old man, distracted from watching a fifty-inch TV.

"Anton's the name. Willby General sends its belated congratulations," he said, placing a vase of white Oriental lilies on the night table to the patient's right.

"I've had enough of flowers," grunted Barklay.

"Enough of everything, it seems," said Anton, "judging by all the unopened presents."

"What's it your business?"

"Check out the card in these lilies, and I'm sure you'll understand."

Barklay drew in a deep, rattling breath, looked sharply at Anton, and with shaking hand reached for the white envelope propped on the rim of the vase. "I think I know what's in here," he said.

Anton shrugged his shoulders.

Barklay opened the envelope and drew out the card, a playing card, the ace of spades. He nodded. "I've delivered a few of these in my time, too," he half-whispered. "Once to a good friend. Neither of us ever knew the other was a member of the Club."

"What we swore to," said Anton. "One of the conditions of membership."

"And as to that other condition… you look close to eighty yourself, Mr. Anton. When your time comes, I hope you'll be as ready as me."

"I've never regretted joining the Club. I was grateful when they asked me to join," said Anton, annoyed at being reminded of his age. "When I reached sixty I was a so-called success, but my health was in the toilet. I didn't have the strength to stay on top of my game anymore."

"I know the story," sighed Barklay. "You didn't think you'd last till eighty anyway. So you didn't see how you could lose."

"The Club has given me all I've wanted, success piled on success, correcting for all my mistakes," said Anton, "preventing me from being the failure I rightfully should have been—and they will collect only half my piles when I'm gone."

"And what will you do with the other half?"

"Probably will that to them too. I don't have family worth a damn. A deal's a deal. I can't lose."

"Yeah, if you disregard that one little proviso... that if you do manage to last till eighty, you've agreed to their putting your lights out."

"Painlessly, Mr. Barklay. Painlessly. The Club needs to collect. The Club has to go on. Faustian deal or not. A bargain's a bargain."

"So tell me, Anton, how many days—or is it hours, minutes?—till you take *me* out?"

Anton shook his hands out in front of him. "Not me! I'm not the agent. I'm just the messenger. The messenger delivers the card. I can't tell you precisely when. All we both know is... soon."

"My only regret," said Barklay, "is that a year or so ago I had this thing put in my chest. Delayed my general collapse. I should've just let nature take its course."

"We all want to hold on," said Anton. "Don't beat yourself up." He didn't want to admit that he'd had the same "thing" put in his own chest—and for the same reason too, expecting, like Barklay, to die of natural causes before reaching eighty and thus avoid a face-to-face with the inexorable Bill Collector.

3

On his way out of Barklay's room he ran into a tailored lab coat containing a distracted female. Literally bumped into her, or she into him, in any case knocking her over. His instinct was to tell her to watch where the hell she was going, but instead he reached down to help her up—and crashed down onto the tiles right beside her. Their heads were so close that they stared at each other for a long motionless moment. And then they burst out laughing, her clear treble to his coughing, phlegmy bass. It was she who got to her knees first and helped pull Anton up. He didn't think he needed her help, but it felt good—her pressing him to her chest. Close enough to hear her thumping healthy heart and to read the name-plate on the breast that was unencumbered by his head: Leila Sapori, Chief of Medicine. Mid-forties, he thought. Tall, slim. Tawny complexion. Rich, dark, shoulder-length hair and heady odor of sweat-tinged perfume with an overlay of disinfectant.

"My fault," she said. "I'm getting clumsier by the minute."

"I'm sure it is your fault," said Anton, exaggerating the difficulty of getting to his feet. "Better than being run over by a guernsey, though."

"A gurney?" she suggested.

"How the hell would I know?" muttered Anton. "I practically own this place, but no one's ever showed me around."

"Be assured, Mr. Malevich," said the doctor with a humorous smirk, "that no one here ever accuses you of medical expertise."

"Oh, so they think I'm a fool?"

"On the contrary, we think you're very smart to stay out of everyone's way."

"You sum me up exactly."

"Oh, I'm sure there's lots more to you," she said, patting his arm as he adjusted his tie, "that it's just as well we don't know."

"Is that so?" said Anton, quashing an involuntary grin. "I think it would be better, Dr. Sapori, if people saw the real monster behind the Halloween mask."

"Leila to you, Mr. Malevich."

"Leila then. Good. And what would you do if I revealed to you the monster within?"

The doctor paused to think. "I haven't met any real monsters. I think I'd find you entertaining."

"I'd scare the bejeesus out of you."

"Try me."

"I will. You owe me a cup of coffee for rattling my bones like you did."

4

Over coffee, and then a hospital cafeteria lunch, and then a dinner out together, Anton tried his best to fulfill his promise to Leila. He made it clear that money and power, now that he had them, meant little to him; that what truly turned him on was destroying his competitors and coming out on top. It annoyed him, however, to have to admit that this revelation failed to distress her. "So what's new?" she seemed to say, opining that all men at the top were ruthless, vengeful, selfish, and rotten to the core. And when he gleefully confessed to using his own surveillance merchandise to spy on rivals in order to outmaneuver them, Leila clicked glasses with him and praised him for his malevolent consistency.

"Why aren't you repelled and disgusted by me?" he asked her.

"Who said I'm not?" she replied.

"Then why are you willing to go out with me?" he demanded. "Are you attracted by my money?"

"I earn more than enough on my own," she said. "And anyway, compared to the truly rich, you're a piker, Anton. Nothing more than a piker."

This stung him to the core, causing him to find her ever more fascinating. "Then what is it?" he persisted. "An ego trip? Are your lady friends jealous because you're hobnobbing with the boss?"

"On the contrary, they think you are revolting and can't see me wasting my time on you."

"Revolting, eh?" Anton trembled with rage but demanded to know *why* he was regarded as so revolting.

"We don't know each other intimately enough—not yet, at least—for me to provide you with details," she coolly responded.

"So what do you see in me?" he growled at last with a slap of his palm on the restaurant table.

"Not much."

"Not much?" he spluttered.

"Your one-dimensional simplicity is rather restful," she murmured, patting her full red lips with her napkin.

Anton clenched his fists beneath the table, barely restraining himself from pushing it over on her. His heart pounded enough to kick his ICD into play. *Bitch*! he said to himself. Tears flooded his eyes. He couldn't believe he was actually falling in love.

Anton's fear of intimacy, however, acted as a brake upon his impetuous plunge into the abyss. He hadn't had a so-called "relationship" for over a decade. That affair, with a wily gold-digger, had chilled him into impotency, his growing distrust of her talons progressively quenching desire. The effect on him in the years that followed was to plague him with uncertainty about whether his seemingly physical problem had more to do with his mind than with his body.

Although desire had lain dormant in Anton for years, he now felt himself stirred to the quick in the presence of this irritating, insulting witch of a woman. Elegant and beautiful, she was also that rare being he could trust completely to tear the veil off the things in him that he most detested about himself.

He became again the Alpha male in relentless pursuit of his quarry. Since Leila had no qualms about telling him what she thought, she presented no threat. Rather than scheming to deprive him of his assets, she seemed to regard them with more indifference than he did. On the positive side, they shared many tastes. They both preferred the sedentary to the pleasures involving physical exertion. They liked dining out, watching movies, playing cards, and even playing chess—at which she repeatedly skewered him. Skiing and skating—well, she'd tried them for a while, but she lacked coordination, was a self-described klutz. Nothing could have suited Anton better. No threat of discovering her having an affair with some sun-tanned Apollo of the slopes! Occasionally they'd go out riding together for a slow jaunt along beaten country paths on the backs of a couple of semi-tranquilized quadrupeds, but that was the limit of his physical daring, and Leila never galloped on ahead of him to vaunt her superior horsemanship. Brimful of confidence, Anton courted Leila as impetuously as if twenty years had magically rolled off his back.

His increasingly aggressive behavior was just "what the doctor ordered" (what she, Dr. Sapori, managed literally to elicit). He pursued her with all the old energy he used to use in taking over a business. Leila began to compliment him on his single-minded, self-centered lasciviousness in total disregard for her own unpredictable mood-swings. Inflaming each other, they achieved a sort of mindless intimacy. One evening, out of more than curiosity, Anton worked up the post-coital courage to ask her what she could possibly see in such an animated scarecrow like himself.

"I love making love so much," was Leila's instant reply, "that even when I'm with you, Anton dear, I don't have to imagine being in bed with someone else."

Sarcasms like these served only to redouble Anton's ardor, but as the weeks panted on, the one nagging thought that he had managed for a while to suppress began to assail him in the form of terrifying nightmares. He lived under a sword of Damocles. His new life with Leila was only six months young, but his candle would soon be snuffed out. He had a year and a half left, by contract, but instead of experiencing deteriorating health, he felt stronger and more virile than ever. So what could he do about his commitment to the Club?

To those guardian angels of death he owed almost all he was worth. There was no going back on his word, no begging for release from his contract. He did not personally know, and would never again meet, the masked members of the Executive Council who had initially invited him to join.

But why must he consider them invincible? he thought. Hadn't he broken contract after contract—surely with their tacit approval, and perhaps their secret enabling—in his business affairs when it would gain him some major advantage? And didn't he have the equipment and know-how to secure himself against agents they might send to try to assassinate him? But to evade them he'd have to live in a place as invulnerable to attack as was possible. His current abode in the city, and his various houses and villas and condos in other locations as far-flung as Europe could not be made as impregnable as he would require.

His only real option then was an island. To own his own island. And to make it, through a technological network of the most advanced design, into an impenetrable fortress. There were, in fact, several islands for sale off the nearby coast. One of them, three miles from land, was thirty-seven acres of woods and meadows and came with a large house and boat-dock and stables. He would describe it to Leila as a vacation getaway, and he would enlist her advice regarding turning the old house into as beautiful a home as she could imagine. They'd spend weekends remodeling, furnishing, redecorating, sprucing up the grounds, and so on. On other days he'd be out there with a different crew—creating a tight web of warning devices to protect the island from incursions by sea or air, a mini-NORAD. Would Leila be willing to join him there when the time came for him to make his fateful move?…

5

Contrary to what Anton feared, Leila threw herself headlong into transforming the big old mansion and grounds into a fashion-plate fit for the home-beautiful monthlies. Leila's taste for understated elegance prevailed over Anton's for the dramatic and the tacky. Money was no object. In fact, Anton was glad at last to have something meaningful to spend it on, and he gave Leila carte blanche in acquiring whatever she decided upon—with the intended result that she fell in love with the place. One day she even let slip the remark, "Wouldn't it be great to leave everything behind and just *live* out here, without a care in the world?" How literally to take that remark, Anton didn't know. Was it a hint? He couldn't be sure. Nor was he ready to take her up on it and risk scaring her off prematurely. He knew she was tired of working at the hospital and looked forward to early retirement—but out here, so soon, with him?

When his island fortress was near completion, it was the height of summer, his woods were dense with sensor-speckled foliage, his elaborate surveillance system fully operational, and they celebrated his seventy-ninth birthday on a marble terrace with a view of green hills out to the sea—facing away from the mainland. As to the mainland, which Anton regarded with mounting apprehension, they communicated with it in a twenty-five foot deck-boat docked at the rear of the house. To Anton's great pleasure, Leila had become an enthusiastic pilot. At first she had dreaded even climbing into the boat, so precarious was her balance. Those immensely desirable legs of hers left much to be desired at sea. But over the course of two or three months her infatuation with the island transformed her into an avid helmsman. Hoping against hope, Anton dreamed that when the time came, Leila would agree to chuck everything, move in with him, and act as his sole liaison with the mainland, bringing in supplies, even his non-electronic mail. One way or another, he would solve this supply problem. That solved, he would have managed to become entirely self-sufficient.

As to his annual heart-health checkup, now, at seventy-nine, he again sat in front of a computer to have his wireless reading done, but from the PC stationed in his office on the island, the office that served as his surveillance-control center. And to Anton's immense satisfaction, he proved to be in such good shape this time around that hardly a "string" or two had to be "tweaked." Mitch, whose financial health depended on his brother's continued well-being, was as delighted with the result as Anton. But as to Anton's health, the one thing he did do that caused him some discomfort was to get rid of his remaining teeth, which were capped stubs anyway, and have himself fitted for a full set of dentures. His teeth, over the years, had caused him frequent distress, so that freedom from having to see a dentist was essential to his overall security plan—not to mention its freeing him to enjoy without hindrance Leila's expert cooking.

But his whole desire to flout the Club and live on indefinitely was based on one thing only—the spell that Leila had cast over him, the hope against hope that she would stay with him forever (though he would never have put it to her in such blatantly poetic terms as that). To be left for very long in a state of uncertainty was not an option for a man like Anton who had always come out ahead in even the trickiest business dealings of his career. He therefore, unbeknownst to Leila, put into motion a strategy that, if successful, would incline her to accept his forthcoming proposal—namely, that she move in with him permanently on the island. As the *éminence grise* of Willby General, he saw to it that Leila's workload gradually increased—more paperwork, more staff review, more clinical involvement, and so on. It was to happen in such a way that Leila should have no legal grounds for complaint, but instead would have to suck it all up and become, he hoped, disillusioned and embittered—and ripe for escape to "their" island paradise.

The plan seemed to be working. Leila seemed more tired, more eager to leave the mainland, more reluctant to return. There was now little more than a month left before Anton turned eighty. One evening, on their moonlit terrace, champagne glasses in hand, Anton told her he had discovered a plot by enemies of his to assassinate him shortly after his forthcoming birthday. He was terrified, he admitted, but the security precautions he had built into "their" island would guarantee him the maximum protection. He said nothing about his contract with the Club.

"That's awful," she said, her voice subdued, "but you probably deserve it."

"I was hoping you'd be more supportive," said Anton, his glass trembling in his hand.

"I could bring you supplies, but if you think I would also be in danger…"

"No, no! I can assure you they would never try to harm you. Do you imagine that I would ever put *you* in harm's way?"

"If it's to your advantage, Anton?"

"No more joking, Leila. And I won't beat around the bush. I want you to come out here and live with me. You've had it up to here with Willby, so why not—"

"Anton!" shouted Leila, rising to her feet. "You narcissistic bastard! You expect me to be your live-in concubine?"

"But—but—I mean…" Anton stuttered, his stomach sinking, his world about to collapse as he wondered why what he said was wrong and how to make it right.

"If you can't think of something better to ask me, I'll pour this wine over your bald, empty head and demand that you accompany me back to shore."

A dim, fluttery light went on in Anton's head. "I mean—I thought it went without saying—that I want you to… be my wife."

"Went without saying? Anton, you are an idiot! A completely insensitive numskull!" Leila flung her champagne into Anton's face. The rejection was enough to stop any normal heart from beating. Anton, hardly breathing, looked up at her like a beaten dog.

"Okay then," she said, drilling him with ice-cold eyes for several agonizing seconds. "I accept."

It took him the space of a dozen erratic heartbeats to take in what she had said. Filled with joy, Anton licked at the expensive drips that trickled down his face. Staggering to his feet, he clasped Leila to him like a shipwrecked sailor clinging to a liferaft.

6

They were secretly married by a JP a week before Anton's birthday. Leila had already shipped in most of her personal effects. But to keep up appearances till the last possible moment, she agreed to make the final break with Willby and come out to join him on the very day he turned eighty. On that sunny summer evening, she arrived with the makings of Anton's favorite dinner—a Kobe steak that she knew how to sear and serve practically raw in order to bring out its optimum flavor. She also brought two bottles of a rare Veuve Clicquot.

Anton had checked and rechecked every alarm system on the island, from its camera-surveilled circumference to the electrified gates surrounding the mansion itself. His cellphone afforded him minute by minute security updates so that he didn't have to enter the office that served as surveillance center if he wanted to monitor any particular sector of his domain. As to *internal* security, in the physiological sense, Anton made sure to have his annual ICD exam in the privacy of his office, before Leila's arrival. After a flurry of buzzes and squeaks emanating from the monitor, the resulting report was one-hundred percent positive, followed by a congratulatory email from Mitch containing a picture of two clicking wine-glasses captioned "Cheers!"

Dinner on the terrace was, as he fully expected, delicious. Expected also were Leila's remarks warning that his decadent appetite augured ill for a man of his delicate constitution, but her digs served only to further tease his palate. After clearing the table, Leila returned from the kitchen with a tray holding an ice-bucket and a pair of tulip-shaped glasses of a very fine crystal worthy of fine champagnes. Adept at the ritual, she poured an inch of the precious bubbly in each, let the foam settle, and then continued to pour until each glass was two-thirds full. Sitting down, she raised her glass. Anton did the same. They clicked. "I hope I've made you happy, Anton," she toasted.

"Happy! Leila, you've given me the only reason to—"

"Oh cut the baloney and drink. We're playing blackjack tonight?"

"Whatever you want." As the sun dipped low toward the sea, bathing the terrace in a golden glow, Anton felt as content as ever he'd felt in his life. Downing half of the superb champagne, he wanted no more out of life, no more than more of this splendid now. But he was at a loss to express what he felt. It demanded a vocabulary he didn't possess.

Leila, meanwhile, distributed the plastic chips, sipped at her bubbly, and got ready to deal. "You're such a lousy player," she said, "that I think I'm going to win this island from you tonight."

"That's what I like about you, Leila," he said. "You keep on wanting things. Me, I already have all I could ever want."

After laying down two hidden cards, one for herself, one in front of him, Leila dealt Anton his first face-card. The ace of spades.

Anton's insides shriveled at the sight. "Bitch!" he shouted. "You are one of them!"

"One of whom?" she replied coolly, setting down the deck of cards and looking at him expectantly.

Anton blinked at his half-empty glass, stared over at hers, and switched them. "Let's drink from each other's," he demanded. "Indulge me, sweet. It's a gesture of trust."

"You fool!" she retorted. "You think I was trying to poison you?"

"Drink!" he insisted. And Leila did, gulping the rest down without a twitch, without the least sign of fear. Anton gaped unbelieving. His body trembled, his mind was in utter confusion.

"My time isn't far off either," she said, refilling their glasses.

"W-hat do you mean?"

"I'm not so steady on my legs. You've noticed?"

"So what?"

"Huntington's disease. I've inherited the dominant gene. I've got at most fifteen years."

"You've kept this back from me?" Anton emptied his glass in one gulp.

"Because, as you've said, I keep on wanting things. In the time I have left I want to reach the top of my profession. I want renown, I want wealth, I want… this island."

"And that's why you married me?"

"I've made you happy. I've paid you for your island, Anton. But if you think I've sold myself to *you*, you're wrong. I've sold myself to a much higher bidder."

"The Club!" Anton mouthed with a shudder from head to toe. "The Club?… You *are* out to kill me."

"I'm only the messenger, Anton. Messengers deliver their message, and then they turn around and leave, don't they?"

"What do you mean? Where do you think you're going?"

"I have someone waiting for me back home."

"Home? This is your home. The whole damn island is your—"

"My lover is waiting for me, Anton."

"And who pray tell may that be?" Anton sneered.

"Your brother Mitch."

It took Anton several seconds to find enough breath to cry out, "Mitch? Behind my back? The two of you…"

"Think of how unselfish he's been. To allow me to share myself with you. A regular saint, your brother!"

"That conniving traitor!" Anton rose shakily to his feet. "Just this evening, after doing my test, he has the *gall…* to send me his *congratulations!*"

"He found you in tip-top shape, didn't he?"

"Yes, he did."

"Hardly a tweak needed?"

"Absolutely right."

Leila looked at her Rolex and sighed. "Your implant has been reprogrammed, Anton. In exactly twenty minutes it will deliver a powerful shock. It will induce ventricular fibrillation. It will be painless, Anton. I promise." Leila refilled his glass. "Drink up."

Hannibal's Victory

Erica's "See ya later, Hel!" thundered through the door. Helga could now set down her paintbrush, peek out of her bedroom, and scan the living room for signs of disturbance that she knew she would find in her housemate's wake. The television stood like a toothless mouth retracted against the wall, silent now after disgorging its bellyful of morning news that garnished Erica's habitual breakfast of eggs and fried onions. The smell took time to go away, but go away it would, and Helga could then count on several hours of olfactory freedom till Erica's return from work at 5:30—not to mention day-long deliverance from the TV, a birthday gift, kindly intended, from Erica. Its ostensible purpose was to provide Helga with a "window on the world" to supplement her stock of visual vocabulary with a store of contemporary idioms. Last week it had intruded with that obituary clip of shriveled old Maurice, a writer she'd slept with eons ago. Yesterday it had dumped images of dead pigeons into her living room. They were being smitten by some contagious new disease whose ghostly threat now hovered about within her very apartment, flapping its batwings somewhere over her head.

Helga took a step forward into her living room—*their* living room for a month now since she'd invited her young admirer to move in with her. She was under no illusion about the modest size of the room—indeed, of the whole two-bedroom apartment—but it was strange how the presence of that TV, unlike a "window," seemed to shrink the room even further. Some things took getting used to.

Hannibal, meanwhile, his eyes narrowing above a set of frayed white whiskers, glared at her from the cushion of one of the four high-backed chairs that belonged to the glass-topped, circular living-room table. That antique table—Third-Empire French, originally with marble top, upper legs still graced with bronze griffins—had been with Helga time out of mind, for many more years than old Hannibal bore on his scruffy black back, accompanying her, like Hannibal, in a Manhattan odyssey from one successively smaller apartment to another. If Hannibal looked put out, the reason was immediately clear. Erica had piled books on his favorite chair, the one flattened with his grungy, indelible imprint.

"Don't look at me like that, Hannibal. She's young, in a constant dither, and occasionally forgetful." She had been such an assiduous student, Helga remembered, respectably above-average in talent. And she had such *lovely* white teeth.

Helga crossed the room into the narrow kitchen to the left. Sunlight filtered through the metal bars and ageless grit that covered the single window. "Look," she said to the cat, who followed at the hem of her housedress, "Erica cleaned the frying pan and also her plate and fork. She's learning. She means well."

"You certainly are quick to defend her," said Hannibal, looking up as he rubbed his chin against the refrigerator.

"She needs no defense," countered Helga, planting her fist on her bony hip and eying Hannibal askance. "She is a young person with her own needs and habits and we all have to learn to adjust to one another."

"Yes, accommodate, learn to compromise. How often do I have to listen to this bullshit, Helga?"

"You're cross because you haven't eaten. Why don't you let her feed you?"

"I told her once what I wanted to eat. A slab of liver and nothing more. But she has the gall to tell me it's no good for me!"

"But maybe she knows better than I do, and that you ought to have more variety in your—"

"Ha! We'll see how *you* feel when she starts cooking in for the two of you and decides what *you* should eat."

"A highly unlikely scenario," said Helga.

"Oh, really?"

"Really." Helga opened the refrigerator to retrieve a plastic container of cow's liver.

"Open the meat and vegetable bins. You'll see what I'm talking about," said Hannibal.

Helga was surprised to see tomatoes and green peppers and sausages and ground beef from D'Agostino's. Apart from the expected onions and eggs. "I don't know what in the world she intends to do with all this," she said. "Make herself lunches to take to work?"

"Dinner, more likely," said Hannibal, following the trajectory of a juicy slice of liver as Helga forked it out of the plastic and into his bowl.

"That's absurd!" said Helga. "We agreed to eat dinner out. It's my one meal a day and my chance to see people and enjoy the city a bit."

Hannibal mounted a stool from which he was able to jump to the countertop. He chewed savagely at his liver, in utter self-absorption, and Helga watched and listened with a deep, visceral satisfaction.

"Let's face it, you don't need her companionship," said Hannibal, stopping for a bloody-jawed break. "Did you take her in because she slobbers all over you? Young as I was, even I didn't fawn all over you when we met—or at any time after."

"I took her in because she needs a place to live. When she can fully support herself—"

"Thousands of people need a place to live. Why her?"

"She is the best of my former students."

"And she worships you, yes. But I still can not believe that for such a petty reason you are willing to share what precious little space we have with this... this clackety young woman."

"What do you mean, 'clackety'?"

"She makes a racket wherever she goes. Clack, clack."

"I am too quiet. I've spoiled you, Hannibal. Young people tend to be doing, moving, flitting around a good deal. I remember, back in Paris, when *I* was twenty-three—"

"You're all generosity, aren't you? No 'What's in it for Helga?' in all this, is there?"

"Just what do you mean?" said Helga, her hand retreating limply to her chin.

"You don't mind living alone," said Hannibal, licking his lips. "But you're afraid of being *left* all alone, to die all alone. Frankly, I don't see why you need company to die. Dying takes a minute or so, and for that you would give up months, maybe years, of precious privacy?"

"Hannibal, I assure you..." His whiplike words drew tears to Helga's eyes. "I assure you that my personal demise is the farthest thing from my mind."

"Sure, like yesterday, when you combed me, and another big clump of hair came out—and what did you say? You said, 'Hannibal, what if one day I have a stroke and I can't get out of bed? Or what if I'm mugged in the hallway picking up the mail? Who will take care of my darling?'"

"Is that so odd? I was expressing my concern for you."

"You were expressing your concern for yourself. I'm not that stupid, Helga. I've been sniffing for quite some time now—in you, of all people—embarrassing whiffs of weakness, of abject fear."

Hand thrust to hip and head held high, Helga marched out of the kitchen. "You refuse to grant me even one generous thought," she shot back.

2

The click of the deadbolt sent a shudder through Helga's shoulders as she bent over the glass-top table, now puffing at an elegantly poised Gauloise, now gluing sequins to the tiara of a cold-eyed Minerva that she had painted on a plywood panel.

"My God, it's so warm in here, how can you stand it?" shouted Erica, depositing her attaché case on the chair next to Hannibal's, from which those trespassing books had been removed. Her flower-pattern dress exposed the sweaty upper slopes of her small, firm breasts—breasts on which Helga had modeled her Minerva's.

Helga never paid much heed to fluctuations of temperature and humidity—at least not when she was working, not when absorbed in the pain and pleasure of making esthetic decisions—like whether or not she should paint in eyeballs or leave the divine orbs stone-blank. She could have continued for several hours more—work obliterated the dimension of time—but now she was party to a Social Contract. Reluctantly, she capped her tube of glue.

"Warm, Erica? It's the middle of August. Wasn't it warm in Ohio in August?"

"You never turn on the air conditioner. Like I said, all you have to do is open my bedroom door and it's strong enough to cool the whole apartment."

Helga did not want to admit how much she disdained air conditioning. She had got through life without such a disease-causing "convenience" and could only deplore the fact that young people had come to regard such a groaning, hissing beast as indispensable. "I'm better off without it," she said. "It causes my paints to dry too fast."

"I *love* her!" said a wide-eyed Erica, staring at the wooden panel. "Her brow is so cold, but that sly mouth of hers contradicts it, doesn't it?"

"Really? I didn't intend that. Perhaps I ought to—"

"Please, please don't change it, Hel. It's so much richer that way. This is one of the best of your mythological pieces."

"Wait till it's finished before pronouncing judgment," snipped Helga. "Right now you can get me a glass of white wine. The Riesling will do."

"With pleasure!" said Erica, disappearing into the kitchen.

"And please, bolt the door. I know you're from the Midwest, but this is New York, darling. Besides, the door swings inward just enough for Hannibal to pry it open with his paw. We wouldn't want you running out, would we, Hannibal?"

"Why in hell would I want to?" said the cushion-sprawled Hannibal, jerking his tail and opening one lazy eye.

"Did you find those books on classical statuary helpful?" yelled Erica.

"Quite inspiring, particularly the one on Egypt, *ma chère*. I thank you for running to the library again, but I would not have discovered these newest treasures if Hannibal hadn't knocked them off his chair."

"Oh, shit! Sorry, Hannibal," Erica shouted. She emerged rolling a chilled beer-bottle over her breast.

"I propose to begin getting drunk *chez nous*," said Helga, accepting the wine-glass from Erica's long, slim fingers, "and then to complete the process when we go out. What do you think, Erica? Chez Jacqueline for dinner?"

"This evening? No, Helga. Actually—"

"La Ripaille, then?"

"I'd really like us to eat in tonight, Helga." Erica squeezed her Bud with both hands.

"Eat in? But sweetheart, you know I never eat in."

"I'm not saying to make a habit of it, Helga. Just occasionally. You'll love my sausage and peppers."

"I hardly think so, *ma petite*." Helga folded her arms across her chest and cast a stare at her young friend as cool as the look on her Minerva. "My last lover, Alberto, was chef at the Tea Room, but I never let him cook for me at home. He adored me. After a while, as I recall… he became unable to perform."

"You should have let him cook."

"Sweetheart, I think that during the time we cohabited we were both undergoing a spiritual transition beyond bodily desire."

Erica knitted her brows. "I know I'm nowhere spiritually, Hel, but—"

"There you go again," said Helga, shaking her head, "taking what I say personally."

"—but if you really think of it, Helga, cooking at home can be a far more spiritual experience than impersonal dining at restaurants."

"Sweet baby, you and I have an agreement. You pay no rent, only the utilities, and we go out to dinner together. We split the bill. It isn't as if I ask you to pay for me."

Erica sat down across the table and took a swig of beer. "Helga, in the beginning I thought that would be fine. But we linger in those restaurants for hours, and the more we drink, the more the waiters fawn over you, and then we drink even more—and the bills we rack up…"

"You resent the few social pleasures that I have?"

"No, no! That's not it. But if I ever expect to save enough to stand on my own two feet, well, a beginning programmer's salary for a city agency doesn't leave me much room for continuous high living."

Helga made a face, dreading the prospect of yet more cooking odors than those of egg and onion. She exchanged a glance with Hannibal. "And how often, darling, are you proposing to—"

"Helga, if we could eat in just once or twice a week… Honestly, I'm not such a bad cook, but of course, compared to Alberto…"

"I don't understand," sighed Helga. "Here I am, sparing you from having to share the rent."

Erica stared at the floor. ""I know, Hel, and I'm truly grateful, but our month of dining out has wound up costing me the same as paying a *full month* of your rent."

"Oh, dear!" said Helga. "I just never think of toting things up."

"I know," said Erica. "And that's one of the things I love about you. If I didn't have to earn a living, I'd paint all day too and think about nothing else."

"I never meant to squeeze you," said Helga, feeling her face turning red. "You should have told me earlier."

"And if you don't like my food, I'll be serving all your favorite wines to compensate."

"Well," said Helga, wringing her hands, touching her face and neck with her fingers, "what can I say?…"

"Say no!"

"Mind your business, Hannibal," scolded Helga.

"He's stubborn as hell," said Erica. "He won't touch dry food. All he wants is liver. He needs a more balanced diet."

"Cooking smells upset him."

"You smoke all day. Doesn't that bother him?"

"Smoking enhances creativity. Hannibal adores my smoking."

"Okay. How about I'll put a fan in the kitchen and blow the odors out through the window?"

"I didn't invite you to live with me in order to use you as a cook. I wanted a social and intellectual companion. You haven't read a book since you've been here."

"I do. I read computer manuals. And I learn from you—I learn a lot about painting just living with you. Sort of by osmosis. After you left Ohio State, I painted for the next two years getting nowhere. The woman I lived with never encouraged me. I knew that if I was ever to get back on the right track—"

"And so you came to me, and you've hardly lifted a brush since! That computer art you do... that is *not art*."

"I won't argue with you, Helga. But what else do I have time for? If we didn't go out and get sloshed every night—"

"Are you blaming me for turning you into an alcoholic?"

"I didn't say that."

"Young women are not deflowered without at least their passive consent," said Helga.

"I'd *encourage* a challenge to my virtue—if it came from the right person," said Erica with a steady stare into Helga's rapidly blinking eyes.

"Enough!" said Helga, uncomfortable with Erica's innuendoes. "I'm sure you will eventually find appropriate companionship. Meanwhile, as to easing your financial situation... I see I've been insensitive. A mutual living arrangement does require compromise."

"Thank you, Hel. I really need you to understand..." Erica reached out and clasped Helga's hands. Helga allowed her hands to be clasped.

"Hannibal dines with us, of course."

"Of course."

"I mean right here, between us. He shall have his own place setting."

"Helga! An animal? At table?"

"Oh dear! You've hurt his feelings." Hannibal dropped to the floor and swaggered off to the kitchen. "Erica, I've always treated Hannibal as if he were a male avatar of the Egyptian cat-goddess Bast. If Hannibal is an 'animal,' then what, pray, are we?"

"Helga, on my parents' farm we never let cats indoors much less at table."

"I'd like to assume you've come a long way from the farm, baby."

"I'm sorry, Helga. I love Hannibal, you know that. And you know how much I want to please you, how that painting class of yours so completely changed my life—"

"Hannibal hated Ohio, poor fellow."

"It was all those students dropping in all the time," said Hannibal, his head poking out from the kitchen. "The racket they made!"

"He's not so young that compromise comes to him easily, you know." Helga shifted nervously in her chair.

"Okay, Hel. Okay, he eats at the table." Erica dropped to her knees next to Helga and embraced her, pressing a tear-stained cheek to her breast.. "Sometimes it's just so hard… adjusting."

"I know, *ma choute*," said Helga, running gnarled fingers with long purple nails through Erica's silky brown hair. The rich, heady odor of Erica's hair filled her lungs, like a drag on a joint. Fearful of vertigo, she closed off the passage of air through her nose and breathed only through her mouth.

3

"She wouldn't take the hint," said Hannibal, looking up from his chair through the glass tabletop as he spoke and breathed through the gauze face-mask that Helga had modified to fit him. "And *you* wouldn't believe me for a hell of a long time either."

"But we've solved that problem now, haven't we, dear? After today, no more mask, my sweet."

"Did you have to wait an entire month? She damn near killed me, you know."

"You've been grouchy and uncommunicative. You ceased eating at table with us—to my chagrin and to her evident delight."

"My withdrawal from your dinner table was intended as a polite hint, Helga. Her cooking—two and even three times a week, it turns out—is not a result of my grouchiness. It is a consequence of your indulgence."

"My indulgence?"

"Absolutely. You've been too timid to object, so what does she do—strong-minded as she is, self-involved as she is? She thinks you actually *like* her cooking, so now I've put up with those fumes and stinks almost every other day for a month now. And that's not counting her daily eggs and onions! The house smells like a dumpster in back of a greasy spoon."

"That's not fair, Hannibal. How many times did I suggest to her, with you as witness, that her cooking methods were affecting your health?"

"Well, your young idiot of a housemate assumed that it was her choice of oils and spices, so you encouraged her—"

"But that's what I assumed too, dear."

"—so you encouraged her to cook at home even more, to try various permutations and combinations, to perform a series of culinary experiments that have resulted, for me, in a horrible case of asthma."

"You could have more openly voiced your objections yourself," said Helga.

"Me? Do I have the power around here?"

"Instead, what do you do? Throw hairballs up on her blanket, pee on her bedroom rug!"

"Really? I don't remember *any* such things."

"You've been semi-delirious. How could you remember? Anyway, it was I who finally deduced that the cause of your worsening condition was cooking odors in general."

"I've never in all my years been subjected to such an assault," said Hannibal, slapping the chair with his tail.

"Erica will be delighted that I've found such a simple solution," said Helga with an elegant flick of her paintbrush.

"I'm not so sure—but we'll find out soon enough," said Hannibal, cocking his ears toward the door.

Seconds later Helga heard the deadbolt click.

"I smell a stranger," said Hannibal, crouching on his cushion, his ears laid back.

"Hi, guys!" said Erica, shutting the door behind her—but neglecting to bolt it, as Helga was quick to notice. How tiring to have to constantly utter reminders! she thought. Jaunty in beige suit and matching heels, Erica strode up to the table.

"Erica, darling, yesterday I was shocked to see our next-door neighbor staring at me from the hallway. You had forgotten to lock the door."

"Shit! I'm so awful. I apologize."

"He was worried that something might be wrong. But it could have been someone with entirely different motives."

"I'm such an asshole. I'll learn. I promise," said Erica.

"Darling, I'm sure you will."

"Hannibal," said Erica, "you still look so unhappy in that muzzle."

"After this evening," said Helga, "he will not have to wear one."

"I hope not. And how's Actaeon today? Sprouting antlers, I see."

"Hannibal disapproves. He would prefer me to paint the final scene where Actaeon reaps the Peeping Tom's reward."

"And is slaughtered by his own hounds? Yuk!" said Erica, making a face. Pink blooms sprouted from her smooth young cheeks. "In my opinion, when he discovers he's got antlers—that's the true climax."

"The psychological one," murmured Helga.

"Exactly. The moment the poor slob realizes he must be punished for his blasphemous desires."

"You look flushed," said Helga. "Is it still so hot out there?"

"No, Hel, it's just that I have a surprise."

"For me?"

"For you *and* Hannibal." Erica planted a kiss on Helga's brow.

"You hear that, Hannibal? Erica has a surprise for you."

"I'm old but not deaf," said Hannibal, his ears aquiver, his forepaws covering his eyes.

"*We* have a surprise for *you, too*," said Helga.

"It was not my idea," said Hannibal. "You can take all the credit."

"You thought of a… surprise for me?" said Erica, smiling, her lips beginning to tremble.

"I have deduced what has been ailing Hannibal and have done something to benefit the three of us."

"And that would be…?"

"Uh-uh. First tell us your surprise," Helga insisted.

"Well, I'm walking home, as usual, past Tompkins Square Park, when all of a sudden I hear this pitiful voice. I look around and see a young guy leashing a kitty to the fence. He asks me if I want her. He's a Hispanic cook and he tells me she's lived in their restaurant kitchen all her life. But the boss found out she was there and they had to get rid of her."

"And so?" said Helga, stiffening.

"She told me her name. Caterina. She's a skinny orange tabby."

"You *didn't*."

"What would *you* do, Helga?"

"You should not have struck up a conversation—"

"Well, she wouldn't survive in the street. And would you rather someone took her to a shelter? Strays get put to sleep there in forty-eight hours."

"Don't even mention those disgusting shelters!" Helga clapped her hand to her face.

"Didn't you rescue Hannibal from the ASPCA?"

Helga sighed, slouching back in her chair. "So where is this Caterina?"

Erica lanced a smile so bright it made Helga blink. Scurrying back to the door, she slowly pulled it open. A leash was attached to the outer knob, and attached to the leash was Caterina, who hopped over the threshold and took in the scene with a couple of swift glances and several exploratory sniffs at the hardwood floor. As much as Helga wished to resist, the puss overran her defenses.

Dragging her leash, the tabby turned to the right and, with increasing speed and confidence, sniffed her way along the edge of the floor, encountering the base of a bookcase, then slinked past closed bedroom doors, examined the legs of a sofa, nosed along toward the kitchen—then stopped and stared back into the center of the room. Helga had been taking note of Hannibal's behavior as well. Maintaining a low crouch, he shifted around in his seat, following Caterina as a compass needle follows a magnet. As soon as their eyes met, the newcomer bounded to the foot of Hannibal's perch. Stretching herself up a chairleg, she extended the nose of friendship by bumping his gauze-covered snout with her naked little pink one. Hannibal hissed, and the stranger dropped back to the floor. But not for long. They stared at each other for several seconds. Then she raised herself to cushion-level again—as though caution were not in her vocabulary. Hannibal's tail flapped madly as their noses advanced and retreated.

"It's a big download for the two of them," said Erica. "But fear not. They'll be pals in no time." Caterina made a sudden leap but failed to land on the cushion. Startled, Hannibal dove to the floor and dashed under the sofa, extruding his head through its skirts.

"My, she does take liberties," said Helga.

"Hannibal will civilize her. Just give them a little time. And now," said Erica, "I'll introduce Caterina to the splendors of our kitchen."

"Wait a bit!" Helga reached for Erica's arm, but Erica was already making the turn into the kitchen.

"Holy shit!" she exclaimed. "What happened to the goddamn refrigerator?"

Helga drew up behind her. They both stared down at the miniature fridge that now stood in place of the big one that had been there for ages.

"You gave us no time to tell you," said Helga. "About your surprise, I mean."

"Surprise?"

"Yes, I decided that the time had come to do what would be best for the three of us."

"But there was nothing *wrong* with the old one!"

"There was plenty wrong with it, darling. It enabled—and in fact incited—you to do all this cooking of yours. Believe me, dear, while I myself have adored your culinary prowess, the apartment has been reeking with odors that are the cause of Hannibal's symptoms."

"You don't know that."

"I'm sure of it."

"So this is a... surprise?"

"My dear, it isn't as if we can't *afford* to dine out. You did, after all, receive a promotion recently."

"Not all that big of a one."

"Darling, you are becoming a successful New Yorker. New Yorkers don't stint. They live beautifully, in the confidence that their income will eventually exceed their expenses."

"But Helga—"

"Really, sweetheart, I don't see why I ever kept such a big, old, inefficient refrigerator. Your utility bill alone will be significantly reduced."

"Wow," said Erica. "I can't imagine what I'll do with all those savings."

"We now have all the refrigerator we need—for wine, beer, and food for Hannibal. ... And for Caterina, of course."

"Yes, of course. But you forgot one thing, Helga. My friends from work are coming over for dinner tomorrow."

"Oh yes. That couple again. The ones who could talk only computers."

"Bob and Ann are really quite cultivated. You have to give them a chance. They were nervous about meeting you. They were familiar with your work from the early eighties, when you made a big splash."

"And they were familiar with nothing since. Apparently, nothing but splashes attract their..."

"I had planned a great dinner." Erica turned her face away. Her shoulders heaved.

Helga reached out to her with shaking fingers, then pulled her hand back and held it in front of her mouth. "They shall *have* a great dinner! Entirely at my expense. We shall dine out at that exquisite little place in the Village—oh, now, what's it called?—that serves that marvelous *crème brulée.*"

4

"She is rude, uncultivated!" Hannibal complained. On his haunches at the edge of the bed, he stared across at Helga. She looked back at him in the mirror above her bureau, where she huddled at night to read. She had only a desk-lamp on. She'd been browsing through the new batch of library books that Erica had checked out for her. Hannibal looked like a shadow with golden eyes—very narrow golden eyes. And a little golden necklace as well. He looked like a mortuary statue. His stillness made her shudder.

"But Caterina can sometimes be amusing, don't you think?"

"It doesn't matter. I've tried to be friendly to the little twit, but you extend a paw, and she grabs the whole leg."

"But she genuinely likes you, Hannibal. If she's overzealous in courting your attention, it's perhaps because she senses your ambivalence."

"I have no difficulty forming friendships," said Hannibal, "but I simply demand a little more distance than she is capable of respecting."

"Have you voiced your complaints to Erica?"

"What do you expect Erica to do? She's not usually home during the day, when most of the mischief takes place. And you, you're lost in your painting. You know I never disturb you when you're working."

"But something must be done, dear!" Helga glanced at her bedroom door. A blue light of changing intensity illuminated the cracks around the frame.

"We are stuck in here like jailbirds," said Hannibal. "This is *your* apartment. We never used to spend time in here until you were ready for bed!"

Helga clapped her hands over her ears. "It's the sound of that television. The more she turns it down to accommodate me, the louder it seems."

"Well I say go out there and reclaim your ground. Tell her you've decided to work again in the evenings. Or that you'd prefer conversation when you got home from dinner. But, of course, if you preferred conversation you wouldn't let her turn on that box every night."

"She doesn't want conversation. She seems to just want to sit with me and... I don't know what she wants."

"Well, you can damn well get rid of that box! You had no trouble ditching the other one."

"For you I would do almost anything, my love."

"So do it! I can't stand being cooped up in here either."

"Hannibal, I do not believe in countering inconsiderateness with violent behavior of my own."

"Gandhi can go to hell," said Hannibal. "Passive resistance does not apply to the sphere of personal relations."

"There you are entirely wrong, *mon amour.*"

"Really? And what if some mugger threatened you with a knife?"

"I should bare both throat and purse to him," said Helga, lifting her chin and stroking the gold-plated necklace she wore, an exact twin to Hannibal's. "I'd rather he sinned against me than if I, in defending myself, sinned against him."

"Sounds to me like a cowardly bunch of crap," snorted Hannibal.

"You are interrupting my reading, sir."

"Bullshit! I've watched you for almost an hour. You haven't turned two pages since she took over that room."

As Helga considered a foray into the noise- and cathode-irradiated living room, the issue was decided *for* her. "Helga," shouted Erica, "you have to see this special! It's on Egyptian myths and mummies and shit— like the stuff you've been working on lately."

Helga turned to Hannibal and shrugged her shoulders. Hannibal jumped down and bounded to the door, looking back at Helga, who decided to tarry a while and examine herself in the mirror. The necklace, she thought, highlighted patches of wrinkles that might look even ghastlier in the light of the TV. The solution, perhaps, would be that same company's inch-and-a-half-wide "dog-collar" version. Holding herself erect, she finally teased the creaky door open and made a wordless entrance. The sofa crouched against the opposite wall. The TV sat on a cart rolled out on an angle to the right of the sofa, nearly blocking the path to the kitchen. The TV squealed and burped and bleated and lit up Erica's eyes like a pair of blue torches.

"It starts right after the commercials," said Erica. "Sit down. I figured you could use some refreshment." Downing a slug of beer, she pointed to the wine-glass on the fold-up coffee-table. It stood beside a freshly opened bottle of wine and three empty beer bottles that lay on their sides.

"My, aren't you prescient!" said Helga.

"A good servant anticipates her mistress's needs."

"Oh?" Helga raised an eyebrow, then padded up to the sofa. Her glass had an animated window in it. She wondered if the wine had been absorbing all those rays. "Make room, Caterina!" said Erica, giving the tabby a shove. The cat landed on the floor, then dashed toward Hannibal's favorite chair. She arrived an instant too late. To Helga's delight, Hannibal beat her to it. Caterina contented herself instead with Helga's seat, a default behavior that Helga did not tolerate during regular working hours. The felines glared at each other.

Helga settled into the cushion to Erica's right and raised her wineglass, which Erica clicked with her bottle. "I must deposit all these empties in the trash," said Helga. The bottles made her uncomfortably aware of how heavily Erica had been drinking—sometimes late into the night, when she would find her sprawled on the sofa asleep with the TV on and Caterina curled up in her lap.

"Leave them," said Erica. "I like them there. I play spin-the-bottle with them, three games at once—to increase my odds of winning. TV too loud for you?"

"Oh, I pay no mind to it at all."

"Helga, that necklace is beautiful! A gold-link chain. Wow! And look at those matching bracelets! I thought you despised jewelry."

"For myself I consider it vanity. As one transcends the level of ego, one finds such trinkets increasingly inappropriate."

"The Egyptians didn't think so. Anyway, what made you go out and buy—I'll be damned! You got one around Hannibal's neck too."

"It's not exactly jewelry, Erica. Its decorative function is secondary."

"Really!"

"These are magnets. Each 'bracelet,' for example, consists of six evenly spaced magnets."

"I'm attracted to you without magnets, Helga."

"I'm glad that you are, *ma petite* cabbage." Helga pursed her lips. "But these magnets do not have an attractive purpose. They are worn to ward things off. To rid the body of injurious processes and to protect against negative influences."

"Negative influences like what?"

"Like the harmful radiation from this television set."

"Helga, these modern sets have absolutely minimal leakage of radiation."

"So they tell you. But do you really know?"

"And you're protecting Hannibal as well?"

"Being much smaller than we are, he is disproportionately vulnerable."

"It gives him a rakish, drug-dealer look," said Erica.

"That computer of yours is another source of household concern."

"Damn it, Helga, it sits in my room!"

"Baleful radiation penetrates everything but lead."

"Does my CD player bother everybody too?"

"Don't be ridiculous, sweetheart. You've usually been mindful of the noise-level, and anyway, it stays in your room."

Erica shoved her bottle between her legs and stared at it. "Helga, is everything I bring into this apartment a source of contamination?"

"Nonsense. I'm not at all worried about myself. If I were, would I be sitting here beside you?"

"Aren't those mummy images great?" said Erica, her mood suddenly changing. The narrator was explaining the process of embalming. The Egyptians removed the brains and internal organs, soaked the body in carbonate of soda, injected balsams into the drained blood vessels, and filled body cavities with salt and other spices.

"As I was saying," Helga began again, clearing her throat, "I'm not so much worried about myself. What really worries me is Caterina's treatment of Hannibal."

"Really? They seem to get along pretty well. She fascinates him. I've never heard him complain."

"Hannibal," said Helga, refilling her glass, "come over here, will you?"

"I don't wish to."

"Don't be such a curmudgeon, my pet."

"I have no interest in images of dead human beings."

"He is too much of a gentleman to air his concerns in public, my dear, but when his pain is excessive, he spills his soul out to me."

"Pain? I can't believe… Caterina, come here!" shouted Erica. Caterina's eyes gleamed back at her. Reluctantly, she stretched and yawned and then hopped down from her chair. Seating herself on the floor at Erica's feet, she looked up and twitched her ears.

"Caterina, have you been annoying Hannibal?"

"*Límpiame la vajilla, maricón!*" replied Caterina.

"What is that supposed to mean?" asked Helga.

"Her English isn't so good yet. She speaks Spanish," said Erica. "She's repeating one of the phrases she learned in that kitchen. It's not very polite. It means 'Wash the dishes for me, faggot!'"

"And what is that supposed to mean?"

"I think she uses it when she doesn't want me to bother her."

And at that, without another word, Caterina loped back under the table and leaped back onto Helga's chair.

"Perhaps Caterina will admit it to you in private," said Helga. "I'm afraid that some of her behavior can be quite rude. For example, she'll occasionally run up and bite Hannibal's tail. I've seen her do that myself."

"She's being affectionate."

"Tell it to Hannibal."

"Is that all?"

"Well… she can be absolutely raucous during the day. Even when Hannibal does want to play with her, she dances around him making such a medley of noises that he eventually flees. I've seen him cover his ears with his paws."

"Little cats are frisky, Helga. It's natural behavior."

"When he's sleeping, she'll come over and yowl and even slap him. It makes him quite nervous."

"She only wants to play."

"Perhaps."

"Look at that, Helga. That's very interesting." An archeologist, admiring the Egyptians' great skill at embalming, mentioned that the soles of mummies' feet, even thousands of years after entombment, are often still soft and supple.

"Amazing!" said Helga. "But you know… there's something else."

"What else?"

"About Caterina. She eats his food. I've seen her. Not content with the dry food you feed her, she'll snatch away Hannibal's liver. I think the poor chap is getting thin."

"Can't he defend his own food?"

"He's asked me on occasion to allow him—quote—'to teach the little upstart a lesson.' I caution him always to eschew violence. I remind him that *noblesse oblige*."

"I'm really sorry, Helga. If Caterina's busting his balls—"

"*Ma chère*, he lost those pointless accessories shortly after I met him," said Helga. The wine relaxed her, and she was surprised that she had ventured such a joke. Erica smiled, showing her beautiful white teeth. "But sometimes," Helga persisted, "she displaces Hannibal from his chair. She'll pursue him so relentlessly that he'll jump off and hide under my bed. Upon occupying his chair, to add insult to injury, she'll make all kinds of yammering noises to try to draw him out again."

"She doesn't know any better, Helga." Erica's mood suddenly darkened, and she covered her face with her hands. "She just wants a little attention."

"I suppose," said Helga, now wishing she had not decided to act as Hannibal's spokesman.

"I'm sorry," said Erica, bursting into sobs. "I'm sorry, I really am sorry," she kept repeating.

Helga, too, felt her nose get stuffy with tears. Reaching out to Erica, she cradled her in her arms, rocking her to and fro. Erica cried herself out on her bosom. Her jaw felt so sharp it seemed to cut into Helga's sternum. Unlike Erica, Helga wore a bra—out of habit, since for many years it had served no practical purpose. "Don't cry, my pumpkin, my sweetheart," Helga murmured, using words she had often showered upon Alberto, who liked to seek comfort with his much heavier head against the same bony spot on her chest. She breathed deeply of the heavy, seductive perfume from Erica's hair, and when Erica faced upward, she inadvertently tasted the girl's smooth, tear-soaked cheek.

"I love you," whispered Erica. "I need you so much," she said, placing her warm, salty lips on Helga's. Helga was unsure of how to react. She felt invaded and yet utterly immobilized. While enduring the gentle pressure on her mouth, and the probing tip of a tongue that wormed its way through her wine-slick lips to her barricading teeth, she glimpsed the golden slits of Hannibal's eyes. He looked at her in disgust. Helga yanked her face to a side. Erica, however, seemed not to take offense. She turned around and rested the back of her head against Helga's thin shoulder.

While Helga worried that the weight of Erica's head might snap her collarbone, they continued to drink and watch TV. The narrator estimated that the Egyptians had made over seven hundred million expertly embalmed and securely wrapped mummies. The ka, the spiritual twin of the body, depended on the body's continued existence. Without it, the ka could not live on, could not assume its place in the kingdom of the dead.

5

"So what did you solve?" said Hannibal, nestled on Helga's pillow as she tried to go to sleep. "The one who should have listened to you paid no attention. She hasn't a freaking clue how much she crowds me!"

"But she only wants to play." The nightlight showed, along the opposite wall, her frieze of black cats all in a row, their golden eyes aglow as they sat in identical pairs, tails joined between them in caduceus-like twists. "It's her way of saying she loves you, you silly."

"First of all, Helga, you smell from wine. Second, at my age I have no interest in being 'loved' if it means losing my favorite seat and wearing a ridiculous necklace."

"Hannibal, I saw what you did the other day."

"What did I do?"

"Out of anger, you pulled open the door to the hall."

"Your bedmate left it open."

Helga's cheeks stung. "If Caterina hadn't been sleeping, she could have gotten out."

"Can't say I didn't think of it."

"Luckily, I saw it before she awoke."

"It's her or me, Helga!"

"Don't be so apocalyptic, Hannibal. Give her another chance. Remember that people's motives are what count."

"Motives, my ass! You wonder why I hole up in this room most of the day? I'm literally afraid to go out. She'll jump out at me. Or she'll sneak around me and claw at my tail. I *am* losing weight. I am close to a nervous collapse."

"You aren't letting me sleep, dear."

"Nonsense, Helga! It is your conscience that is preventing you from sleeping."

"Stuff and nonsense! Hannibal, promise me you'll try to be more flexible."

"Damn!" said Hannibal, dropping to the floor with a thump.

"Where are you going, dear?"

"Under the bed, where I shall curl up and die."

"Hannibal!"

There was silence, then a tap at the bedroom door. Helga didn't stir. The door creaked open and a slender, robed shadow slid in. Erica dropped to her knees at Helga's bedside. She laid her warm, soft cheek on the thin blanket that covered Helga's thigh.

"I'm frightened," she whispered. "I need to be near you. I'm afraid to sleep by myself tonight. May I?" She waited, and as Helga couldn't find the will either to invite her or send her away, Erica stood up and shrugged out of her robe. In the nightlight her skin glowed as smooth and creamy as ivory. Her small breasts formed perfect cones. Helga watched her move around to the right side of the bed as if Erica were an image on TV. When she slipped beneath the coverlet, Helga did not move a limb. She pictured Hannibal jumping between them, but Hannibal stayed out of sight.

"You're cold, even with your nightie on," said Erica, leaning over her.

"I'm always cold," said Helga. "Aren't you too... like that?"

"I'm always warm. I never sleep in nightclothes. Yes, you *are* a bit cold," said Erica. She sat up, shaking free of the blanket, and passed her right hand over Helga's right leg, slowly, from thigh to toe. Wordlessly, she leaned forward and massaged Helga's feet. The hands felt good on her perpetually cold feet. "The soles of your feet are nice and soft and supple," said Erica. The warmth of Erica's hands seemed to steal up Helga's legs. Suddenly, Erica's face hovered smotheringly near. "Your cheeks need warming too," she said, laying long, languorous kisses all over Helga's face. Helga wanted to speak, to ward her off in some kindly, gentle way, but the words wouldn't come. Her tongue seemed to cleave to the roof of her mouth. A crazy-quilt of odors settled thickly around her—sweet from Erica's hair, pungent from Erica's armpits, and musky from the whole length of the electrifying body that snuggled up against hers.

"It's time to go to sleep, dear," Helga chided, turning away. "Really, my sweet—"

"Your legs are still cold," replied Erica, reaching down to massage Helga's calves, tugging at Helga's silky chemise till it slid up over her crotch.

"We *really* must go to sleep, Erica," Helga heard herself inanely repeat. The naked Diana had beauty to hide from an understandably moon-struck Actaeon. But she? What was it that *she* so dreaded to expose? She caught Erica's hand as it lightly, caressingly cruised to the top of her thigh. What she felt in her belly, produced by Erica's hand, was a powerful, frightening tremor.

"I love you," said Erica.

"Stop, dear," Helga replied in a cracking, pleading voice, a voice that had lost all authority.

"I will not stop loving you," said Erica, bending down over Helga's body, nuzzling her unwrapped stomach. "You're shivering," said Erica. "You need me to make you warm."

Memories of past lovers flashed through Helga's mind. Maurice, the novelist so recently deceased. Chef Alberto, of course. Sandor, the gentle playwright. Wesley, her guru for five years... All had once been beautiful, and so had she, once. They whirled through her brain and sneered! A *woman* in your bed! So this is what you've come to? She tried to beat them back. The past was dead, deserved to be dead, should stay dead. She too was dead—a drunken fool who had momentarily forgotten the shadow she had become. Corpses are of indeterminate sex! she shouted back at them. Love was a charred spot at the base of her belly. Ghosts hovered above her: laughing, knee-slapping specters who regaled each other with the hilarious tale of a bunch of old bones that attempted to ignite but splintered and cracked in the unaccustomed heat of a living flame. The pain in Helga's belly, and now between those sticks of jerky that once had been her legs, threatened to tear her to shreds.

"Stop!" she shouted, pushing against Erica's head. Her parted knees kicked back at the limpet-like body that had fastened itself between them. She felt Erica slide away. She heard Erica crumple to the floor, then lie there quietly weeping.

6

The first thing she felt when she awoke in the morning was Hannibal sprawled on her chest. "About time," he said.

"I'm sorry, Hannibal. Are you hungry?"

"Who the hell knows? I'm too pissed to care."

"You're angry at me."

"At you? Only very indirectly. It's that bitch of a Caterina."

"Hannibal!"

"Don't 'Hannibal' me when I'm trying to tell you something!"

"You haven't seen her all night. What makes you so cross?"

"You mean you didn't *hear* her—all damn night? She sat hollering and moaning right by the door, pleading with me—in that horrible foreign accent of hers—to come out and play."

"I didn't hear a thing, dear."

"Oh, no? Well, after your girl friend left, the little siren kept me up all night. As soon as I'd doze off, she'd be at it again. I'm absolutely exhausted. Lucky for her the door *was* closed between us.... I'm announcing it to you right here and now," said Hannibal, tapping Helga twice on the chin, "I've had it with her—and that's that." He yawned, showing yellow teeth and gaps in dentition, then rolled off Helga's chest and groggily slumped to the floor.

"We cranky old people have been short on patience, haven't we?" said Helga, hearing Erica still bustling about in the apartment. Sitting up in bed a mite too fast, she felt dizzy, then waited until the blood flowed back to her brain.

"This apartment is much too small for two incompatible felines," said Hannibal, warily approaching the door.

"Learn to forbear, sweetheart. And try to be a gentleman." Helga draped her purple bathrobe around her and swung the door open. The sun-filled living room promised a pleasant working day. Erica, in a dark brown suit, was just coming out of the kitchen.

"Hi, Helga. I left you some coffee."

"Erica, dear, I wanted to see you before you left for work."

"What for?"

"To apologize."

"For what?"

"For last night."

"No need to. I shouldn't have come on so strong."

"It was entirely my fault, my dear."

"You don't really believe that, Helga."

"Oh, but I do. I'm a stick."

"I promise to be patient with you next time," said Erica, reaching down to scratch Caterina, who stared at Helga with bright, mocking eyes from her perch on Hannibal's cushion.

"Next time?" said Helga.

"Isn't there always a next time?" said Erica.

"Not necessarily," said Helga, placing her hand against her sternum, over the part which still felt bruised.

"Of course there is, my love." Erica smiled and grabbed her handbag from the table.

"Have a good day," said Helga. What she wanted to say was, Haven't I made it abundantly clear… that there can *be* no next time? Why hadn't *Erica* seen how absolutely clear she had made it?

"I'm giving you fair warning," said Erica with a wink as she marched to the door.

Helga shuddered as though she'd been issued a threat.

"See you later, sweetie." Erica unlocked the door and slipped out into the hall.

"Lock up, sweetheart," Helga whispered after her. But Erica did not lock up. Helga heard the squeal of the front door, then the clack of Erica's heels down the four steps leading to the street.

It was time for Hannibal's liver. She stood guard until he finished it.

"I'm starting to work now," she announced. "And I don't want to be interrupted." Hannibal scrambled to take possession of his cushion. Caterina, on her best behavior, took the seat next to him—but Helga knew what the little vixen was thinking. Putting the pair out of mind, she began to sketch the idea for a new painting. The door to a tomb accidentally left open. The goddess Bast seen through the door, seated on a lofty pedestal.

7

A series of cries coming from the street distracted Helga from her sketch-pad. She glanced at the clock over the sofa. Past five-thirty already! What was the hullabaloo all about? Hannibal jumped from his cushion, scrambled up onto the arm of the sofa, and peered through the curtains behind it.

"Can't see a damn thing!" he said.

"We must clean some windows," said Helga. "Sometimes one does want to peek outside."

"You do know who that is, don't you?" said Hannibal.

The cries grew sharper, and Helga did indeed know the voice. It was Erica's. Reluctantly, she closed her sketch-pad. She threw on a sweater, since it was nippy out there, as she knew from stepping out about an hour before. Or was it five hours ago? she wondered. Objective time and the world of 'reality' meant nothing when you were working. Unable to stop thinking of her unfinished sketch, Helga shuffled in slippers through the still-unbolted door, out into the hallway, then out through two sets of doors and onto the front steps.

Erica knelt at the curb in front of the hydrant some yards to the right. Neighbors that Helga neither knew nor wanted to know were already gathering near.

"Whatever is the matter, Erica?" said Helga, almost *sotto-voce*, as though speaking to herself. She tried again, speaking aloud, but how could she compete with all that commotion? So she climbed down the steps and made her way over to Erica, who saw her and uttered her most agonizing scream yet—blood-curdling, Helga thought.

It did not come as a complete surprise when Helga saw, stretched below the curb, the squashed little body, its bloody mouth open in a silent scream of gleaming-white teeth. Someone had at least had the decency to scrape the poor thing out of the middle of the street, where a stain—overrun with tire-tread marks—showed where the accident had occurred.

"*You* killed her!" shrieked Erica as Helga grew near.

"Whatever do you mean, dear?"

"You killed her!" Erica repeated, then bent again over the broken body, her torso rising and falling in grief. All these strangers, these carrion-sniffing buzzards, began to stare at Helga, then at Erica, and back at Helga.

Helga raised her hand to her throat in dismay. "How many times have I warned you to bolt the door?" she said—but Erica wasn't listening.

"Hannibal did it," Helga explained to her grim-faced neighbors. Among them she recognized the man who had stood in her doorway. "I can't keep tabs on him all day, you know. He loves getting into the hall, if you give him a chance."

The man she recognized stared at her and slowly shook his head. Erica wept. A woman, meanwhile, spoke softly to her and held her to her breast.

"Caterina obviously sprang out after him," Helga continued, rounding out the scenario to be sure that they all understood. "People come and go through the front doors all the time. It could have been one of you let her out."

How dreadful to feel that no one was even listening!

"Who would have bothered to keep her in?" said Helga. Erica, convulsed with sobs, clung to the bosom of the stranger who tried to console her. "I ask you, now, Would any of you have thought to keep her in?"

Facedowns

For several years, about every Friday evening, the four of us would get together for an all-night session of low-stakes poker at Mel Belcher's house, where we'd gorge ourselves on deep-dish pizzas, demolish his racks of Coors, and take turns sharing Jennifer. We never had to worry about Melvin catching us with his wife (who had sampled us all back in high school, by the way) because Mel was so obsessive about playing that he literally wouldn't get up to pee till five or six in the morning.

It's hard to say what mainly kept us coming throughout those years—our passion for the game? the abundant food and booze? the restorative time-outs with Jennifer?—but if it weren't for some or all of those incentives I doubt that any of us would have stood for very long the pompous pinhead that Mel turned out to be. He wasn't like that in high school. A shy, sensitive, B+-average student, he was the only one of us who went on to finish college (much good it did him!), and he was the only one of us who had graduated from high school without ever sleeping with Jennifer. He'd never put on airs during our Friday nights either, in any case not for the first year or so, unless his constant bragging about the Harley he had bought, ticking off Jennifer but merely amusing the rest of us, was a sign of crap to come.

The true beginning, rather, of his irritating behavior only started to show its horns when he began to fancy himself a Writer. While wasting his time endlessly switching majors at the College of Staten Island, where he failed to take a single course that trained him for his ultimate elevation to Produce Manager at Waldbaums, he did sneak in a course in Creative Writing. The only problem with that course, he once told us, was that it

51

didn't teach him how to get *ideas* for stories. The teacher did tell him, however, that literary writers didn't *need* to think up low-brow things like plots, so that if he worked at the skills he did possess, he would one day be crowned with critical success as a writer of the sort of innovative fiction that lasts throughout the ages.

Now as far as all of us guys were concerned, ideas for stories were a dime a dozen. We were hearing stories and going through our own about every day of our lives. Whenever we sat down for a long night of poker, about all we did was tell each other stories that made us croak with laughter or shake our heads in recognition of some timeless truth about human misbehavior. We came loaded with tales, usually about our escapades with women—all of us, that is, except for Melvin, who'd been out of the singles market for years, drew no inspiration from fruits and vegetables, and would generally sit mum and glum as the rest of us matched each other story for story—embellishing here and there, of course, lying a bit to impress each other, but mainly to round out our little reports with some shocker or clincher of a point.

During the course of any one night, we could probably have filled a whole book with our sleaze. In fact, we'd occasionally do a number on Melvin. We'd claim that if we all had had that same creative-writing course, we'd all be published authors by now. Literary-shiterary, what difference did it make? We'd all be rolling in dough. Our cockiness never sat well with Mel, and his usual reply was to grimly insist that without "Technique," which presumably he had in spades, we could never write works of Literary Art on any level whatsoever, not even bargain-basement. Bullshit artists we were; literary never.

Well, these sorry-ass moods didn't upset us in the least, especially since we figured Mel wasn't getting any from Jenny—or if he was, it was a case of few and far between, because he paid so little attention to the modest and reasonable demands she made—such as for new living-room furniture because she was ashamed to invite people over any more ("people" had nothing to do with us, of course), or for a new used car in place of the Model T Corolla they'd got married in. One of us, Josh Harrison, luckily happened to be a furniture salesman and eventually came upon a great deal for Jenny which—unbeknownst to the Belchers—involved his getting the stuff at cost and also forfeiting his commission; but the upshot was that we got Melvin to go for it. And if our own "Dork" Dornberg, ex-footballer and wizard at five-card draw, hadn't been a salesman for Toyota, Jenny would still be risking her life instead of riding high in her clean, fully loaded, silver Camry that came with low-mileage and with barely four years on its back. Even Melvin couldn't sniff at a bargain like that.

But as to shopping in Manhattan for long-overdue new clothes, Jennifer had to wait a good while. Melvin's priority was a laptop computer. "Absolutely essential," he told us one day—the day he announced that he had finally become a Writer—"a *published* writer," he emphasized.

He made this statement quite casually, as if announcing he had bought a new suit, but all of us felt our jaws drop, and we stopped in mid-chew or just about choked in mid-swallow. "What did you publish? Where?" said Dork, who had always, as much as the rest of us, taken Melvin's literary pretensions with a super-size grain of salt.

Brushing back his slick black hair, drawing his hand down over his gaunt, sallow cheeks, Melvin stared across the dining-room table not *at* Dork, but *through* Dork, and out into empty space. "A story, of course. In a literary magazine. Paid quite well, I might add." He had just won a decent-sized pot, maybe eight or ten bucks (we never played for blood) in a round of five-card draw; we had let him win because at four in the morning, after we'd each taken our "breaks" and were all of us mellowed out, we didn't bother calling his bluff.

"What's the story about? What magazine?" pursued Hank Castro, our buddy the gym trainer whose ambition to become a priest collapsed on the day of his first erection.

"What do you mean, 'about'?" sneered Mel. Gathering in the cards, he had already started to shuffle for the next round without first displaying his winning hand, a courtesy we friends always paid each other automatically, without ever having to be asked. "A story just *is*. It's pointless to ask what it's *about*. It is itself and can't be summarized. It exists only in its unfolding."

"So what is it *about* when it unfolds?" demanded Hank from the end of the table to Mel's right.

"Unfolds my ass," said Josh, who'd procured the Belchers the very table we were playing on. "How come *we* all *folded* and you wouldn't show us your hand?"

"Forgot," smirked Mel, unfolding a few fingers to toss at us while staring up at the ceiling.

"Okay, so what did you have then?"

"Forgot," sighed Mel. "Hank was distracting me with his amateurish questions."

"I have a very amateurish question," I broke in finally, staring across the table at our strangely forgetful friend. "How much did they pay you for the story?"

"Just the kind of question I would expect you to ask, George. A property manager *would* be interested in literature only as *property*, not in the life within the literary object itself."

Jennifer had by this time unglued herself from bed to brew us a pot of coffee. She stood off to my left against the doorway to the kitchen, her ratty beige bathrobe falling back now and then from her bare left breast. When I gave her a quick look, she rolled her eyes and shrugged. Twirling a loose lock of her long blond hair, she withdrew back into the kitchen.

The next several weeks went by without much change in the way things had always been with us. When Mel announced that he had sold another story, we all clicked glasses, wished him more power, but none of us asked for details. If he was annoyed at our lack of curiosity, he managed not to show it; but none of us wanted to get sprayed in the face with some literary horse-piss again. If anything emerged as peculiar about the new Mel, Melvin Belcher the Writer, it was his greater generosity about ordering in pizza, a more varied selection of beers—and then there was also the greater attention he paid to all of us, all night long, as we shot the bull and served up our twisty little stories.

Before he had become a literary maven, he would occasionally interrupt with some irrelevant remark, run out to the kitchen for another beer, or nudge the dealer to reshuffle the deck. Now he was all ears, his drink or cards suspended above his chips, and if one of us didn't spin his yarn in exactly logical order, he would correct us or challenge us to fill in details, as if running a class in creative writing and demanding we incorporate "Technique."

With a wink to each other and a nod to Mel, we put up with such chicken-shit comments. We appreciated the fact that for ten minutes at a time now we could get him to focus on something besides the game. He would even go so far sometimes as to try to one-up the rest of us by dropping a "story" like a lead turd into one of our rounds of tale-telling. For example, after hearing what had happened once to Josh in Las Vegas, he came out with a dull summary of a "classic" Russian novel called *The Gambler*. You wouldn't want to read it after the jumbled mess he made of it—you'd never know what the *story* in it was!—but from us he demanded a professional presentation.

While it is true that we didn't care to pester Mel for evidence that he was actually getting published, one of us—myself, actually—would occasionally pump Jennifer for information. Finally, but reluctantly, one night she reached across me to the end-table at my left and drew forth a copy of a men's magazine. It was one of those rags several leagues below *Playboy* that train-station kiosks keep plastic-wrapped on a back-wall shelf out of reach of sweaty hands. Opening it to the Table of Contents, she pointed to a story by one Jock Durango, the pen name Melvin had fixed upon for the stories he'd so far been writing. While I wasn't going to sit down and read it—it would have been imprudent of us to overextend our breaks—I did make mental note of the dumb-ass pen name.

"Did he actually get paid for this, Jennifer?" I asked.

"Three hundred and fifty dollars," she said, her expression switching from a smirk of shameful confession to a shaky grin of pride.

Had she expected me to express disapproval? I wondered. I had to admit it, I really was impressed.

I was so impressed that for a few months thereafter I would casually check out magazine racks, and despite the creepy sensation I felt, I would open copies of *Hustler* and similar tripe, sometimes surreptitiously slitting their plastic protectors. Finally, I hit upon two magazines with stories by Jock Durango. I can't describe the humiliation I felt in bringing them to the girl at the counter. "I never really read these things, but a friend of mine is a writer and has stories in them," I said.

"Sure," she replied. Her pinch-nosed grin made glaringly evident the image we both had of me—that of some two-foot gargoyle playing hooky from his niche.

Back at my office at Hammond Property Management, I instructed my secretary that I was not to be disturbed, and I sat for the next hour reading those stories, my amazement and anger mounting. Naturally, he manufactured lots of details he'd never heard in the original. But stripped to the bare bones, these stories were ones that we his friends had unwittingly fed him during the course of one or other of our chat-filled Friday evenings. Not necessarily the most interesting ones either, but they came out "logical," with full beginnings, middles, and ends, all of which he swiped from the material we'd provided. Not a single important incident had he invented on his own. His professor had been right. Mel was good at Technique, but he couldn't come up with a Story of his own to save his plundering ass. From Dork came the story about the orgasm that was accompanied with an aria from *Figaro*. From Josh, the story about the couple who could only make love after losing at roulette.

After the four of us had read the two stories and agreed that they'd been stolen, we asked ourselves, What should we do? I didn't think there was anything we should do. We were eating our cake and having it too. The others felt quite differently. Not that they wanted any of the money that Jock Mel Belcher Durango was making. The general sentiment was that Mel owed us some sort of acknowledgment. Not in print, but in person. For our indispensable role in helping launch his career.

But how could we possibly ever let on that we knew who Jock Durango was? He'd know that Jennifer had betrayed him. That was an applecart with everybody's apples in it and heaven forbid we turn it over. But was there any gratitude in that snickering heart of his? My friends devised the following method to put him to the test.

We began bringing magazines, including a few of the sleazier ones, to our weekly pokerthons with the excuse that during our breaks away from the game we could catch a snatch of good writing for a change, something to pleasure our souls. This could hardly appear suspicious, since we'd often retired to Jenny's room with a newspaper in our hands. Inevitably, of course, among the magazines we brought we'd slip in an issue of something that featured a story by Jock Durango: the two that I'd discovered and another we later happened upon, further proof of Mel's unconfessed debt to his friends. Also inevitably, one of us—we first picked Josh—mentioned that although he rarely read trash, he'd come upon this funny tale by a guy named Jock Durango. And he waved the magazine in the air—to which all of us pretended indifference.

Except, of course, for Melvin.

"So tell me, what was so good about it?" said Mel. The hand poised to toss in his discards hung suspended in mid-air.

"Well, what's so funny," said Josh, "is that months before this issue came out I told the same story right here at this table—with even the same ending—about a couple whose love life hung on their luck at roulette."

"You're exaggerating," mumbled Mel.

"You tell me if I didn't tell this story," said Josh, launching into a repetition of what we'd all heard earlier. With an air of boredom we all agreed that, yes, we'd heard it before. I agreed, accommodatingly, to read the printed version on my forthcoming "break."

Mel, meanwhile, insisted that it was either a coincidence or a tale that had been making the rounds in Vegas, where Josh and others had picked it up, by which mode of transmission it had eventually reached the ears of a skilled craftsman who knew how to turn crude anecdotes into cash.

He finessed us easily on this first challenge, which he must have seen right through. But he sounded less in command of himself when two weeks later he used the same reasoning to discount the strange coincidence of another Jock Durango story that was strikingly similar in outline to one that Dork had told months back—about a passionately operatic orgasm. We waited another couple of weeks, though, before springing on him a third Durango "coincidence." The story was aptly called "Super Duper." In it a property manager discovers that one of his employees is repeatedly engaging in infra-structure sabotage involving the same apartment building. The man needed to justify those frequent return trips to continue to get it on with the super's wife.

With regard to this story, Mel's insistence on coincidence proved particularly lame... because it happened to be a totally true story that had played out under the nose of Yours Truly.

"This Jock Durango sure gets around," said Hank Castro, reigning in a rising tide of testosterone.

"You're putting me on," said Mel, gesturing impatiently for Josh to deal the second facedown card in a new round of seven-card stud. "I never heard George tell any such story."

Everybody, however, jumped to my defense.

At which Mel slammed the table with his fist. "Listen, jackasses, read any hundred stories and I'm sure you'll pick out ten that you'll swear you first heard here. Just *think* of all the stories we've dumped on each other over the years! You don't remember half of them yourselves."

"But *three* now? And by the same Jock Durango? Isn't that a bit uncanny?" murmured Josh, staring hard at Mel, who refused to look any of us in the eye.

⊙═◄• •►═⊙

That was as close as we ever came to letting Mel know that *we* knew what he was up to. He'd have to have been stupid not to suspect that we, at least, *suspected.* As to why his reaction to such unsubtle pressure was to bury his head in the sand, Dork thought it was his fear of being regarded as unoriginal, while I put equal stress on Mel's potential for shame— shame at being exposed, after all his high-falutin literary vaunting, as nothing more than a scribbler of skuzzy porn. Not that we would ever have put him down for this accomplishment. On the contrary, we were never judgmental. I think any of us would have been proud to be able to turn into gold the screwball stuff that happened to us in the course of daily living. The problem was all in *Mel's* head. Exposure would amount to a severe blow to an elaborately constructed self-image.

Though irked at our failure to get him to come clean, we continued our Friday behavior as usual—except, perhaps, for the style of our story-telling, which at times became pompously theatrical, as if we could already foresee our casual ramblings converted into print. It wasn't *our* behavior that—at first, at least—underwent much change; it was Melvin's.

I may have given the impression earlier that we free-loaded entirely at his expense. The truth is, however, that every one of us always arrived with something in hand—six-packs, a pizza—but that the supply we brought was always generously supplemented by Mel, who made sure we were well sustained through our many hours of play. So that when Mel's support began to wither in the munch 'n slurp department, we knew he'd been taking our disguised accusations very badly. He'd order in some pizzas and then, especially if he'd been losing a few hands, pat his pockets, make believe he was short on cash, and get one of us to foot the bill with the promise—which of course we wouldn't hear of—that he'd pay us back next time (which he never did). And when the beer ran out early we never complained, but it did darken the general mood in the wee hours before sunrise. Our bedrock of dependability through this period of erosion remained the ardor of Jennifer's ministrations, which fortunately never slackened.

I look back in shame at the petty changes that began to show in our own behavior—in reaction to Mel's, no doubt (but I don't mention this as an excuse). Our practice had always been full disclosure: to show each other our full hand, especially incumbent upon the winner when he'd made the others fold. But now we'd sometimes balk at flipping our facedowns up after winning at seven-card stud—or not show our hand at all if we'd successfully bluffed in five-card. This method of needling Melvin became irresistibly tempting if he had just been prattling on about some "classic" we illiterates hadn't read, or after he'd announce how many words of a new story he'd written that very morning, or how many dollars he was negotiating for with some editor in a glass tower on Forty-Second Street. And especially when he'd announce with glee that he'd just made a new sale but brush off our by-now-pro-forma inquiries as to What magazine? and How much?

One day, after weeks of such mean-spirited tit-for-tats, Hank came upon a recent issue of *Screw* or *Hooters* or something like that at the gym, and the first thing he noticed after perusing the visuals was a new Durango story. During an hour break between training sessions he read it—and then passed it on to all of us. To no one's surprise it was a fleshed-out, fully accessorized version of a story that had happened to Josh barely four months prior to the date of the magazine.

Most of the tales we traded on Fridays were perfectly forgettable, but this one stood out. It was a story about his meeting a girl after tracking her down through the wallet she'd left on a recliner in his showroom. He soon introduced her to a vast storage area in the rear, and there, in the inviting jumble of sofas and beds, she turned playful and succeeded in confusing him. While Josh was intent on making a sale, she seemed focused on making the salesman, and when Josh switched gears she would suddenly about-face and show a deep interest in furniture. We all remembered Mel's fascination, his prying detail after detail out of Josh as if challenging the story's authenticity. The Durango version added nothing new, not a single element of importance that was Mel's own invention.

Here was new evidence of ingratitude. How much longer could we tolerate being milked and pumped like a barnful of cows? How much more could we stand being treated like a stable full of prostitutes run by a stingy pimp? Josh suggested that we no longer confide our adventures and such to each other in the presence of Mel. Dork pointed out, however, that we didn't see each other much beyond our Friday nights, so that if we followed Josh's suggestion we'd be depriving ourselves—as much as Mel—of one of the most rewarding features of our friendship. What won the day, finally, was a suggestion of my own that sprang to my mind in a moment of evil inspiration.

⊚━◄ ►━⊚

Few of the stories we told each other could ever have been called memorable, but one Friday night, not long after that pow-wow, we put my plan into motion. Dork had recently undergone an adventure which we had earlier judged well suited to our purposes. We were playing seven-card stud and Dork's face cards looked impressive. He was expansive, raising and raising again, and he chose this opportunity to launch into his story.

"She was a real cute Latina," he said, rubbing his red mustache as always when he was feeling confident, "born with the kind of beach tan that cost my last girlfriend a bundle, dressed to the nines, in a skirt that hugged her ass tighter than O. J.'s glove."

"Cut the poetry," I said, feigning impatience. "Did you finally nail her?"

"Let him tell it the way he wants," said Mel, meeting Dork's raise like the rest of us.

"Nailing her is not the point," Dork resumed. "Point is, every couple of months she'd come in—to buy a *new* car, with a new *guy* in tow."

"How many cars she freakin' need?" said Hank.

"I don't know, but she'd buy the car for *him*, always ask *him* what he wanted, but when push came to shove she always wanted *my* advice—and even though this would piss off the guy, she wouldn't go for anything *I* didn't recommend. I was the only salesman she'd deal with."

"Cool. But who was she trying to impress?" said Josh.

"Now you're getting nearer the point," said Dork. "The third time around I wondered, Who dumped who, her the boyfriend or the boyfriend her? But I wondered more, Who stayed with the car? Did she give one away to each of those morons? And believe me, those guys were nothing to write home to Caracas about."

"So go on. Did you find out?" said Mel, pretending to be studying everyone's final face card. Pretend though he might, I knew by then he was hooked. And I hoped that Dork was enough of an angler to know how to reel him in. Dork paid no attention to Mel. Good going, Dork! I thought.

"Get this now," said Dork. "One day she comes in alone to see *me*. I peek out and what do I see she was driving?"

"Her last boyfriend's birthday present, and he's in the trunk," said Hank.

"Don't get ahead of me. What's she driving? A bomb," said Dork. "A junker. A jalopy. She comes up to me practically with tears in her gorgeous eyes and says she needs a new car. She points at the wheels she's parked outside and she sobs that her *last boyfriend* gave her that one! Do you believe this shit?"

"No," said Josh. "So cut the crap and play poker."

"I agree," I said. "Enough bull. I can't focus on the game."

"Don't listen to these losers, Dork," said Mel with an angry look around the table.

"Sure I'm not boring you, Mel?" said Dork, with a quick wink to me. "Well all right. Next thing I know I'm taking her out for a test-drive—and while I'm pointing out the features of the car, she's crying her heart out about her last romance gone sour. Next day she's back, wants to test a different model. And I oblige. And what does she tell me?"

"I meet your raise, you bluffing bastard," said Hank.

"She tells me, the reason she kept bringing those guys back to buy cars from me is that, from the first, she was attracted to *me*, Dork Truly!"

"You're full of shit," said Josh.

"And soon we're fucking *dating!*"

"Fucking or dating? Make up your feeble mind," said Josh, meeting Dork's raise.

"That's not the point," said Dork.

"Then get to the goddamn point!" snarled Josh.

"Let him take his time," said Mel. "Whatsa matter, got a feather up your ass?"

"The point is that our 'dates' are peculiar. Each date we take a spin in a different new-model buggy. I'm burning with curiosity, among other things, ha-ha, so I ask her one day what happened to the other cars she bought in *her* name for her boyfriends...." Suddenly Dork's attention shifted. "Whatsa matter, girls? Who's left in the game? Only George? I don't even need my facedown, George. I already beat your ass with the first five."

Everybody watched me as I contemplated folding. I folded.

Dork raked in his winnings and proceeded to gather up the cards.

"You gonna show what you're hiding?" said Mel.

"No more than you," said Dork. Giving us all a raised-eyebrow look, he turned everybody's cards face down and stacked them together to prepare for a new deal.

"Dick!" said Josh.

"Asshole!" said Hank.

"Reminds me, I gotta use the john," said Dork.

"Hey wait," said Mel. "You were in the middle of telling..."

But Dork was already on a run to the comfort station.

"He was bluffing," said Josh

"You don't know that," said Hank.

"He doesn't want to reveal his strategy," I said.

When Dork returned, he began dealing out a hand of five-card draw.

"So," said Mel, "you were saying about that, uh, Latina chick…"

"I was saying?"

"Who cares what you were saying?" said Hank. "Just deal from the top of the deck."

"Did you wash the piss off your hands?" said Josh.

"I saved a little for everyone," said Dork.

A few times through the night, trying to sound casual, Mel pried Dork for the conclusion of the mystery of the car-addicted Latina, but one or another of us would immediately intervene with some piddling and pointless car-related anecdote of our own. Mel's features would stiffen. At times he appeared distracted. He was shrewd enough to know that if he reverted too often to Dork's unfinished story, we'd all grow suspicious. He seemed to have only one thing on his mind.

⊚══⊰⊶ ⊷⊱══⊚

During the following weeks, the four of us poured out bunches of new stories. They might not have been laced with much intrigue, but Melvin seemed to pay our chitchat much less attention than usual. He was much less alert to the course of an anecdote than he'd been for a good many months. His appetite for beer and pizza seemed to fall off as well. If we asked what was bothering him, he'd shrug off the question, or grunt, or say nothing, or sometimes he'd glare askance—at Dork. When we left his house as the sun came up, we'd chuckle at the effect we were having.

That was during the first few weeks. But as Friday followed Friday, we noticed further changes in Mel. He made stupid mistakes in his play. Further, he'd open a new beer, forgetting he'd just opened one ten minutes before. Or he'd call out to Jennifer to make us some coffee—and that could be disturbing if one of us happened to be out on a break—but seconds later he'd forget he'd even asked. We tried telling stories as funny as we could make them, embellishing as never before, but Mel seemed to be with us more in body than in spirit, and what truly drew our concern was that he seemed to be losing weight. We pushed pizza at him. He'd take a bite and leave the rest. And if Dork were to offer him anything, he'd reject it out of hand. His complexion, which had never looked rosy, looked more and more like dried parchment every week. We'd occasionally lose a hand to him on purpose, but he now greeted winning or losing with indifference. He completely abandoned the practice of bluffing, and we now wondered why he bothered playing at all.

One night, when taking a turn with Jennifer, I saw that she was unusually distracted. My friends had earlier remarked a change in her demeanor. Jennifer had always been delightfully predictable, a touchstone of emotional stability—so we all began to feel threatened, as if the ground were giving way beneath our feet. "Is anything the matter?" I asked her gently, stroking her cheeks and shoulders.

After lots of hesitation, she said, "You know how obsessive Mel can be?"

"Of course. That's our Mel," I replied.

"But this is I believe unhealthy. I think he's pining away with unrequited love."

"Love? Mel? A check-out girl at the supermarket maybe?"

"That's what I was thinking. Some sort of Latina."

"What!"

"That's what he's been shouting out in his sleep. He mumbles something and all I can make out clearly are two words, Latina and cars. Do you think he's been screwing some bitch in his car? If he has, she's driving him crazy."

I shuddered. "No," I said. "He's not been screwing some Latina bitch. He's trying to write a story about a Latina and her cars. He heard it from us months ago, but I don't think we had a chance to tell him the ending. He's brooding over the ending."

Jennifer stiffened in my arms. "For God's sake, that must be the story he's been trying to finish for months. I read one of the drafts he keeps leaving around the house. It's got no Latina in it, but it's about some chick who keeps on buying cars. I once asked him if he finished it, and he told me to shut the fuck up."

"Listen, why don't we just tell him the ending?"

"You'd better *not* tell him the ending," she snapped. "*I* know and *you* know where he's been getting all his stories, but if you even hinted at it—I did once and he flew into a rage—he'd have a fit and accuse you of denying him originality."

"Are you saying he's never admitted, even to you, the use of materials we supplied?"

"Never, George. The day you accuse him of that is the day your friendship is *kaput*."

"None of the guys want *that* to happen." I grazed Jenny's lips with a kiss."

"George, not only does he *deny* his sources, but I believe he actually, honestly, totally *forgets* where he gets his ideas, and that he thinks they're completely original."

"Okay, I have an idea, Jenny. It was Dork's story. Dork could repeat the story—right through to the ending—and we'd all pretend we hadn't heard it before."

"Are you nuts?" She wriggled out from under me. "He'd immediately assume that I put you up to it! He'd hear the end of it, all right, but I'd *never* hear the end of it."

"But he'll never figure out an ending on his own."

"Why not?"

"Trust me. It won't happen."

We gazed at each other in utter bewilderment, and then I had to return from my break.

During the weeks that followed Mel underwent a rapid decline. He showed not a spark of interest in any of our stories anymore. His face turned jaundice-yellow and his clothes seemed to drape over a skeleton. We hoped he was not using his Harley to get to work—or, to put it bluntly, for any reason whatsoever.

After the Friday nights ground to a halt, Jennifer'd have nothing to do with us anymore. She wanted true love. A household pet. Devotion. Obsessive would be fine—so long as it was an obsession with her.

You're asking what happened?... To whom? In which story?

If it's this one, that's a whole other story in itself.

The Fetal Position

Jamie's mother was so sure she'd be having a girl that she tagged her son with the name long reserved for her dream-daughter. Continuing to give the finger to embryological destiny, she further ignored convention by refusing to change the pink décor, which she'd spent months blissfully assembling, to the gender-appropriate blue. She could have reserved that name Jamie—fortunately for the son a sex-neutral choice—for a second child, on the fifty-fifty chance that her luck would turn around, but Carla Pendleton Masters had already suffered two miscarriages and now, in her mid-thirties, had little faith in her gestational future. Besides, her husband had skipped out on her, smack in the middle of her pregnancy with Jamie, and after six years of marital hell she did not look forward to playing the genetic lottery with yet another loser.

Compounding her disappointment at giving birth to a male child, a doctor had told her, on the basis of an early sonogram, that he thought she'd be having twins—that he saw two fetal sacs, one smaller than the other, even suspected a second heartbeat. An elated Carla was immediately certain that the smaller had to be female. Later, however, the doctor in charge disputed that reading of twins, hinting wryly at the existence of long-standing problems with the now retired previous doctor's sense organs. Subsequent tests did in fact turn up one fetus only—a male, as Carla suspected.

A nurse, in order to console Mrs. Masters, confidentially told her that strange things sometimes happened in the womb, that a twin could "vanish," could be reabsorbed by the mother, and could sometimes even be enveloped, swallowed up, by the aggressive surviving twin. By no means could Carla imagine that her own body would snatch back the little girl of her dreams. Far easier was it for her to assume that the greedier fetus, like the good-for-nothing spouse who had lived off her selfless bounty, had gobbled up his womb-mate while wolfing down all else he could snatch beneath the placental roof.

Jamie himself had absorbed with his mother's milk—figuratively speaking, since he'd never sucked on other than silicone nipples—the sense that his mother regarded him as a cuckoo egg, a changeling, an Ugly Duckling foisted on her by a father he would never know, a husband who had left only two things behind: the cigarette burns on her furniture and the brand of his likeness on her son. But not necessarily on the boy's personality. It was Carla's belief that nurture outweighed nature in character formation and that, with proper maternal guidance, she could divert into socially positive channels the predictably negative energies that had yet to emerge in the son.

As a teenager Jamie could not exactly remember how and when his mom had let him know what a prenatal predator he'd been. All he knew was that his occasional acts of disobedience would cause her to throw a fit. Rarely, however, during the course of any such bitter tantrum, would she actually lift a finger to him. Instead she was likely to withdraw into herself and tearfully address the peeling ceiling about how his vanished sister, whose name he disgraced, would never have misbehaved as he did, or left such a mess in her room, or refused to eat what her mother had cooked. And if it had to do with eating, she might not hesitate to remind him of the ravenous hunger he'd had in her womb, an appetite so beastly that he had swallowed up his sister during the months before he was born. He never thought to argue about the absurdity of such a suggestion. The graphic image of his cannibalism had been ingrained in him since childhood, and all his mother had to do was allude to the ugly deed, and right after dutifully licking his plate clean he would often feel the urge to throw up.

Which he sometimes did outside in the yard, out of range of his mother's hearing. He hated to upset her, but what made him feel worst of all was not so much the tongue-lashings as those reproachful, self-pitying looks of hers. They told him that his guilt was irremediable, that his petty instances of misbehavior were in themselves nothing much, but symptomatic rather of some profound, innate deficiency that resisted all her efforts to expunge. Sometimes she would seem to relent, approach him with a shake of her head, give him a brief hug, then leave behind the impress of narrow, pendulous breasts and, most memorably, the cool, strong scent of freshly crushed flowers.

Particularly alarming to Mrs. Masters was Jamie's growing interest in sports. She refused to enroll him in Little League; a playing field, she explained to him, was a minefield full of accidents waiting to happen. The kids soon called him "sissy," "Momma's boy," and "faggot." Jamie shrugged off the insults as well as he could. Keeping his room extra-neat, Jamie tried a few times to get Carla to relent, but she remained deaf to his pleas. She hardly had to say a word. The look she gave him made him swallow his voice, pushing it down his throat and into his stomach, which burned for hours afterward.

The vomiting and stomach pains, Jamie well knew, were not so much caused by his mother as by the sister he had swallowed and still resided somewhere, intact and not very friendly, in his intestines. And if his mother tried to prevent him from participating in sports, Jamie also knew—without her having to say so—that it was not so much for his own safety's sake as to protect her trapped daughter, who had already endured so much, from the further harm that could come to her through the violent rattling of her cage. He had a name for her: Amy. And his bouts of abdominal discomfort he called "having the Amys."

More than out of concern for his safety, his mother's opposition to Little League stemmed from her firm conviction that male team sports were good for nothing but to exacerbate men's inborn tendencies toward mindless cruelty and reckless ambition, whose combined effect led unsurprisingly to various forms of childishly destructive and antisocial behaviors when later in life men encountered failure, refused to recognize their limitations, and inevitably took it all out on their loved ones—and who knew all this better than she?

Mrs. Masters worked as a secretary in the local high school, and if not for being a single mother, she would have gone back to school to become a guidance counselor. The students sorely needed good guidance, and Carla harbored secret contempt for the guidance counselors she'd seen come and go, their minds poisoned by the ideology of the football field. Her educational ambitions thwarted, Carla took pride in adjusting to her modest position in life—the result, she knew, not of limited talent but of grinding external circumstance.

Jamie's first serious clash with his mother came when, at age fifteen, he tried out successfully for the high-school basketball team. He was tall, agile, and skillful at the game, having played informally with neighborhood kids for years in parks and schoolyards. He would play without her suspecting, often before she got home from work, and at other times employing various excuses like going over to a friend's house to help him with his homework. To enforce her prohibition, Carla used what leverage she thought she had—after all, she worked at the very school Jamie attended—but her appeals on up from the coach to the principal proved fruitless. Feigning sympathy, they saw no merit in her argument that Jamie's involvement in sports would detract from his academic performance, in which he already excelled across the board. She told them about his unusually sensitive stomach, but they would not buy into her claim that the mental and physical strains of such a demanding team sport were bound to wreak havoc on the poor boy's gut. Grudgingly backing down, Carla dropped hints to Jamie of some dire Nemesis waiting in the wings, and she increased his schedule of household chores in the hope that they would cut into his practice time.

A couple of months into his period of delinquency, a second and far more serious clash occurred between Jamie and his mother. Jamie got interested in a classmate named Trisha. When Carla found out that he was spending time with a girl—no matter if a Trisha, a Grisha, or an Alicia—she felt a wrenching pain as if her womb were being despoiled all over again. When Jamie made the mistake of inviting Trisha to the house, Carla treated them both with cold suspicion and refused to allow them to do "homework" together upstairs and out of her sight.

Jamie had no idea why his mother would react as she did. She had never objected to his doing homework with male friends of his. So the next time he hung out with Trish they did their homework at Trisha's house. But on walking the half-mile home he began to feel sharp, pinching pains in his stomach. It was a windy autumn afternoon. Clawlike leaves scraped at his feet and the descending sun followed him behind rows of half-bare trees. At first he thought that Trisha must be following him too—she grew silly at times, even while they did their homework—because he heard a girl's voice whisper his name, a voice close by, as close as the whisper of wind in his ear, but not of the wind… and he turned to see who might be hiding behind the trunk of a maple to his right. No one was there, and now he doubled up with an agonizing cramp as the voice came right up behind him together with the wind that whipped his neck. "Jamie," she said, in a voice much sadder than the wind's, "you know who I am. You know me very well, in fact."

Jamie spun around. The street was deserted. He even went so far as to scan the overhead branches, but he knew already, knew very well, that the voice came not from above—but from directly behind his back. And yet there was nothing behind his back—except, of course, his backpack. Which contained, in an outside pocket, his cell phone. A device he alternately loved and hated. Loved when chatting with the very few friends he had, especially Trisha. Hated when it was used like an implanted chip for his mom to keep track of his whereabouts—the only real reason she allowed him to have one in the first place.

Determining where the voice came from gave him a moment's relief, respite from the creepy sensations that prickled the back of his neck. But an instant later that hot flush of fear, that instinctive reaction to the uncanny, returned in spades, burning his neck and ringing in his ears. "Ringing" was the problem. The phone, though always on, had not *rung*, had not needed to *wait* for him to answer. That was not possible. Swinging his bookbag around to his left, he yanked his phone out and flipped it open.

"You still there?" he said, his hand trembling as he waited for an answer. "Trisha?" he said hopefully, knowing the voice had sounded nothing like hers.

There was no answer. Examining the lit-up face of the phone, detecting no caller ID, he was about to flip it closed again when he did get an answer—one he did not want to hear.

"If Mother knew what you were up to, I doubt that she'd approve."

"Say again?" said Jamie.

"You've got that girl too much on your mind," said the small sad voice with a sigh. "You call her your 'friend,' but you'd like to do much more than 'homework' with her, wouldn't you? A different sort of *home-work*, am I right?"

"Who the hell are you?"

"Am I right?"

"It's none of your business!"

"Am I right, big brother?"

"My mother put you up to this. It's a pretty stupid joke."

For answer he felt a knot in his gut, another touch of the "Amys."

"I don't enjoy making you feel uncomfortable," said the voice, "but when I think of the pain you've caused *me*—and *Mom*—"

"You're a nut case! Who gave you my number?" shouted Jamie.

"Oh, I've had your 'number' for quite some time."

"I didn't hear a ring. How come you—"

"Ex*cuse me!* Next time I'll be more polite."

"Polite?" gasped Jamie. "What's this got to do with being—"

"Listen, big brother, in spite of everything, I guess on some deep level I still love you. Otherwise, why would I bother to warn you?"

"Warn me about what?" said Jamie, holding the phone out at arm's length in front of him.

"Restrain your animal instincts—or you'll wind up having an accident."

"Who the hell do you think you are? I guess I'll just… shut you up," said Jamie. He clicked the button for ending a call, then snapped the phone shut and glared at it.

The wind kicked up. It was not a cold wind, but Jamie shuddered as if freezing. His thoughts ran to Trisha, to the warmth of her arm against his, to the slide of her hand over his as they both held up the book they were studying. The click of that button had restored the world to normality, to the reality of trees and cracked pavement and creeping leaves—but not for long.

"I see you can't lift your thoughts out of the gutter," said the voice, unaffected by Jamie's hanging up, "and I don't doubt *she's* leading you on, but it's up to *you* to break it off. Stop seeing her. Stop sneaking, big brother. Out of love for you, I give you advance warning. Good night."

"Warning about what? What 'accident'?" Jamie stared at the clam-like object in his hand as if it were alive, as if it could at any moment fly off like a witch in the night. "Don't call any more," he threatened the inert phone, sounding stupid even to himself, "or I'll have you traced!"

He thrust the phone back into his knapsack and walked on home feeling quivers aplenty, but no outright pains, in his stomach. Trying to put aside the threatening content of the call, he focused his thoughts on the technical shocks it gave him—the discovery, for example, that his cell had a built-in speaker-phone function that he hadn't known anything about.

⊙━▌◄·   ·►▐━⊙

Jamie, of course, never for one moment entertained the idea of not continuing to see Trisha. After another week of doing homework together they exchanged their first mouth-on-mouth kiss, Jamie's first ever. He could not tell who initiated it, but the sweet shiver it sent through him was followed by a pang of guilt—and an accompanying knife-like stab in the gut—which he ignored as they kissed again. His face felt flushed, and Trisha felt very warm in his arms. He wanted to hold her even closer, drink in the heady odor of her hair, run his fingers down her back… but just at that moment his phone began to ring. His backpack lay on the rug within reach of the couch where they sat.

"My mother!" he snarled, shaking his head.

"Do you have to answer it?" said Trisha, breathing unevenly.

"I'd better. But it's always the same shit," said Jamie, shrugging his shoulders yet plucking the phone up anyway. "Yes, Mom?" he said after clicking the receiver button.

"Hello, Jamie. I listened to you, see? I *rang* first, just as you wanted me to."

Jamie looked up at Trisha, who clearly could not hear the strange voice. It had opted this time not to use the speaker mode, a function not even mentioned in the manual, which he had scoured from cover to cover.

"Leave me alone. I'm in the middle of homework," he said.

"I listened to you, Jamie. But you did not listen to me."

"Hello?" said Jamie. "Can't hear you. Lost the connection."

"I gave you fair warning, brother. You've done *too much* homework. Gone too far. I do love you, Jamie… but now I'm sad for you, big brother."

Hanging up, Jamie rammed the phone back into his pack. All week long he had wondered whether that voice would ever contact him again. She sure knew how to choose the right moment! he thought, pissed with himself for having answered the phone at all. But it could have been his mother—she once *had* called while he was with Trisha—and he did not want to appear to be avoiding her probes. It would only lead to another evening of dinner poisoned with punishing silences and a subsequent bout of retching. Next time, however, especially if he was with Trisha, he'd let it ring its damn head off!

"That was short," said Trisha.

"Thank God."

"Do you have to go now?"

"Not right away." He would have liked to pick up where he'd left off with Trisha, but the mood was broken. He'd also have liked to let Trisha know about this stalker who'd ruined their first moment of intimacy, but if he did, she might think he was crazy.

"Is your mother coming to the game tomorrow?"

"You've got to be kidding," Jamie snorted.

⊙═╾ ╼═⊙

The game with Allbridge High was to be a turning point in Jamie's high-school basketball career. Allbridge was his school's chief rival, but the coach had developed such confidence in him that he assigned him the position of center, where he'd be literally bumping up against some of the toughest players in the circuit.

Bumping was one thing, but a serious collision that would dislocate Jamie's right shoulder as well as sprain his right knee was another. Thus it happened that ten minutes into the second half of a game that Jamie's team was winning, he found himself suddenly on the floor beneath the basket, writhing with pain, and looking up into the worried eyes of his coach and players from both sides. Soon people ran up with bags of ice, and a few minutes later an EMT team trundled him off to an ambulance, his coach running beside him yelling, "Don't worry, Jamie, you'll be fine."

He wound up in a hospital emergency room. Someone, probably his coach, had thought to send along his clothes and backpack from his locker. The attending physician who made the preliminary estimate of his injuries laughed when Jamie, somewhat dizzy and temporally disoriented, asked how soon he could get back into the game. "You'll be okay," he said, "but you'll be out for the rest of the season." After bandaging Jamie up, he left the curtained bay, and Jamie wondered if anyone had let his mother know what had happened. His body pulsed with pain. He had no doubt that she'd be there soon, shaking her head, mouthing the expected I-told-you-so's, letting him know in uncertain terms that he had hurt her far more than himself.

She was certainly taking her time, thought Jamie. Tears came to his eyes as he pictured her deliberately staying at home, making him wait, giving him time to fully assess the results of his disobedience. When the phone rang, he grabbed for it from the bedside console with his good left arm, flipped it open and clicked. "Hello?" he said, holding it to his ear.

"You could have been killed," said the voice he had hoped never again to hear. "Maybe the thought doesn't bother you, my brother, but doesn't it occur to you that you would have killed me as well?"

"You're already dead. You were never alive. You're a phantom!" Jamie shouted, deciding to end the call.

But *she* wasn't ready to end the call. "Your stomach hurts too, Jamie, doesn't it?"

"So what if it does!"

"I might just have more than one way to get *through* to you, brother." The voice was clear but fainter now that he'd retracted the phone a hand-span from his ear.

"For shit's sake," said Jamie, "why didn't I think of it before… to get rid of you…" Using his thumb to dislodge the knurled cover from the back of the phone, he disconnected the battery and tossed it onto the floor.

"You okay?" said a passing doctor, peeking in.

"I'm fine!" said Jamie, staring at the blank, dead face of the phone. He pressed various buttons with his thumb. Nothing, of course, happened. The little unlit window reflected the ceiling light. He snapped shut the eviscerated phone.

"How much more do you want to make Mother suffer, Jamie?"

The voice that emerged from the little sandwich now sounded somewhat muffled.

Jamie dashed the phone to the tiled floor.

◖══◦◦ ◦◦══◗

No more did Jamie spend sweet afternoons with Trisha. They remained casual friends through high school, but given the fact that their relationship had hardly gotten started, neither wound up missing the other very much. Though Jamie had had few friends at the time of his accident, as time went on he had even fewer. One reason was that he had gotten rid of his cell phone (much to his mother's unavailing dismay). More to the point, he tended to avoid his former teammates, with whom he felt no longer connected, and thereby sacrificed abundant opportunities to develop relationships with girls. He would often enough hear his former locker-mates brag about their conquests, and in truth, he envied them deeply, picturing the hot bodies of girls in his classes in poses of nude abandon, deliriously making love with guys no more attractive than he was.

When he did get the chance to make out with a willing girl, however, the raw images of sexual encounters that friends of his had described to him would pop into his head and, instead of urging him on, *prevent* him from using simple kissing as a springboard to serious petting. It was not that such moments of sizzling temptation would always be accompanied by abdominal distress, but sometimes they did seem to bring on those dreaded pains—even when he wasn't with a girl. Sometimes it just took *thinking* about a girl, about unleashing on her beautiful body the ravenous wolf within him. Among girls, therefore, he soon developed a reputation for being, at best, a perfect gentleman, but far more likely a crypto-queer. Some girls even made bets to see who could get him to drop his pants, and though he could sense their stalwart efforts and even secretly wish them success, the unhappy outcome for Jamie was always that no one managed to undo his mental zipper.

Even after recovering perfectly well from his injuries, Jamie could not be induced to engage in contact sports of any sort whatsoever. Now and then he was powerfully tempted to try out for baseball or football, but the very idea would unleash butterflies in his stomach that seemed to have razor-tipped wings. He continued to excel in his studies, however, with particular strength in biology. By his junior year he had decided that in college he would major in Phys Ed and become a high-school gym teacher. Working out at the gym provided a much-needed outlet for all his pent-up physical energies, and soon he found himself seriously committed to body-building. Not only did he enjoy the discipline involved, and the macho rhetoric of "no pain, no gain," but he felt on some deep level the need to barricade himself behind a solid wall of muscle from the glancing smiles, arched brows, and whispered insinuations of his schoolmates both male and female.

To his mother this new passion of his seemed harmless enough. No threat of brutal collisions here, no need to fear for the life of her precious flesh and blood. As for Jamie, devotion to a sport that gave his mother no cause for worry—why, could a better compromise be found, one that satisfied everyone, even himself? Carla even allowed him to have a small basement gym at home, even paid for the equipment, but most of Jamie's evenings and weekends, after his homework was done, he'd spend at the local World Gym, where he picked up endless tips on exercise routines and dieting schemes that would further a new ambition now knocking around in his head. He was determined to get in shape to enter a state-wide body-building contest.

Almost everyone at the gym was older than he, and as Jamie put on muscle he drew proportionately more attention and was treated with more respect—particularly by the "elite," that small circle of workout freaks who hung out together and would deign to take note of the existence of others (all those soft-bodied, chit-chatting jokers) only when others got in their way, used *their* machine, occupied *their* bench, and tested the limits of their patience by making them suck up, as Jamie saw it, doses of much-needed *wait*-training. The elite included several men and two or three women who themselves had competed in local or regional contests, and these few began to regard Jamie with an almost proprietary air. They noted his seriousness and would talk to him in part because he paid no undue attention to them, did not try to enter their magic circle, asked no amateurish questions—certainly none intended to start conversations—

and yet visibly took to heart their casually offered advice while mostly he stayed walled up within the double cocoon of his workout routine and the hypnotic beat of music from his MP3.

The most prominent distractions were those leggy, tight-bunned beauties who flooded the gym with pheromones, loving all the attention and therefore shunning the Women's Section. While many of the guys would freeze in place, swiveling their heads like compass needles to track the lilt of their shorts, Jamie would work all the harder. His utter dedication would often draw an admiring comment from precisely one of those shapely babes to whom he'd been paying no mind. The mirror-clad walls existed for him to check on himself, not to sneak an oblique peek at a frontal view of some girl with a tear-drop butt burning rubber on a treadmill. He knew that once he succumbed to such distractions his energy output would fall and he would fail to achieve that tough last rep before "failure" (which in gym-speak means success).

Developing those much-desired "washboard abs" was Jamie's most difficult challenge. Try as he might, those rock-hard ridges would no more than hint at their presence beneath that stubborn last layer of teenage belly fat. To his aid came a member of the inner circle. Lisa, a honey-blonde older woman (age twenty-one) was also in training for an upcoming contest. Having previously won in a state-wide competition, she was now gearing up for the regionals—not for one of those tits-and-ass "fitness" affairs, as she put it, but for a serious women's body-building contest where muscle-mass mattered most.

Since their workout schedules jibed, she was happy to suggest the right kinds of protein supplements and exercise sequences to help him reach his goal. Soon they began working out together, each encouraging the other to squeeze that last rep out before caving in with a triumphant groan to "failure." When Jamie looked at Lisa's body he saw it as she wanted it seen, as a sculpture in progress, not as an object of feminine allure. The thought did cross his mind, of course, that she was deliberately undercutting her femininity, of which she still could vaunt plenty because she'd been out of serious training for nearly a year, and he could not help noticing the sweet sweat-smell her underarms exuded when he hovered over her, spotting her on her bench-press.

Jamie struggled valiantly to focus on their mutual goals, but at times each seemed to be homing in a lot more personally on the other, and it did not help when Lisa took advantage of his growing susceptibility by hugging him upon his successful completion of a particularly grueling set.

While Lisa's femininity proved unnerving enough, far more worrisome was Jamie's recognition that no matter what he did, those coveted six-pack abs refused to materialize.

A week before the competition Lisa tried all she could to help Jamie conquer that last hurdle to a perfectly shredded figure. He took all her advice about sodium and carbs and water and diet. Increasing his cardio, Jamie ran the treadmill till he was ready to faint. Two days before the contest, with Lisa on the machine beside him, and the music from his MP3 drumming at his ear, a dehydrated Jamie was pushing himself well beyond his normal point of exhaustion.

A voice, however, interrupted the stream of Latin-accented rock, and it said, "Go for it, big boy! Knock yourself out!" Jamie assumed that it was Lisa being ironically supportive, and that his MP3 had conked out.

He looked to his left at Lisa, who winked and smiled back as "her" voice continued, "Look at that hot body, all for the asking, why don't you ask, big brother? Afraid you'll lose your primary focus—on your desire to kill yourself?"

Jamie's scalp bristled at the shock of recognition. Each stinging, sneering sentence arose like a whiff out of a long-abandoned sewer.

"Killing yourself is one thing," she continued, "but you've got family to consider, big brother, and if I didn't love you as much as I do—though I can hardly say you deserve—"

"Die, bitch!" Jamie blurted, stumbling off the treadmill.

"What?" said Lisa, scrunching her brows at him.

Jamie pointed to the MP3 strapped to his bicep. He pulled the plug from his ear, then from the base of the device, and stuffed the unruly player into the pocket of his sweatpants. Lisa shrugged her shoulders, having no idea what he was motioning about. "Come on," she said, "another five minutes!"

As Jamie prepared to re-board, his stomach muscles decided to twist and contract. Pulling up his shirt, he could literally see them moving. There they danced, the six-pack he'd been living for, taking on a life of their own, completely out of his control. Suddenly they seemed to knot together into a single ugly lump, and the pain was so unbearable that Jamie slumped unconscious to the floor, rapping his head against the metal base of the treadmill to his right as he fell.

"You never told *me* you were training for a competition," his mother complained at his hospital bedside as soon as he could manage to sit up without fainting from vertigo.

"You'd have done all you could to stop me," he replied with bitterness. He had suffered a concussion bad enough to rob him of any hope of entering the contest.

"There you go again, thinking only of yourself," she snuffled, "never thinking how you could have hurt me."

"Or your daughter?" said Jamie.

"What could you possibly mean?" said Carla, raising her hand to her chest.

"Why won't either of you ever let me be myself? Why?" demanded Jamie.

Mrs. Masters stepped back from the bed, on which she had deposited a couple of news magazines and a box of cheap chocolates from the ground-floor gift-shop. "Well," she hmphed, "you certainly *aren't* yourself—at least, not yet. I'll be back for you when the doctors say it's okay for you to come home."

"But Ma, all I'm saying is—" A sob rose in his throat as Jamie glanced after the frail, stumbling, retreating figure of his mother. She left behind a strong, cool whiff of flowers, of fresh-mown flowers. He loved that smell, but in a different way from the way he loved the smell from Lisa's armpits. He didn't think he'd get her so angry that she'd leave without giving him a ceremonial embrace or at least a couple of pats on the head.

"Get well, dear. See you soon, dear," she said with a long-suffering shake of the head, her lips pressed thinly together and her eyelids brimming with hurt as she slipped with a sigh through the door.

Jamie tossed the box of chocolates after her, hitting the closed door, then gripped both magazines in his veiny fists and tore them neatly in two.

❦

Although continuing to work out at the gym, Jamie lost the ambition to train hard enough to get into shape for any future competitions. Lisa focused on her own forthcoming ordeal and worked out exclusively with one of the "inner-circle" guys, a contest veteran himself. Jamie now stood aloof from the whole pack. How could he have become so self-destructively obsessive, he wondered, just to lose a final two pounds of fat? His goal now was to work even harder at his studies—with the aim of winning a scholarship to some top-rated college for Physical Education—preferably, if he could help it, some very far out-of-state college. If so highly disciplined a life left him little time to hang out and get something going with girls, he had already decided that he would much prefer older, more mature girls of the sort he would meet in college. And anyway, he had little in common with girls of about his own age. They were all into music and rock stars and this or that marginal or upcoming "group," and Jamie had lost interest in all that. It was "typical teenage crap," in his opinion, and he had left all that behind when he had retired his MP3.

But Jamie's hermit-like devotion to studies backfired on him in the middle of his junior year. He would find himself staring at the same page for an hour, his mind thousands of miles away. After a while, he discovered that the only way to shake off his trance was to slouch in front of the living-room TV. But this growing habit soon brought him into conflict with Carla, who resented having to sacrifice any of her favorite evening shows, like the food-channel and home-make-over programs that gave her lots of "ideas," she'd tell Jamie, but never resulted in her re-arranging furniture or cooking a single new dish. Jamie's specialized tastes—war movies and full-body contact sports—did not garner Carla's approval either, and occasionally she would taunt him as well, asking him why his own viewing habits hadn't inspired him to join the NFL or charge a machine-gun nest. Remarks like that did not sit well with Jamie. He still envied former friends of his who numbered among the school's top athletes. In reaction to Carla's gibes, it took all the self-control he could muster to keep from knocking the snack tray over or to dam up a retort that he knew he'd come to regret.

The viewing conflict resolved itself when Carla got him a TV for his room. It was a decision she found rather difficult to make because she clearly had good reason to be concerned about its effect on his studies. Jamie reassured her that all was going well at school, but in fact, academically, he was sliding downhill. His applications to various colleges resulted in his not receiving a single scholarship offer. No longer could he hide from either his mother or himself the depths to which he had sunk. Worse yet, right after he graduated, his eighteenth birthday sneaked up on him and found him totally clueless about what to do with his life.

Pressed by his mother to get a job, Jamie did not want just any old job. He wanted to do something meaningful. Ironically, Carla's stinging little taunts together with the news about the conflict in Iraq had been propelling him to fantasize about front-line combat duty against America's terrorist enemy. Certain that one man *could* make a difference, he explored a host of military sites on his laptop computer, homing in finally on the toughest of the services, the Marine Corps. But would *they* be interested in *him*? To find out, he visited the local recruitment center. The clean-cut, bullet-headed officer in charge treated Jamie like a customer with a million bucks to spend. He assured him that a smart high-school grad like himself—and in top physical shape, no less—would make a great addition to the Corps. What's more, he'd have a whole year—after signing up and committing himself, of course—to stay at home and prepare himself in body and spirit for the rigors of Recruit Training that would transform him in a mere thirteen weeks from an ordinary civilian Joe into a world-class Warrior, the pride of a grateful nation.

"Talk it over with your parents," the dapper recruiter suggested, loading Jamie down with reading materials that would answer most of his questions.

"I want in. I know I want in," said Jamie, gushing with enthusiasm. Then, just as suddenly, his shoulders drooped and his voice trailed off. "But I know my mother won't let me."

"But you're eighteen, Jamie. You don't need parental consent."

"I don't?" said Jamie, straightening up. Disbelief evaporated under the rays of a dawning smile. "Where are the papers? I'll sign."

<hr/>

Jamie made new friends among his fellow recruits. He met them periodically during the process of instruction and physical conditioning prerequisite to actual boot camp. To support himself during this year of preparation, Jamie took a low-paying maintenance job at a gym where few people knew him. He preferred to work evenings, to keep from having to deal with his mother, who often stared at him reproachfully as though she knew he had something to hide. He knew what she was thinking: that he was going out behind her back with some slut, just like his father. It didn't matter whom he went out with, nor how respectful his behavior and even his thoughts, his mother's tight-lipped face would be there hovering over his shoulder, and he was sure the girl could see through him too and was all set for his next "move"—which he managed to refrain from making, but at great cost to any budding relationship.

He could have gone out with any number of girls, and he was often sorely tempted, but wouldn't that have undermined his concentrated devotion to becoming a United States Marine? That true secret of his, vowed Jamie, his mother would find out only on the day he left for camp.

When Jamie did spend time with his mother—for he could not avoid her entirely—her presence made him feel queasy, and his stomach began to translate what he knew could be nothing but an exaggerated sense of guilt. His abdominal distress, "the Amys," increased over the next several months. They seemed to go away during his frequent, prolonged workouts, but then began to invade even those bouts of heavy training that were absolutely essential if he were to meet the expectations of the Corps. Diagnosing himself with various stomach ailments that he read about or saw in TV commercials, he began to medicate himself with any number of over-the-counter drugs. They didn't work, however, and perhaps even worsened his condition. "No pain, no gain," however, and he persisted in toughing it out. Tears would spring from his eyes during a set of squats or crunches, and sometimes he'd just drop a barbell in a panic and run to the toilet to puke.

Jamie hid his condition from his recruiter, passed his final mental and physical tests, and then, only a few weeks before boot camp, noticed a lumpy swelling in the region of his stomach that did not go away when the pains went away. On the contrary, the distortion grew larger, and though he tried to cover it up by wearing long black T-shirts, he feared that by now his workout buddies had noticed and were whispering and chuckling behind his back. At first he would spin around to confront them, but either he did not turn fast enough to catch them, or else there would be no one there at all, and the only thing to do was to chalk it all up to stress.

Alone in his room, Jamie now dreaded to check himself out in the full-length mirror that up till now had witnessed only his uninterrupted progress toward Marine-quality perfection. He was looking into a fun-house mirror now, and the canned sounds of cackling seemed to accompany his self-disgust. But the worst was to occur only a week before his planned date of departure, when the expanding abdominal lump caused him such severe pain that he cried out in agony and dropped, writhing, to the living room floor in the presence of his horrified mother. Carla, wasting no time, and paying no heed to Jamie's garbled objections, summoned an ambulance.

Lying once again in a hospital bed, his mother sitting with folded arms in the far corner of the room, Jamie felt another sharp quiver as the white-frocked, gray-haired doctor returned holding a large manila envelope from which he extracted some papers and a couple of outsized pictures.

"The good news is," Doctor Bellman smiled, "that you do not have a tumor, as we feared.... Instead, you have something quite operable."

"And the bad news, doctor?" said Jamie, gripping the metal rod at the side of his bed.

"Oh, it's not so much a matter of bad news, young man. It's what you might call weird news. These pictures show"—and he held them up before the uncomprehending eyes of Jamie and Carla, who stepped up to take a look—"that the growth in your abdomen is a fetus."

"A fetus?" cried Jamie. "Are you saying I'm freakin' pregnant?"

"Not at all!" the doctor laughed. "This is your twin—a second fetus that never had a chance to develop on its own because it got trapped inside of *you*."

Carla grasped the bedrail. Her face turned white. "Then what they told me at the hospital... eighteen years ago... it was all true." Stifling a sob, she waved away the pictures and sank back in her plastic seat.

"Are you okay, Mrs. Masters?"

Carla, lost in thought, wouldn't answer.

"That's Jamie," said Jamie, pointing at a foot-long oval object of contrasting areas of light and dark that occupied the center of one of the photos. "That was supposed to be Jamie. Do you get it?"

"Sort of," said Dr. Bellman, glancing once again at Carla, who sat stone-faced and rigid and stared up at the ceiling.

"When you were nothing but a blastocyst—and that's pretty tiny," said the doctor, "you wrapped around your twin, who grew up inside you in its own sort of placenta and has been feeding itself from your bloodstream all your life. Sometimes it doesn't get noticed for years, but eventually it causes serious problems, as in your case, and has to be removed."

"Is it... a human being?" asked Jamie.

"A partial, stunted wannabe," said the doctor.

"Once you remove it, can it grow up into a—?"

"No, Jamie. It cannot grow outside of you. It's essentially a *parasite*."

"Like a tapeworm?"

"Sort of," said the doctor. "Totally dependent on its host."

At which Carla rose and strode toward the door. "I'll be waiting outside," she said, spitting the words through her teeth, slamming the door behind her.

"I can understand why she'd be disturbed," said Bellman.

"I doubt it," said Jamie.

"She needs to be reassured. You're going to come out of this just fine," said the doctor. "If it gives you any comfort, you're going to go down in medical history."

"I couldn't care less about medical history."

"Cases like yours are extremely rare. Not even ninety in the whole literature. Normally this growth would have been noticed and removed before your second birthday."

"I think it had good reason to act up just when it did," said Jamie.

"Really?" grinned Bellman. "Perhaps they finally need to stretch their legs." Jamie didn't laugh. The doctor continued: "In case you think your case is strange, there's one on record of a man in Italy who didn't find out he had one till he was forty-seven years old."

"Do they have… intelligence?" asked Jamie, squinting from the jab in the gut that his "parasite" had just then inflicted.

Bellman laughed and examined the pictures. "This one has a clearly developed torso, four stumpy limbs, possibly some hair and facial features too, like teeth."

"A face?" said Jamie, shuddering, unable to see anything like a face— an Amy/Jamie face—in those blurry prints.

"But it doesn't have a heart," said Bellman. "They never do, since your own arteries supply them with blood—and it's doubtful that any of them ever develop much brain tissue either."

"But she could be hooked into *my* brain, couldn't she, Doctor?"

"She?"

"Isn't it a she?"

"The sex organs," said Bellman, "never had a chance to develop. But a *fetus in fetu*—that's what they call this, a fetus inside a fetus—is always an identical twin, always the sex of the successful twin, which is you."

As Jamie tried to adjust to such an improbable bit of news, he felt as if a strong hand was trying to uproot his intestines. Bellman saw right through his stoical façade.

"That thing in you has no mercy, Jamie. It'll take you down with it if you let it, and very soon."

"And you're telling me it has no intelligence?"

"Does a cancer have intelligence? You'd better get this removed real quick."

"How soon can you operate?" said Jamie. He'd been having a vision of himself lagging behind his platoon, but now he suddenly saw himself catching up.

"I can fit you in tomorrow evening."

Just one more day, he said to himself, and he'd be rid of that bloodsucking parasite that had plagued him all of his life. He knew very well why she had chosen just now to act up. Soon she would meddle no more.

"Yes, I definitely… I'll talk it over with my mother," Jamie mumbled.

"Of course," said the doctor. "It's only about noon now. Here's my card. You can get dressed and go. And don't forget these pain pills. One every four hours and two to get you through the night. As soon as you decide, call my office—but no later than five p.m."

Bellman left the room and Jamie sat up in bed. His clothes lay folded on a bedside chair, and as he reached for them, the phone on the bedside table rang. Calling to tell him where she was, he supposed.

"Hello?" he said.

"Hey, big brother. You really aren't going to swallow that bunk—that I'm not even human, are you?"

Jamie slammed the receiver down. He waited many seconds. Silence! Finally, unable to resist picking it up again, he stealthily put it to his ear.

"You know *better* than Bellman, Jamie," the indignant voice exploded into his ear.

He thought he would just hang up again, but anger trumped common sense. "Who cares if you're human? They found your ugly ass," he shouted, "and you heard what the doctor said. You're nothing but a goddamn parasite!"

"A parasite? But I've earned my keep. I've always kept you pure, and safe from harm, haven't I? And now because I care for you *so much*, Jamie, because I love you so much that I'm signaling you again, signaling the best way I know how, trying not to let you get killed—now you want to *turn* on me!"

"I'm going to boot camp. You're not going to stop me."

"I'm not thinking of myself, Jamie. I'm thinking about Mother. It'll kill her, what you're planning. One of us has to think about Mother."

"Mother only thinks about herself."

"She loves you, we both love you, brother."

"You love me so much that you're ruining my life. I'd rather die in battle than be killed by you."

"It's okay to be angry at someone who only wants to protect you, brother. But don't go through with it. Tear up the doctor's card, Jamie, my love, my one and only—"

Jamie slammed down the receiver, bent forward and pulled on his jeans. The effort hurt, and he fell back on the bed. Just as he tried to push himself up, a female nurse (or doctor: he couldn't tell which) wandered into the room, saw him in distress, and rushed over to help him sit up straight. Jamie was doing fine on his own, but her golden hair and strong sweet scent made him fake sudden weakness... so that she hurried over, caught him around the shoulders, and crushed him against her white-coated breast.

But just as her soft bosom nuzzled his chest, his "Amys" acted up again. He groaned and pushed the woman aside, breathing through his mouth in order not to be swamped by her overpowering scent. Doubled over, Jamie pressed his forearms into his churning, raging middle.

"Should I call for Dr. Bellman?" she asked.

"No, no. I'm fine. I don't need help. I'll be dressed and out in a minute."

"You sure?"

"It was just a twinge. I'll be fine."

⊕═‹‹ ››═⊕

Jamie's mother hurried to her car in the emergency parking lot. Despite the wrenching pain, Jamie kept right up behind her.

"Mom," he said, "isn't that what I *have* to do—get it done right away?"

She didn't turn, she didn't answer.

"I'm covered by your insurance, right?"

She rummaged in her bag for her keys.

"Aren't you glad it isn't a freakin' *tumor*?" he shouted.

"I've had enough of that vulgar language," she muttered without turning around. "What must that doctor think of me? That I raised you in a pigsty?"

⊕═‹‹ ››═⊕

For a couple of hours Jamie paced in his room, the pain subsiding, but always letting him know it was there, ready to flare up at whim. To inform himself as much as possible as to the nature of his condition, he resorted to his laptop and called up several Web pages devoted to *fetus in fetu* —usually in medical mumbo-jumbo—and detailing several cases resembling his own. All required surgical removal to save the life of the host.

There was nothing more to be said, then. Jamie picked up Dr.

Bellman's card. As he got up from his desk to go downstairs for the phone, he noticed a lone Web site among those he'd googled that he hadn't yet checked out. He clicked on it, and in place of the search page got a blank, black screen. No doubt a dead page, he thought—except for the sounds. Nothing visual, only sounds. Infant cries followed by gurgling, choking noises as of someone gasping desperately for breath. Mesmerized, Jamie expected he'd soon see some corresponding images.

Instead: "These aren't sounds that would come from *me* when they start to cut me out of you, Jamie. Oh, no. You are listening to your own baby, as I imagine it drowning in its own little pool of blood—the baby *you* planted inside of me."

Jamie's scalp tingled as if his hair had caught fire.

"Haven't you known for a long, long time, dear brother, dear lover, that I alone have harbored and protected and nurtured those precious vital juices of yours that all those little flirts you've known, those selfish little tricksters, have never been able to extract from you?... So now you have a baby of your *own* to raise, and if you kill its mother, your sister, your wife, you kill our love-child too."

This is absolutely crazy! thought Jamie. Who could "love" something that was killing him? One or the other's got to go! And now, a fetus *inside* a fetus in fetu? The idea of some kind of gastrointestinal incest—could anything be more ridiculous?... but could he deny that his sperm ducts were so close to that lump, that deformity, that...

"So think twice, then, dear brother, dear lover."

Lying, self-serving leech! thought Jamie.

And the monitor suddenly displayed another normal medical site—which again pointed out the only course of action available to the afflicted host.

So Jamie did *not* have to "think twice." Dr. Bellman's card in hand, he rushed downstairs to make the call.

⊛━← →━⊛

"Is she gone?" were Jamie's first words on awakening and staring into Bellman's bright gray eyes.

"Completely. It'll take you a while to heal, but you'll be as good as new in a couple of weeks."

"A couple of weeks!" Disappointment dropped like lead on Jamie's chest. "How long have I been out, Doctor?"

"A few hours. You still have time for visitors. It's six o'clock now. Visitors can stay till eight.

"My mom? Where is *she*?" Jamie strained his neck to search the corners of his room, where he saw an empty chair. He also noticed, standing at the foot of his bed, the same white-frocked blonde who had happened in on him and smothered him in her scent the day before. This time, as he basked in the memory of her smell and the soft press of her breasts, no demonic hand reached out and twisted the coils of his gut. Was it the result of anesthesia? Then he wished the anesthesia could be permanent.

"Ah yes," said Bellman, "as to visitors… your recruiting officer dropped by. He left you a copy of *Marine* magazine and told me to tell you you'll be welcome for training at Parris Island as soon as you're fully recovered and fit for duty again."

"He said that?"

"Yes he did."

"I called him before I came here," said Jamie. "I told him I was having some surgery but should be able to ship out with the guys at the end of the week."

"Well, he knew better, and I guess he didn't want you to worry."

Tears blurred Jamie's eyes. He'd *kill* for that man, for *all* those gung-ho buddies of his! A distressing thought, however, snaked across his mind. "For Pete's sake, Doctor, was my *mother* here when he came by?"

"As far as I know, they didn't cross paths."

"She came by and left *before* he showed up, then?"

"Well, yes," said Bellman, exchanging a funny look with the blonde.

"What's going on?" said Jamie.

"Your mother came by to *object* to the operation—when we were halfway through. I'm sure she was just worried about your well-being."

"I'll bet she's on her way right now," said the blonde assistant.

"She has a thing about hospitals," said Jamie, desperate to conceal his shame. "A phobia."

"Oh?" said Bellman.

"I have a dumb question," said Jamie, eager to change the subject. "When you took out my… parasite, was there anything peculiar about it? I mean, was it just another normal *fetus in fetu*, or was there…"

"Funny you should mention it," said Bellman. "It did have sort of an attachment… pressed so close up against it that at first it seemed embedded in it."

"An attachment?" said Jamie.

"A squooshed-up sac containing parts of another—but comparatively very undeveloped—fetus. Most likely what we call a dermoid cyst. Not all that uncommon. What made you ask?"

"I thought I felt it kicking," Jamie quipped. The doctor and the blonde burst out in brief laughter.

"Well, I'll look in on you later," said Bellman, reaching out and shaking Jamie's hand. "Ouch! Hell of a grip!... Okay, I'll leave you in the much softer hands of Miss Burton. She'll make sure you're comfortable."

⊕=◄∘ ∘►=⊕

When Bellman departed, Jamie began to stare in fascination at the momentarily captive blonde, running his eyes, over and over, from her full red lips down to her full curvaceous hips. Miss Burton, replying with an increasingly forced smile, then turned aside to putter with objects on the bedside table.

When her back was to Jamie, who couldn't stop staring, he rolled up his *Marine* magazine into a cylinder. He felt suddenly free—to think, and to feel, any damn way he pleased! With his right hand he reached out beside him for a plastic cup of water with a bent straw protruding. But instead of lifting it to his mouth, he "accidentally" knocked it over so that it would land just in front of the blonde while her shapely back was still turned toward the bed.

Predictably, Miss Burton bent down to pick it up. Leaning to the right, his timing perfect, Jamie thrust his paper poker into the crack of her behind.

"My God!" she shouted, springing up, her face almost as red as her soft luscious lips. "Behave yourself, you little jerk!" Slapping the unspilled cup back on the table, she strode out of the room shaking her head. Jamie stiffened, expecting any moment to feel that punishing knife in the gut... that *should* have stabbed him *before* his thoughts issued in thrilling action.

He waited and waited, slowly relaxing, finally to realize that at last he was *free*!

By way of confirmation, he grabbed the remote and clicked from channel to channel, giving "her" plenty of time to commandeer the tube, to speak, to chastise, if she still had the power. But the news remained the news, and Rambo remained obstinately Rambo.

⊕=◄∘ ∘►=⊕

Apart from the TV, the room remained silent and unvisited. As daylight dimmed through the window slats, Jamie felt a rising tension in his chest. Breathing was hard and came out tremulous, like extended sighs. As the hands of the clock on the wall in front of him crept along to eight, his lungs seemed about to burst. He strained to catch the least movement in the corridor behind the glass of his cubicle's door. She still had not come. Had she gotten into an accident—caused, of course, by him? Was she already there, wandering about the hospital, unable to find his room? But no, all she had to do was ask at the front desk.

At eight-fifteen they let her in. They saw he was still awake and winked at the rules.

"They say you'll be fine," she said, standing a few feet from his bed. "I suppose it had to be done," she whimpered. Her reddened eyelids trembled with tears. She carried no gifts in her hands, only her old brown leather purse, which she seemed reluctant to set down.

"Put your bag down on the bed, Mom," said Jamie. After a moment's hesitation, she drew closer in and complied.

"Aren't you going to ask me how I feel, Mom?"

Looking down at him, pursing her lips, she said, "Have you thought of asking how *I* feel?"

"Aren't you going to at least give me a hug, Mom?" asked Jamie, lying back on his raised pillows. He stretched out his arms to embrace her.

Carla glanced at the door as if to make sure there was no one loitering outside who could spy on an intimate act. As she bent stiffly down, Jamie grabbed her around the neck and pulled her hard against him. He hugged her fiercely, unremittingly, her face against his chest, her mouth pressed closed. She tried to emit sounds, but Jamie pressed even tighter. He pressed and he pressed, minutes on end, and tears sprung to his eyes at the thought that she'd finally come, and at that wonderful scent of hers, that cool, earthy scent of freshly crushed flowers.

Lyonel Unbound

Lyonel Lambert sat sipping coffee in the quietest corner of the lounge, his battered briefcase on the floor to his right, and a black plastic bag, into which his wife had tossed his clothes, to his left. Near the refreshment table, in the busiest corner of the lounge, sat Rod Stillback, pretending not to have noticed him, while knowing full well he had Lyonel's fate in the grip of his gym-callused hands.

It was awkward to be handed a bag full of one's clothes by one's departmental secretary upon returning from lunch, but the same thing had happened to Lyonel a couple of times before. He had almost expected it would happen again, though not on the very day when his whole professional future hung in the balance.

This time, when handing him his bag of clothes, the demure, gray-haired secretary, Madeleine, avoided his eyes as she repeated Laura's icy request: "Would you please remind my husband to deposit these clothes at the Salvation Army drop-off up the street?"

Lyonel was grateful for her studied casualness. He knew she felt especially bad for him today because she knew what else was facing him.

A sympathetic woman, Madeleine looked him over and noticed the purple bruise that bedecked his left temple. "You poor man, where'd you get that?" she asked.

He gave the traditional answer, that he'd bumped into a door. She already regarded him as enough of a schlemiel, so what would he gain by admitting the truth, that Laura had landed a right to his skull?

Left holding the bag, he slouched across the hall into the Rudolph Giuliani Common Lounge, where he always had coffee before his two o'clock class. To avoid looking like a garbage man, he could have first taken the elevator five flights up to his seventh-floor office and stowed the bag there, but his class was on the sixth floor. There was no point running up to his office, then down for a coffee, then dashing back up to the sixth, wasting the precious minutes he needed to prepare himself mentally for the oncoming ordeal—the observation of his two o'clock class by his department chairman, Stillback.

Stillback's tenure recommendation to the Dean would decide whether Lyonel would be kept on for life at this new Brooklyn branch of the university or be dumped, like his clothes, out of the only security that he'd known for the past five years.

Two added irritants now approached from across the room: Charlie Spaso, and that even bigger lug, Tim Buckley, students in the Intro to Poetry class that Stillback was about to observe. After each exam, they wheedled and moaned to get Lyonel to up their grades. Only once did they persuade him to raise a D to as much as a C-. It distressed Lyonel that professors could not have their own watering hole, out of bounds for students.

"Hi, Professor," said bald, thick-necked Spaso, fingering a little gold ring in his ear. "Looks like today's the day, huh?" He winked and tossed an over-the-shoulder glance back toward the corner where Stillback held court.

"We're rootin' for you," said big Tim Buckley, sucking the tuft of hair below his lower lip.

"Big day for you, right?" said Spaso. "Word gets around, and we'd like to do our part to make you look good."

"Really?" Lyonel smiled.

"Sure, why not?" said Buckley. "But, like one hand washes the other, you know? I mean, like—"

The approach of Madeleine put a halt to the conversation.

"Catch you soon, Professor," said Spaso, shuffling off with Buckley across the room.

"Excuse me," said Madeleine, "but I should have offered to hold that bag for you in the office."

"No problem," said Lambert, shaking his head at the unbelievable impudence of those two big-mouth losers.

At the last class meeting, he had announced he'd be observed today. In fact, they would all be observed, but those bozos seemed to know a lot more about its importance for him than it was any of their business to know.

"I've got twelve minutes before class and I'm heading upstairs now anyway, Madeleine."

Gulping down the rest of his coffee, he grabbed both bag and briefcase and hurried out into the corridor. He cut a right towards the nearby elevators and he slipped into one just as the doors began to close.

A female student, seeing that his hands were full, pressed the number seven for him. As the elevator slowly ascended, Lyonel wondered why Laura had decided just this morning to blow up at him when she could have held off for at least another day, knowing what he was up against. He understood the daily stress she was under, counseling battered wives, but that couldn't explain her timing.

Considering himself a reasonably good amateur psychologist, having double-majored in English and Psychology, Lyonel attributed Laura's timing to the near-certainty she felt that he was due for a thumbs-down and she wanted them both to suffer in advance to ease the pain of the inevitable. Now in his mid-forties, having bounced around the city from job to job, he did not offer her very much hope for stability. Nor did he hide from himself that her timing stemmed also from his prolonged neglect of her as he prepared his dossier—in defense of his claim to tenure—to present to a tenure committee headed by Stillback. If there was justice in this world, thought Lyonel, his several articles and one monograph amounted to enough evidence of scholarly competence to impress even a modernism-hater like Stillback, who thought that poetry had pretty much died after Donne.

Stillback had intimated over the years that Lyonel's primary problem was his teaching—a Student Evaluation of Teaching record that had become tilted toward the negative—but he did give Lyonel a specific reason for hope.

"Lambert," he had told him recently, "it would stand you in good stead if the student evaluations of your teaching this semester showed some mild improvement."

What Lyonel did not expect was that Stillback, in an effort at fairness against the murmurings of a cabal of colleagues, would be taking on this last observation himself.

"Seven, sir."

"Thanks," mumbled Lyonel, barely squeezing out with his baggage through the elevator's closing doors.

His closet of an office was packed to the hilt with two chairs, a gray metal desk, and two gray metal bookcases so crammed with dust-covered volumes that the shelves buckled in the middle. After doffing his winter coat and tossing bag and briefcase onto his jammed desk, Lyonel checked the time. Nine to two: time for a visit to the men's room on the sixth floor near his classroom. Rather than enter that class one minute early, he'd have a few minutes after relieving himself to rehearse the introduction to Robert Frost that he had especially designed with Stillback in mind—a succinct and elegant Lambertian refutation of windy anti-modernist prejudices.

Emerging on the sixth floor, he turned right to the men's room halfway down the hall, but not before noting, several doors to his left, a small gathering of students waiting to enter his class.

Inside the restroom, both cubicles were occupied. *Damn*, thought Lyonel. If he was annoyed with lounge facilities that invited the intrusion of students, he found far more upsetting the school's failure to set aside bathrooms for the use of faculty only. He'd have to use one of the wall fixtures, but just now only the middle one was available. It distressed him to think that either of the tall students flanking him might want to sneak a sideways peek to confirm some adolescent judgment of his manhood. In any case, what he couldn't conceal was his bulging, middle-age midriff. While Laura's was a good deal plumper, it matched her overall generous proportions. His own, however, stood out in dismaying contrast to the rest of his lax-muscled, small-boned body. He could suck in his stomach, but he could not repress the thoughts that slowed the flow of his urine. Impeding him more, however, was the disturbing recollection of what he had noticed this morning while seated on the toilet at home: normally, the level of water managed to graze his scrotal sac, but it hadn't today. The implication of such a surprising shortfall was either that (a) a plumbing problem was causing a decline in the water level, or (b) his testicles had been imperceptibly shrinking; if choice (b) were the case, there was no one to blame but that castrating bitch of a wife who had now gone so far as to humiliate him publicly on the day he could least afford it.

He managed to empty about half his bladder when a voice behind him shut him down completely.

"Hi, Professor, we were looking for you," said Spaso.

"We were rudely interrupted downstairs," said Buckley, who stood so close that Lyonel felt his breath on his neck. Looking over his shoulder, he saw not only these two smug assailants, but a gaggle of their equally studious confreres. Though he couldn't pee, he pretended to do his business in total disregard of their presence.

"We've heard about this tenure thing comin' up," said Spaso. "I mean, like, it's all over the school."

"And professors in your department are saying your teaching record could really fuck you over," added Buckley.

"Oh, is that right?" asked Lyonel.

"That's right, Professor. And we think we can help you get through," continued Buckley. "There's five of us here, and another three outside—not your best and brightest—but today we can make you look good."

"Now, that's a laugh!" said Lyonel.

"But you do know we can make you look *bad*," said Spaso. His remark occasioned a general round of snorts, grunts, and sniggers.

"What are you louts driving at?" said Lyonel. "What *you* do in class today won't matter a damn! It's what *I* do that counts."

"Even if you're right about today," said Buckley, "next week you have to administer the Student Evaluations. You could use a really good set, now, couldn't you?"

"That's what we hear," said Spaso.

"And in return," muttered Lyonel, "you want…"

"Well," said Buckley, "we'll even do something for extra credit, but all this shit with those Fs and Ds we've been getting, you know…"

"Can you imagine," someone blurted, "getting an F in a fuckin' poetry course?"

There were murmurs of indignation.

"High Cs and low Bs," said Spaso. "Deal?"

All Lyonel wanted was to get them to leave, to leave him in peace to finish up. Weakly, he shrugged his shoulders and nodded his head.

"That's a yes?" said Spaso. "That's a yes, guys! Thanks, Sport. See you in class."

A slap on Lyonel's back caused the release of a squirt of urine. The mob behind him shuffled out and clattered down the hall.

Zipping up, he felt utterly demoralized. Had he really caved in to their unethical demands? And could he count on those thugs to honor their half of the bargain? And if they did, could they really do him any good? But what about the *principles* involved? What about *integrity*?

Lyonel despised himself. He looked at his protruding little stomach, asked himself what he'd done wrong to reach middle-age and wind up in such a bind, then undid his belt and yanked on it to tighten it back a notch.

And to Lyonel's amazement, the square brass buckle tore off and it clattered down into the urinal.

He scooped it up, unmindful of hygiene, and tried to slip it back on the belt, but there was nothing to hold it in place. The brown leather belt was one he had worn for years; it had become practically part of his body.

Lyonel had hardly recovered from his surprise when, as soon as he ceased sucking in his belly, his pants slid down over his hips. Fortunately at that moment, there was no one around to observe them at his knees, or to watch him jerk them back up and clutch them to his waist under the flap of his brown, tweed jacket.

Leaning against the sink, he washed and dried his hands and his buckle, deposited the buckle in his jacket pocket, and strutted out into the hallway, hitching his pants up with one hand. Under the eyes of students waiting outside his classroom, he turned nonchalantly back into the stairwell, bounded up the echoing steps, and skittered back into his office.

He had the hope that Laura, in her attempt to degrade him, had provided him with the way out of his plight. Rummaging in the plastic bag, he tossed out shirts, pants, shoes, underwear, even those black Victoria's Secret panties that turned out to be three sizes too small which he had recently got her for her birthday.

A belt? No belt, damn it! Ties, then? Sure, why not? A tie would fit. And it would be hidden under his jacket as he lectured. No goddamn ties either! Why couldn't she at least have been logical and thrown him out with a full set of clothes?

Now what to do?

He remembered that there was a gym in the basement, and in the gym, a foul-smelling locker room.

He would be late for class, but how late was the question. Lyonel remembered with relief what certain colleagues had reported about Stillback's observation routine: namely, that he always showed up late, even ten minutes late, presumably to avoid all the attendance-taking and other administrivia that wasted the beginning of most classes.

Lyonel had not a second to spare. Gripping his pants by the waist, he made a lopsided dash out to the stairs. He gripped the cold metal railing and took a deep, tremulous breath. Using the stairs, at least, he was likely to encounter no one. Scurrying down, flight after flight, he swung himself around by the newel at each landing until his twirling descent made him dizzy.

The stairwell stopped at the basement in the corridor outside the gym. He put his ear against the door, heard the floor-pounding of a class in session, and pushed on through.

A class of young men was bouncing through an aerobics routine. With luck, he should run into nobody in the locker room down below.

With a tight grip on his pants, Lyonel scurried towards the exit to the lockers.

Dimly lit, peeling, ochre walls surrounded row upon row of tall, green lockers placed back to back with long benches between. The dank air reeked of sweat.

He stepped down the center aisle with confidence and an increasing sense of urgency. He examined every lock in the hope of finding one open. On some lockers, the full-length doors stood invitingly ajar, but they proved empty. Lyonel knew, though, that in spite of the constant security harangues, he'd soon find one carelessly left open.

He checked his watch. Three minutes past two. If Stillback's behavior conformed to his reputation, Lyonel might even beat him back to class.

He randomly fingered all kinds of locks: padlocks, combination locks, finding them always shut. The quicker method was to zero in only on any that was visibly open, like the one farther down, in the center of the row, that hung away from its hasp. In hurrying, he rapped his shins on the central wooden bench. He froze, breathing heavily. Apart from the pounding in his head, he heard nothing but the low rumble of underground pumps that kept the building alive.

Advancing to the targeted door, Lyonel opened it with hardly a squeak. He peered inside. Above a tumble of shoes and underwear, a hanger dangled from an overhead crossbar, and draped over that hanger were a sweatshirt and a skuzzy pair of jeans.

Lyonel's heart leaped. He yanked the black belt free of its loops. He would have preferred brown, but wrapped it around his waist.

It was about four inches too short. He dropped it on top of the underwear.

But within arm's reach hung another unclasped lock. As in the other locker, suspended from a hanger was a jumble of clothes. Ambushed by essence of jockstrap, Lyonel turned his face away, probed blindly beneath a light jacket and a Harley Davidson sweatshirt, grasped a belt, and pulled it off.

It consisted of metal studs connected by strips of leather, but what could he care? Testing it around his waist, he found it a perfect fit.

It was now five minutes past two. With luck, it would only take him another five to get to class. At worst, he would begin to teach a bit out of breath.

As Lyonel passed the belt through a loop or two, unexpected footsteps came down the aisle to the left, headed in his direction.

A gruff voice bellowed, "Who's there?"

With neither time nor inclination for an embarrassing confrontation, Lyonel backed up sideways into the stuffy, smelly locker, stepping on a pile of pestilent under-things. A tight fit, but it would do until the danger passed. He pulled the door as close to shut as he could, taking care not to rattle the lock that hung from the handle.

Menacing footsteps approached. Lyonel held his breath. With hardly a rustle, his pants fell down to his ankles, but there was nothing he could do about that now. The footsteps grew closer and so did the sound of a hand slapping at doors and locks.

Not far from where he stood cocooned, the steps ceased for a second or two, and Lyonel could hear the distinct snapping of a lock. Another minute and the security check along his aisle would be over. Stillback might beat him to class, but there was a good chance he might interpret a late entrance as an artful expression of greater confidence.

The footsteps moved on again and stopped directly outside Lyonel's locker. The light from the ventilation slits was obscured. Lyonel dared not breathe. His muscles twitched at the thought of the door suddenly being jerked open.

The hand slapped at the door and, to Lyonel's great relief, instead of pulling it open, slammed it tight. Rather than move on, however, the hand then snapped the lock into place. And then came the click of receding footsteps, and the rattle of other locks and doors as the man made his way down the line.

As soon as Lyonel was sure that the man had left his aisle, he pressed gently against the door, which gave part of an inch, then stopped. He tried to bend down to pull up his pants, but there was not enough room to maneuver. Far worse, Lyonel felt an urgent need to pee.

Two-Time Losers

Jeremy Hightower did not mind students' addressing him as
"Professor" even though he wasn't yet a *real* professor—but the closer he
got to earning the Ph.D., that coveted stamp of academic authenticity, the
more he resented the time lost eking out a living teaching hordes of night-
school lummoxes the essentials of written English. It wouldn't have been
so bad if the Administration had at least once deigned to recognize the
depth and scope of his intellectual capabilities by offering him something
other than the lowest level writing courses to teach. Yet the plums, even
the intro-to-literature courses, were continually awarded to the same
group of middle-aged hacks who had long ago given up working toward a
doctorate but were valued for their many faithful plodding years in harness
and rewarded for their abject willingness to plug up gaps in emergencies,
to teach anything at any time whether competent in the *materia* or not.

Jeremy nursed hopes of breaking through this wall of privileged
mediocrity. Occasionally, in the hallway, he would run into the Vice-
Chair of the Department, Wilfred Glick, the bushy-browed, knuckle-
walking flunkey in charge of the part-time staff, and in answer to Glick's
casual "How's it going?" Jeremy would not hesitate to corral him, stop
him in his tracks, and leave him au courant on the status of his research
into medieval bestiaries, the topic of his projected dissertation. Despite
the man's nods of incomprehension, and the jerky body language that
revealed a desire to escape, Jeremy felt it imperative to impress the fellow
with the measure of his mind in the hope of standing out from the herd.

One evening, then, at the start of a new semester, when he found in
his departmental mailbox a message from Glick about switching to "a

97

different course," Jeremy instantly surmised that all those buttonholings were at last to pay off and that a literature course had fallen vacant suited to the employment of his talents. What else could it be but a lit course, he thought, since there was no course lower than the one he always taught, and all courses above that included at least some sort of literature component? Did he mean, rather, that he wanted to switch him to a different *section* (of the same old course) or a different time-slot? Approaching Glick's office, crumpling the note in his jacket pocket, Jeremy shrugged off such unwelcome interpretations. Whereas in other uses of language Glick was as slovenly as a sophomore, when it came to administratese he was always very precise.

"Have a seat, Jer," said Glick, and Jeremy did so, swallowing as always his resentment at being addressed by the diminutive of the more common Gerald. Properly speaking, a diminutive for Jeremy did not really exist, but how were semi-literates to know this? "I know that you're a flexible, cooperative guy, Jer..." –and while Glick sat back, tenting his hands, thinking no doubt of how to deliver the good news, Jeremy silently agreed with that assessment, for he had never ceased adhering, with cynical indifference, to an unwritten policy of the night school, namely, do not fail more than ten percent or award more than ten percent Ds in any class, no matter that one's conscience insisted on one's failing over half.

"So," said Glick, "we're switching you over to the only section of a newly created Special Course we're sure you are more than competent to handle on short notice."

"I appreciate your confidence in me," said Jeremy, leaning expectantly forward in his seat, knowing of course that Glick's "we" was the use of the royal plural and did not involve the approval of anyone else. "As you know, I've only recently passed all my doctoral exams—with High Distinction, as I may have mentioned—so that on the very shortest notice I feel adequately prepared for just about any literary specialty—"

"Jer," interrupted the Vice-Chair, also leaning forward, "this opportunity calls more upon your superior *pedagogical* skills." At this Glick cleared his throat. "We're assigning you to a select group of Exceptional Students, the pick of the entire night school, in fact."

"Really?" said Jeremy, his cheeks aflame as if reacting to the kisses of the bare-breasted Statue of Justice herself—or of his girlfriend Celia, whose most recent devastating threat to leave him had caused him to sacrifice an entire weekend of productivity at the New York Public Library. "A special seminar, no doubt?"

"You can look at it that way," said Glick, picking his nose.

"Am I to have complete curricular freedom, then?"

"Sure," said Glick. "Whatever it takes to get a bunch of two-time losers to write a single coherent paragraph by the end of the fucking semester."

"Two-time losers?" mumbled Jeremy, his scrotum twisting in a painful knot—as when Harriet, his only girlfriend prior to Celia, one day suddenly ditched him claiming an infinite preference for solitude.

"Yep. Failed 101 twice. They're out on their ass if they fail a third time. We'll allow them to bypass 101 if they pass your English X, though.... 'Smatter, Jerry? You look upset."

"It's Jeremy, not Jerry," said Jeremy.

"Look, Jer, if you don't think you can handle it..."

Reacting to the implicit threat of future unemployment, Jeremy was quick to shift gears. "It's a matter of... justice. Justice." He meant the justice long denied to Jeremy Hightower, but he cleverly turned the notion away from himself. "It seems a little unfair that these students should get special treatment."

"Ah, but these are special people," said Glick, cracking his knuckles. "Was justice on their side when it endowed them with their special handicaps?"

"But do they really need a college dip—"

"Let's not get into philosophical debates that have long been discarded as socially irrelevant. Let's focus on keeping our numbers up so this goddamn night program will keep getting funded. Kapish?"

"Capisco," muttered Jeremy, replying in correct Italian. "Do I know any of these students?"

"You might have had a few," said Glick. "The lamp-shade woman?"

Jeremy shook his head.

"Little Old Miss Five Times?... The Fun-House Mirror?... Mr. Tourette?... No? You have an interesting semester ahead of you. We appreciate your cooperation, Jer. But the challenge is bound to be its own reward."

That was just what Jeremy was afraid of. Finally, picking up the new roster, he mumbled something about trying to do his best, then deliberately showed his anger on leaving Glick's office by refraining from closing the bastard's door.

◦━◦ ◦━◦

Since the fifteen students in English X were required to turn out only a single decent paragraph, Jeremy quickly slapped together a syllabus consisting of famous opening paragraphs, models of rhetorical perfection by masters such as Kafka, Proust, Hemingway, and Orwell. He felt a bit nervous on meeting his class for the first time, fearing confrontation with a troupe of circus freaks, but a quick, sweeping glance revealed only the normal mix of working-class and lower-middle-class adults ranging widely in age, about equally divided as to sex, and as tired- or bored-looking at the end of a long day as any bunch of night-schoolers he'd ever had to deal with.

After introducing himself, he proceeded with the routine of reading off the roster and connecting names with faces. But when he came to Beulah Lamotta he saw not only the upraised hand, but a squat stump of a woman with skimpy gray hair and a solemn gray face rising from her front-row seat to his left as though he'd called on her to stand to attention. Snickers surrounded her to which she paid no notice.

"Aren't you gonna ask us to innaduce ourselves?" she said.

"Not right now, Miss Lamotta. Why not just sit—"

"It's still *Missus* Lamotta, but you're right, I shoulda gotten rid of that S.O.B.'s name as soon as I recovered."

"Really?" said Jeremy. "Well, Missus Lamotta, for now why don't you—"

Cutting him off, she stepped forward to the left of his desk and stood facing both him and the class. "I'm Beulah Lamotta," she trumpeted, "and I stand here by the grace of God though my husband shot me five times." Rude mutterings broke out from various corners of the room. Beulah gave them no heed. "I didn't fall," she continued. "Then he shot *himself.* One bullet to the brain and he dropped down dead, may he burn forever in hell."

At this she resumed her seat, the murmurs ceased, and Jeremy managed to run through the roster without further interruptions—except that a timid-looking middle-aged student with a bowtie (an accountant, fancied Jeremy) named Timothy Perkins got up from his seat near the shut classroom door and opened it wide, sitting back down again without uttering a word. Ignoring Perkins, Jeremy proceeded with the rest of the Introduction, distributed handouts, invited questions, and at the end felt satisfied that things had gone reasonably well, even felt that, in general, this class of presumed losers accorded him greater than usual respect—out of fear, no doubt, of a further failure not one of them could afford. True, some odd noises peppered the session, but refusing to be distracted (unswerving focus was essential to maintaining authority), Jeremy paid them no mind.

By the third class session Jeremy had ample reason to suspect that the simple notion of a *topic sentence*—the general statement that began a model paragraph—was a concept that baffled all but a handful of his charges. In addition, his efforts were rudely interrupted, and not for the first time, by noises coming from he knew not where. This time, however, halting in mid-sentence, he looked all around in an effort to determine their origin. Adding to his irritation, all the students but one seemed to notice nothing at all. Every few minutes there was a sharp report as of a baseball bat connecting with a ball. At first the noises seemed to come from outside, beyond the windows to the right—and that made sense since baseball season wasn't yet over.

When Jeremy looked up and squinted out through the windows, young and hyper-serious Arnold Memmelman in the second row right-of-center acknowledged Jeremy's distress by swiveling around and craning his neck to search out through the windows too, evidently disturbed even more than Jeremy by what failed to draw the least reaction from his peers. Jeremy almost wanted to thank Arnold for thus reassuring him that he wasn't experiencing auditory hallucinations.

A few minutes went by with no further distraction—except for Timothy Perkins bobbing up and slinking over to reopen the door. Jeremy now had to go over and shut it for the second time in fifteen minutes, hoping that a behavior-modeling non-verbal reproach would engineer a change in Timothy without embarrassing him publicly. But before Jeremy could get up to close the door, another explosive snap rang out, this time apparently from the corridor.

Though Jeremy was sure that no one could be out there in the hallway batting out balls, he dashed to the door to check, saw nothing, and slammed the door shut—casting a look at Timothy as if to suggest that it must all be his fault. This look too sparked an angry supporting grimace from Memmelman, who spun around and shook his head violently at a completely unfazed Perkins. Memmelman's exaggerated gestures of support now troubled Jeremy more than Perkins's door obsession or the mysterious cracking noises. Was this gesturing of Memmelman's a passive-aggressive display of hostility againt a symbol of Authority? Turning back to the business at hand, trying for the tenth time to demonstrate the function of a topic sentence, Jeremy heard not a baseball bat but a distinctly uttered phrase: "Stupid piece of shit!" He pretended, of course, not to notice either that or the flurry of muffled giggles that followed.

A couple of days later Jeremy snagged the Vice-Chair, who was loping down the hallway a few yards ahead of him though Jeremy knew quite well that he was typically trying to avoid him.

"How's it going?" said Glick.

"It can't be worse, so I'm sure it'll have to get better."

"You're the man for the job, Jer, and we're sure you'll do a bang-up job at that."

"Speaking of bangs," said Jeremy, tagging along behind the speed-walking Glick, "I wanted to ask you about certain disturbing noises that others must also have brought to your attention. They sound like someone whacking out balls with a bat, and I can't exactly tell where they're coming from. How can we be expected to teach—"

Glick stopped in his tracks and spun around. "That's Babe Ruth. I didn't tell you about the Babe? He's that sleepy whale with the Yankees cap who's always dressed in black."

"Harold Bickel?" said Jeremy. He pictured the enormous Bickel who walked with a limp and usually sat with no one around him in the middle of the third row. "That's impossible."

"It's Bickel, it's Bickel! He makes an incredibly loud *thuck* with his tongue." Glick demonstrated. "I can't do it nearly as well. You place your tongue up against your palette then suck the tip back explosively."

"But the noise is coming from outside the room!"

"Sounds like it, but he has this uncanny knack of projecting his thuck like a ventriloquist."

"Nobody seems to notice except me—and, oh yes, one student who seems to know exactly how I feel and then makes faces and gestures mimicking my emotions to the point of caricature. It's like looking into—"

"The Fun-House Mirror," said Glick. "Didn't I mention the Fun-House Mirror?"

"I don't exactly recall."

"Poor Memmelman has this neurological disorder, the result of a car accident, I'm told. Otherwise he's quite normal. I mean—"

"I know exactly what you mean," sniffed Jeremy. "Thanks for the information."

"Any time. Just ask," said Glick, charging ahead toward his office.

⊫← →⊨

By the first class meeting of the third week of the semester, Jeremy thought he had come to understand why the concept of a topic sentence, essential to the logic of paragraph construction, still eluded the grasp of most students. The reason was that they had no idea of what constituted a *sentence*—any sentence—in the first place. So Jeremy began to work with them on the recognition and production of sentences. He began with the simple exercise of asking everybody to write a single sentence, then asked for a volunteer to read his or hers out loud.

Beulah Lamotta, without waiting to be called on, stood up facing the class and read: "My husband shot me five times, then he turned the gun on himself, I'm glad it was him not me." Looking smugly around as if daring anyone to challenge her, she plopped back in her seat and stared at Jeremy with arms folded across her sagging breast.

"Beulah," said Jeremy, "that's three sentences, not one sentence." Shaking his head, he smiled sadly and ignored the dizzying head-swinging of Memmelman, who sat just behind her.

"You said a sentence was a single idea," she shot back. "That's a single idea."

"Actually, Beulah, it's three closely connected ideas. In fact, all you need to do to make it into a para—"

"But I'm tellin' you," insisted Beulah, "it all happened in one single flash, no breaks, between whippin' out his gun and splattin' the mirror over the chest o' drawers with his brains."

At this very moment an angry muttering arose from Julia Fenton, a normally quiet, hatchet-faced woman who looked in her mid-forties and dressed in a kind of Granola-chic of potato-sack beiges over mud-colored clodhopper boots. Jeremy didn't catch at first what she was spewing out, in a rage, across the empty seat that separated her from Timothy Perkins, who fingered his bowtie and shrunk back in his seat trying neither to look at her nor to listen. But it appeared that she was accusing him of making improper advances.

"...disgusting men are all alike. You think I didn't hear you? Why would I be interested in a twerp like you when I was married to one of the biggest names in show biz? You sicken me with your ogling and your filthy whisperings, you undersized dirtbag, you ought to—"

"Piece of shit, drop dead!" cracked a voice from the row in back of her and two seats to her right. Jeremy had come to recognize and ignore the occasional blurtings of "Mr. Tourette," a middle-aged postal clerk named Edwin Seidenham who was not responding to the drama being enacted in front of him—even though it might seem that he was. Julia turned around, made a face at Seidenham, then slumped back in her seat. Timothy, still fumbling with his tie, got up and stepped over to the door, which again he opened wide.

Wearily, Jeremy walked over to close it when in stepped one of the strangest sights he had ever seen except for some of the fanciful illustrations in bestiaries.

"Hi, Helen!" shouted several of the students.

"It's okay, Helen, you can come in," coaxed another.

The first thing Jeremy noticed was a rod or rapier pointed toward his chest. Stumbling backward, he recovered quickly, taking note of the woman's head. It was crowned by a faded yellow lampshade with a square cut out in front. The woman stopped still and froze in place, staring confusedly with watery blue eyes down at her clunky brown shoes, apparently undecided as to which foot to move forward first.

"The left foot," urged a couple of voices.

"No, the right one, Helen," said others.

Attached to the wire ring at the top of her headpiece, two foot-long metal antennae reached up in a V.

"It's okay, you can come in," said Jeremy, recalling Glick's mention of the Lampshade Lady.

Sighing with relief, Helen thrust her left foot forward and followed it with her right. "I forgot which one I stepped in with," she explained, "because if you don't use the correct foot, there's the *rays*." She pointed to her quivering antennae, then lowered her silver-gray rapier, which on Jeremy's closer examination turned out to be a collapsible curtain-rod. "I'm Helen Wheaton. I registered late. I apologize."

"Have a seat, anywhere," said Jeremy, reaching into a manila file and handing her a copy of the syllabus.

"She's *always* late," sniffed Beulah.

"Goddamn crock of shit!" spouted Mr. Tourette, but by now almost no one, Jeremy included, bothered to take notice of Edwin. Instead, Jeremy smarted from a reawakened sense of insult and injury as it occurred to him once more how Glick had mistreated him. His syllabus was now worth less than Edwin's crock. He found himself caught in a downward pedagogical spiral, failing to impart the idea of a paragraph, failing to impart the idea of a topic sentence, now about to crash trying to explain the concept of a sentence, any sentence. It was not his fault. His conscience was clear. But Glick expected him to pass them all, everyone, with a C or better.

That was the rub! Well Glick be damned! Financial security be damned, too! He would no longer lie to shore up Glick's precious "numbers." And if that meant putting off finishing his doctorate for another five years, so be it—but of course that depended on the slim possibility that Columbia would grant him extensions.

But Celia would be sailing through her degree in two more years at most. With a specialty like hers—in "Modernism"—any fool could get by in no time, thought Jeremy, but as a self-respecting scholar he had never once considered such an easy way out. What if, however, Celia did not appreciate his sudden onset of conscience? Celia kept telling him again and again that she wanted "to get on with her life." And if she left him again—as she did recently for a full two weeks upon his picking her up late after he'd spent a couple of hours chasing an obscure reference in Isidore of Seville—he knew she would never come back.

Celia was all he had in the world. She was the only one who admired his integrity, no matter how much, as she put it, it "irritated the shit" out of her. Losing Celia would be hell.

Living a lie—betraying all the values on which his beloved Literature was founded—would also be hell.

⊷ ⊶

By the fifth week of class Jeremy had regressed from attempting to teach the composition of a paragraph to defining and illustrating the grammatical bits and pieces that went into the making of a sentence. Knowing that his efforts were hopeless and that few of his students would wind up worth even a C, Jeremy felt deep down in his soul that he'd be doing society a favor if the buck stopped with him and he awarded honest, Glick-defying grades— though it cost him the only job he might ever have that both paid his rent (his parents lived hand to mouth in some Florida retiree slum) and afforded him the leisure to advance toward his degree. Though he trembled also at the thought of a life without Celia, he convinced himself finally that a man had first to be able to live with himself, to be able to face himself in the mirror.

Whenever Jeremy now thought of mirrors he could not help thinking of Beulah Lamotta's horrifying mirror, but he had managed by now to stiffen himself against the shock of her obsessive-compulsive outbursts. He had managed by now also never to look directly at Memmelman the Fun-House Mirror, to treat as mere sounds signifying nothing the ballpark blasts of Harold Bickel, the same for the involuntary burps of filth from the mouth of Edwin Seidenham, and ditto regarding the lengthily disruptive tirades of Julia Fenton, whose drug-impaired brain created paranoid fantasies of leering men (and not just the innocent Timothy Perkins) that a vicious tongue-lashing would put in their place. As to claustrophobic Perkins, Jeremy hardly bothered any more to get up and re-close the door. Lampshade Helen was only a visual distraction, so that her habit of almost always showing up late for class—having frozen several times in stairwell and hallway to confound alien signals by correcting the order of her steps— no longer threw him off in the middle of a sentence.

Everything was now routine, a dismal routine of darkening days not only due to the season, but to Jeremy's obsessively trying to picture to himself that bleak moment of confrontation when he would announce to Glick that ten of his fifteen students would be receiving Fs and Ds. What redeeming virtues did these poor losers have that could convince him to surrender his integrity? he wondered.

◖◗◦‹‹ ››◦◖◗

The course of action Jeremy would take became absolutely clear to him during the seventh week of class. The gloomy Brooklyn night poured like a cold liquid into the spiritless classroom, multiplying the gloom within. Swallowing his despair, Jeremy collected the homework on gerunds and participles and began to make comments on each student's exercises, scribbling examples on the board.

Hardly had he finished discussing the first two examples when a pair of strangers burst in through the open door. They were two hoods barely out of their teens. The short, skinny one in the black leather jacket brandished a large hunting knife, while his tall, heavy-set companion, whose jeans barely clung to his backside, flicked open a switchblade. Nervously, they pointed their weapons first at Jeremy and then at the dead-silent roomful of stunned, wide-eyed students. As the bigger brute kicked the door closed behind him, the rat-faced little guy announced their demand while dangling a brown canvas bag out in front of him. "Trick or treat," said Rat-Face. "I want all your wallets and handbags up front."

Response was underwhelming. Nobody moved, but several students creased their brows—as was their irritating habit when unable to reply to some of Jeremy's simplest questions. Jeremy, face to face with the little guy, tried reasoning with the pair. "Look," he said, "no one here is carrying much money, so why don't you—"

Rat-Face lifted his blade to just under Jeremy's chin. "Get those wallets up here quick or asshole gets it in the neck," he said.

Jeremy stumbled back against the wall. Though Fear loosened his bowels, the intestinal fortitude born of Shame luckily prevented a mishap.

"Give us a hard time and I'll cut yiz up good," echoed his beefy partner, swishing his knife at the first row of seats.

"Drop dead, you piece of shit!" snapped Edwin Seidenham with a dazed, blank expression from his seat in the middle of the third row. Jeremy wanted to explain to these thugs that Edwin meant nothing personal, that he probably didn't even know what was going down, but he didn't get the chance.

"What? Who the fuck was that?" said Rat-Face. "Joey, show 'im we mean business."

"Who's the wise guy?" said Big Joey, glancing around the room.

"It's the dick-head over there," said the little guy, pointing with his knife at Arnold Memmelman. Arnold, in response to Rat-Face's glare, squinched his features up into a triply-menacing mad-dog expression with narrowed eyes and lips stretched back over his teeth.

"Teach him a lesson, Joey," said Rat-Face, shuddering.

But before the Golem could take a step forward, Edwin, whose symptoms seemed to worsen under the stimulus of nervous excitement, followed up his earlier exclamation with another: "Goddamn bastards, you can all go to hell!"

"Oh, so it's you!" said Rat-Face. "It's that asshole in the back, Joey. Get him!"

Again, Big Joey was about to move forward when he was distracted by a sudden movement along the wall to his left. Timothy Perkins stood up, and, while the two hoods watched in suspended animation, sidled forward as he always did and quietly re-opened the door. Golem charged toward the door to prevent Perkins from escaping, but Timothy had already headed unhurriedly back toward his seat.

"Did we say anyone could get up?" shouted the little guy, now red in the face.

"No one tells *me* when to get up or sit down!"

"What!" said Rat-Face, pointing his knife toward Beulah Lamotta, then back at Jeremy, and then again at Beulah as she stood up, stepped forward, and planted herself, arms akimbo, right in front of the outstretched blade, forcing the pint-sized hood to back up.

"Get the fuck back in your seat, bitch!" he croaked.

"See this scar here?" she said, oblivious to his command. She fingered a spot on her neck. "That's a bullet wound. I got four others. Wanna see?"

"Back off, bitch!" shouted Rat-Face. "If I have to cut up a woman—"

"Beulah," blustered Jeremy, trembling now with fright as if the seriousness of the situation had finally dawned on him, "do what he says, sit down!"

"My husband shot me five times," she said, ignoring Jeremy, "and I didn't fall down, and if you think a *zhidrool* like you can scare me..."

"You crazy old douchebag, I'm warning you..."

"They're *all* fuckin' crazy," muttered Rat-Face's partner.

At that very moment, just in time to deliver the smaller punk from a potentially violent confrontation with an immovably stubborn Beulah, there exploded a familiar *thuck* that even to Jeremy sounded as if it came from out in the hallway.

While Big Joey ventured a cautious step toward the door, the little hood backed away from Beulah, producing in Jeremy a tremulous sigh of relief. Still with knife-blade held out in front of him like a crucifix to ward off a vampire, Rat-Face stopped his back-stepping when he stood alongside his partner. Craning his neck toward the hallway, he was startled by a second thuck. To Jeremy it sounded like a pistol shot.

And then appeared Helen, late as usual, ditzily decked out in lampshade and all, with both antennae quivering. Unable, however, to halt the progression of her calculated sequence of steps, she lunged ahead with her curtain-rod directly into the belly of the bear-like figure in front of her. Big Joey, taken aback, dropped his jackknife and clutched his stomach. But before he could realize that he had not been skewered, his friend had already registered an entirely different impression. Letting out the strangest sound, something between a shout and a gargle, the little hood dashed out through the door and clattered to the left down the hallway.

"Hey!" his partner yelled down the hall, but the little punk wasn't returning. Not bothering to retrieve his knife, Big Joey hitched up his floor-scuffing jeans and stumbled on out after him.

His stomach vibrating like the antennae of the utterly clueless Helen, who stared in amazement at her fully collapsed wand, Jeremy scrambled to the door for a glimpse of the retreating duo.

And then he took a deep breath, shrugged his shoulders, and solemnly returned to his desk. Beulah, back in her seat again, folded her arms across her chest and looked at him expectantly. Helen, once more sure of her footing, clumped over to her place near Bickel in row three.

"We have work to do," mumbled Jeremy, searching his desk for the next example he'd intended to write on the board. But what he had in mind, yet couldn't tell them, was that he'd decided then and there that he'd be giving every one of them an A.

Double Occupancy

1

The life of Harris Trimmel was completely regular and predictable until one day he came home from work and smelled a faint odor of incense in the apartment. Jennifer, who had come home a little earlier, said she couldn't smell a thing because of a winter cold she had coming on.

"Maybe the pilot is out in the stove," he said.

"They don't spike natural gas with incense, Har. They want it to smell bad if it leaks."

"To me, incense smells bad," said Harris.

"It didn't use to, dear, *did* it?"

"That was back in our dormitory days. Since college my nose has undergone considerable maturation."

"What exactly *does* it smell like?" Jennifer removed a cup of hot water from the microwave and dipped a bag of Earl Gray tea into it. "Does it smell like the apartment did when we took it over from that gay hairdresser? Remember those black drapes of his—literally *stapled* onto the windowframes? Remember the black incense candles?"

"Maybe *that's* what it is!" said Harris. "Maybe the walls are so steeped in the stuff that two aging coats of paint can't hide it anymore."

"Think it could be from Billy's room?"

"C'mon, Jennie, the one thing I would not indulge about his craze for sixties memorabilia was anything that stank."

"He did burn a few joss sticks."

111

"And you can remember how quickly I put a stop to *that!* But for all I know he's burning 'em again now—asphyxiating his dorm-mate, doing his homework, and watching television all at the same time."

"I wish I could smell what you're smelling," said Jennifer, inhaling steam from the teacup to clear her nostrils.

"Billy never burned enough incense to stink up the place more than a day." Harris waved her idea away like a fly not worth the swatting. "Soon as I saw he was using the stuff to cover up the smell of pot, that was the end of that."

"I still think we should have allowed him to smoke a little weed now and then, together with his closest friends, in the shelter of his own home, instead of forcing him to smoke *behind our backs*, in company and circumstances that were quite possibly *dangerous*."

"Indulging in a little vice is okay if it's in your own house, is it?"

"Is there a better place?" She winked at him. It annoyed him when she did not take him seriously. "Do you remember twenty-plus years ago the games *we* played," she said, "that would've given our parents coronaries if they knew?"

"Come on, Jennifer! Nobody thought much about *anything* back in the Woodstock era."

"I think I do smell something," said Jennifer, leaning back from the kitchen table. "Patchouli oil, I think."

"It can't be patchouli. Patchouli smells nothing like incense."

"Don't tell me what patchouli smells like, Harris. It wasn't you who used to wear it."

"You're smelling a *memory* of patchouli oil."

"And you're smelling a memory of incense."

"I am not. I have a perfectly functioning shnozzola." Harris began pacing up and back, from the small kitchen table to the refrigerator. "And by the way, I've been meaning to ask, how come you've been leaving the toilet seat up lately when that's exactly what you used to scream at me for doing?"

"I *am not* leaving the toilet seat up. You must be, and you're forgetting!"

He wanted to tell her that at forty-seven, though in marvelous *physical* shape, she was suffering from incipient Alzheimer's, but why get into a fruitless argument?

"And what about *you*? Leaving the light on in Billy's room?" she continued. "I've put it out two or three times in the past couple of weeks."

"I have not left the light on in Billy's room. I have not even *entered* Billy's room! I have no business that brings me there. You, however, for nostalgic reasons—"

"I am not nostalgic about the sixties!" she protested.

"About Billy, I mean. About the cuddly kid he was in his early high-school years."

"Oh, he was a lot friendlier then," she conceded. "But then you started hammering away at the kid for not doing his homework, for smoking anything, pot or not, for having girl friends in his room, ta-da, ta-da, ta-da."

"I did not want to pay for another abortion. Yours was nightmare enough, back in the days when you didn't know whom to trust—over or *under* thirty."

"God, how thoughtless we were!" she said.

"We never thought our bodies could betray us."

"It's we who betray our bodies," she countered.

"You're right," said Harris. "For example, why the hell did I pay to join a gym if I hardly ever use the damn—"

"Now stop it! I'm sick of that litany from you, Harris."

"I'm blaming only myself."

"Well, if going to the gym regularly would improve your *memory*... Listen, let's go check whether the light is on *again* in Billy's room." Jennifer got up from the table with a smug look on her face. As though she could prove it was *his* fault, thought Harris, even if the light *were* on.

2

Taking a right out of the kitchen, they marched down the hall past the bathroom to the first of their three bedrooms. Harris pushed at the slightly warped door that always arched open a crack (just enough to have enabled him to monitor Billy during his green-haired, black-jacketed punk phase). The light was *not* on, as Jennifer could very well see. "The smell is stronger here, I think."

"Nonsense! I'm going back to my tea."

Harris switched the light on. "Don't you smell it?" he said, entering the room.

Jennifer lingered in the hallway. "With you it's psychological," she said.

"Sounds like you've been reading too many of those books you sell in your little bookshop," he retorted.

"The world of so-called facts, Harris, is not so hard-and-fast as you think."

"Tell that to my accountant at income-tax time. He's never inventive *enough*, as far as I'm concerned." Harris took a quick survey of Billy's oppressively "period" room. The purple curtains were drawn, as usual, against mundane images of the street below. Psychedelic posters shouted Day-Glo obscenities at all who entered here, and the harsh yellow ceiling lights glinted off a rack of buttons on the wall behind Billy's old computer. Harris couldn't read them from where he was standing, but he knew them by heart: "Make love, not war," "America has gone to pot," "Draft beer, not boys," "Love is a many-gendered thing"... A color print of John F. Kennedy, framed under glass, hung above the button display.

He looked to the right, at the shelves above Billy's bed, and noticed something missing from the bottom shelf. As expected, there sat the white plastic Zenith radio, the old black plastic record-player and the collection of 45's that went with it. But the doll was gone. Harris glanced around, puzzled. Opposite the bed a big old wardrobe—hand-painted by Billy in garish swaths of uncomplimentary colors —took up half the left-hand wall of the room. Harris yanked open both of its misaligned, louver-style doors and found the doll face-down at the bottom. "Why'd you take Billy's G.I. Joe off the shelf?" he said, holding aloft the rifle-toting doll and straightening out its ruffled army fatigues.

"I never even noticed it was gone, Har."

"Why should you? It's one of the few things in this room that *I* bought him."

"Billy must have moved it, not me." She shrugged her shoulders and wandered over to the desk near the window where she examined the yellowing print, tacked to the wall next to JFK, of flower-children sprawled over the ground at Woodstock. As she looked at the print, her hand reached out and covered the Mexican onyx ashtray on the desk. But Harris had just seen a small white object squashed into its green concavity.

"What's that?" he said.

"What's what? Oh!" She pulled her hand away and almost toppled the tall Lava-Lite lamp that stood nearby.

Harris came up for a closer look. He bent down and sniffed. "A roach!" he said. "Who the hell's been smoking pot in here?"

"It must date way back. I guess we just never noticed it," she said.

"Smells pretty fresh to me!"

"What makes *you* the expert in fresh versus stale marijuana?" she countered. "How many years ago was the last time *you* ever indulged?"

"Why were you reaching for the ashtray?" he snapped.

"Out of habit, I guess."

"You were about to empty it into the wastebasket."

"I suppose."

"Without noticing what you were dumping?"

"I suppose."

He shook his head. "What the hell's going on here?"

"I still can't smell a thing," she said. "Except maybe a whiff of patchouli?" She turned around, looked at Billy's bed and ran her hand over the quilt to smoothe it.

3

At work the next morning Harris couldn't keep his mind off that roach—and that peculiar, almost surreptitious gesture of Jennifer's as her hand swooped over the ashtray to empty it. But why would she do pot behind his back? And *when*? Would she come back home from the bookstore just for a joint? He remembered her smoothing Billy's bedcovers, too. Had they been rumpled? Was there more going on here than he'd really care to know about?

In the dining room that evening, over a plate of leftover spaghetti that Jennifer had heated up in the microwave, Harris blurted out a part of his suspicions. "I believe that someone—maybe more than one person—is using our apartment while we're at work."

"That's absurd, Harris. How could they get in?" Jennifer's spaghetti slowly unwound from her fork as she held it before her heart-shaped, still-very-kissable mouth.

Harris swept back at the ghost of unruly curls that tumbled down his hairless forehead. "Someone could've copied your key. You have the habit of leaving your purse unattended... as if you *wanted* someone to take advantage of you."

"That's *absurd*, Harris!"

"'That's absurd Harris, that's absurd, Harris!' Is that all you can think of to reply?"

"Now look, Harris, not that I would credit your theory one iota, but Billy could have given someone a key, for that matter."

"Billy, huh?" Now why, he wondered, was she so quick to deflect his suspicions onto Billy? Why didn't she simply stick to her Theory of the Absurd?

"Look, Har, if you're so sure our premises are being invaded, why don't we set some little traps to find out?"

Harris rose to the challenge. During the course of the next several days he watched as Jennifer put a dent in Billy's pillow, or left the light on in his room, or set Billy's door open an inch wider than usual. At the same time, unbeknownst to Jennifer, Harris set his own little springes: the toilet-seat left up, pencil-marks showing the positions of the front row of water-glasses in the cupboard, crushable candies set under the rug beside Billy's bed.

Sometimes they noticed a change, but then they couldn't agree on whether one of *them* had unconsciously turned off the light or accidentally nudged the door; and once, when Harris found a crushed candy, he couldn't be sure that he hadn't stepped on it himself. And if he noticed something new, like a half-empty bottle of Coke in the fridge that he could swear had been nearly full that morning, Jennifer got him to doubt his own recollection.

No, this method would never work. What was going wrong between them, he wondered, now that Billy had been away at college for little more than six months? For the first couple of months, the unaccustomed privacy acted on them both as an aphrodisiac. They pleased and embarrassed each other with amorous advances made spontaneously, even in the midst of a shower. Then the embarrassment seemed to deaden the spontaneity and they fell back into their old routine of making love by appointment—except that now they approached each other fully aware of how, ideally, it *should* be.

Was Jennifer secretly smoking pot with some friends, then covering up the odor by lighting incense? Had she taken on a lover, perhaps? A rather remote possibility, he thought. But she *was* looking nice and trim these days, took lots better care of herself than she used to; and those flare-ups of passion after Billy had left, those headlong "sexsterics"—were they simply a passing fever of which she was now definitively cured? At the bookshop, after all, she did have plenty of opportunity to "meet" people. And she could duck out whenever she wanted to, leaving her assistant in charge...

4

Obsessing for three days over the hypothesis that Jennifer, like the pop-tune's Mrs. Jones, had "a *thing* going on," Harris Trimmel went to work one morning and told his partner he was feeling ill and would be leaving for an appointment with his doctor. Business was running slow at their little computer-graphics firm, so Harris felt he could afford to take the day off— even work on an account at home on his laptop. So he turned right around and drove the half-hour back from Manhattan through heavy traffic to his building in Brooklyn Heights, a four-story red-brick walk-up dating from the twenties. It was located on a grassless but tree-lined block of buildings, mainly newer and taller than his own, interspersed with a few brownstones.

Harris left his car in its reserved parking spot. Skirting poop deposited by the Afghan of a certain notoriously uncooperative neighbor, he hurried upstairs and tiptoed along the third-floor corridor to his apartment. After catching his breath, he placed his ear against the door. He didn't hear a thing. Not knowing all of the people who lived on his floor, and fearing that one of them might peep out and mistake him for a burglar, he did not linger long in the hallway. He turned the key in the lock, nudged the door inward, and entered.

No one besides himself was at home. Not *yet*. That was exactly as he wished it to be. His was the apartment at the end of the corridor, farthest from the stairwell, so that he could easily detect whether footsteps were approaching *his* door. It felt eerie to be home alone when he should be at work. He felt like an intruder in his own house. A thief, or even a ghost! What if the phone should ring? Should he answer it? Should he run the water, use the toilet? He felt absurd to be sitting in the living room, playing with his laptop, waiting, waiting… and what if there *were* visitors, why would they be coming along *today*, just when he, Harris Trimmel, decided to spy on them?

Footsteps did come. Harris tucked his laptop under the sofa and slipped off quietly toward Billy's room. But the steps stopped about halfway up the hall. Harris returned to the living-room sofa. It was not long, however, before other footsteps—at least two pairs of footsteps— shuffled and squeaked down the thin-carpeted corridor, this time heading straight for his apartment.

His heart knocked at his chest as he closed Billy's door behind him. Dim daylight filtered through the purple-curtained window. There was plenty of headroom in the closet. Harris hid among hangers thick with clothes. If he leaned forward, he gained a clear view of the lower half of the room, especially the bed, through the down-slanting louvers. But this was ridiculous! Even if they did enter his apartment, why would they necessarily come into Billy's room? He could be standing here for hours and still be left clueless as to the identity of the intruders.

It was a notion that quickly vanished as Harris heard nearby footsteps, then voices, then the creaking of Billy's door. He blinked as a hand he could not yet see flicked on the ceiling light. As they entered his field of view, the sight of them stopped his breath.

Two young women. Two attractive young women!

The taller, a brunette, strode across the room to turn the Lava Lite on. Her honey-blond companion meanwhile stretched out like a cat at the foot-end of Billy's bed, to Harris's right. They seemed quite at home, seemed to fit in perfectly with the décor. The beauty on the bed wasted no time kicking off her sneakers. Her dark-haired friend sat down next to her and pulled off her short leather boots. "It'll be warm in a jif," she said, looking back at the lava lamp.

"I already feel deliciously warm," said the blonde, in an extraordinarily musical voice. With a mischievous smile, she leaned back on the bed to wriggle out of tie-dyed jeans. "Kevin doesn't like to join us anymore. Do you think he could actually be jealous, Sarah?"

"No, Nina," said Sarah, helping her friend out of her jeans. "Kevin knows we both love him, but I think he's trying to work out his feelings toward Josh lately."

"You could be right," said the dusky-voiced blonde named Nina. "I hope it works out between them, but Kevin can't handle his bisexuality as comfortably as Josh."

Harris noted that Nina wore no panties under her jeans. The sight hammered a spike into his groin. Carefully, he angled his head behind the down-slanting louvers to take in all he could. When she cast off her tassled leather jacket and squirmed out of her green woolen sweater, he was not surprised to find that she was braless as well. Her honey-colored hair rippled down below her shoulders to where her breasts began to swell out under her collarbone. The smooth, solid cones tilted upward, each nipple erect over its small brown base. His mouth dry, his throat parched, Harris knew exactly how those outstretched nipples felt to be free of restraints.

Dark-haired Sarah had meanwhile removed her necklace of shells and animal teeth, had stripped off her heavy silver bracelets, and now stood up to peel herself out of a pair of faded jeans and a thick-knit, off-yellow fisherman's sweater. Harris took note of Sarah's lacy little panties, but like Nina she sported no bra. Her breasts were softer and fuller than Nina's, but Nina's pert and pointy ones were the ones he fantasized fondling. The bodies of both were lithe and slim. Neither of the two wore makeup. Their skin was perfectly smooth, a detail that, twenty years ago, he would have taken for granted as he had once taken his own young body for granted, but now he found that flawless, glowing skin of theirs utterly ravishing. His heart thundered in his ears. Could these two weather-sprites *hear* the mini-tempest they had set off in the closet? he wondered.

Sarah curled up next to Nina, who lay on her back with one knee raised. She reached out to Nina's hair, her fingers slipping through waves of gold till they traced the curve of her breasts.

Nina caught Sarah's fingers in hers. "The lights," she said—or sang, rather.

"Of course!" Sarah sprang up, crossed the floor, and switched off the glaring overhead light. The change in mood was startling. Harris had forgotten why these Lava Lites had once been so popular. Through melting yellow lumps of wax that rose and fell in the water-filled lamp, a forty-watt bulb projected strange forms onto the walls and ceiling— bulbous, bubbling, ever-shifting, biological forms. The undulant light wafted flowers over their skin as Sarah nestled beside Nina. It rippled along their flanks as they kissed and stroked and pressed each other's flesh. It painted them with the contours of exotic fishes as yielding limbs and searching mouths interlaced, and as they swiveled and moaned with abandon upon the bed. Harris tried to imagine how the Josh they had mentioned fit into the picture, but he could see only himself, wedged in between them, voluptuously entangled among the eight writhing limbs of a soft-skinned arachnoid with four stabbing breasts.

5

When the closet door swung open, exposing him, Harris groped wildly for something to cover the bulge in his pants. The women sat up, clutching their knees, their backs against the wall. For a long, breathless moment, no one said a word.

"Hi!" said Nina, managing a crooked smile. "You look pretty stupid just standing there."

"Especially," said Sarah, "with that jackhammer in your pants."

"Why don't you join us?" Nina invited. She tapped a spot between them at the edge of the bed.

Harris hesitated a moment, then removed his hands from his crotch. "I apologize," he began, "but..."

"Would you rather we just left?" said Sarah.

"No, no, of course not! I'm awfully sorry, but you see, I suspected—"

"Burglars?" said Nina. "It's just us, and we're pretty harmless."

"Did we upset you?" said Sarah.

"I'll say we upset him!" said Nina.

Harris's ears were on fire. He made an absurd move to cover his crotch again.

"Come join us, Mr. Trimmel," said Nina, tapping more insistently at the bed. "If you don't want us to leave, then that means you'd like to be our friend. Correct?"

"I'm Harris," said Harris.

"I'm Nina," said Nina.

"I'm Sarah," said Sarah.

Harris tripped on the throw-rug as he neared the edge of the bed. Nina sprang forward, caught him under the arm, and eased him onto the bed. The naked flesh, the psychedelic lighting, the sloshing of blood in his eardrums —all of it made him dizzy. "How can you breathe with this *thing* on?" she said, removing his tie. "You do want to get comfortable, don't you, Harry?"

"Harris," he said to her pouting left nipple as her breasts jiggled just below his chin.

"Then if you want to join us, you can't keep those clothes on. Right, Sarah, dear?"

"Absolutely," said Sarah, reaching around from behind him and unbuckling his belt. "I like your back." She ran her hands around under his shoulder blades. "I love men's big broad backs."

"How did you… get in here?" said Harris, his voice barely a squeak as they began methodically to undress him.

"With a key, of course," said Nina, looking him innocently in the eye as her hands unzipped his fly.

"With a key? *With a key*?" he repeated an octave higher as he felt cool fingers sting his thigh.

"Yes, with a key," said Nina as her dark-haired friend behind him pulled his arms out of his pin-striped shirt.

"I like hairy chests," cooed Nina, her soft fingers raking him from his shoulders down to his waist.

"How did you *get*… your key?" said Harris, lifting his butt obligingly as Nina tugged at his pants. The sweet smell of Nina's sweat, of the mingled flavors of the sweat of both of the women, swamped all his senses like a drug. And wasn't there a faint taste of patchouli, too, among all those unnamable spices?

"A friend gave us the key," said Nina, propping his leg over her knee to untie his shoe. Once his pants had come down to his knees, Harris felt that shackles had been snapped from his body, and he sat there throbbing between the two women as if that were exactly what he ought to be doing, as if workaday time had been suspended, and as if he had stepped through a magic door into a realm of rhythms that had neither beginning nor end, into the heartbeat of Nature herself.

"A friend?" croaked Harris. "You mean my son Billy?"

"Don't know any Billy," Nina pouted. "Do you, Sarah?"

"Nope," said Sarah, who had bent over so far to undo his other shoe that Harris could see dark hairs in the crack of her ass.

"Then it must have been a friend of Billy's who gave you the key," said Harris.

"I guess so. We never ask," said Nina. She helped him shed his boxer shorts, of whose pattern of little gold alarm clocks he suddenly felt ashamed. "Think Kevin or Josh would know who gave them Harry's key, Sarah?"

"Kevin and Josh have a key *also*?" said Harris, ignoring Nina's calling him Harry, a name he detested.

"Does that upset you terribly?" said Nina. Her voice was low and resonant, as though her larynx were some marvelous sort of echo chamber. It was a sensually lulling voice the like of which Harris had never before heard. Up close it was hypnotic—soothing and exciting all at once.

"I'm not upset by... you," said Harris, feeling Nina's hand stray down his flank. "But wouldn't *you* be concerned if your home was being used by a bunch of—by people you hadn't even met—as some kind of social club in your absence?"

"No," she answered simply, "if we *had* a home, no."

"Me neither," Sarah breathed against his neck from behind.

"Let's have a smoke," said Nina, bouncing suddenly to the floor to dig into the pocket of her jacket. Out came an awkwardly rolled joint and a book of matches.

"What do you mean if you *had* a home?" asked Harris. "Where do you normally live?" He felt annoyed that after exciting him so she would ignore him for a lousy *toke*. Was that her way of teasing him? he wondered. Then again, she seemed just to want to enjoy *everything*, as though everything gave her equal pleasure—men, women, nakedness, dope—no one pleasure having to compete with any other; and she seemed to expect that he would feel the same.

"We don't live 'normally' at all!" laughed Sarah, tickling Harris's ribs.

"We crash whoever's pad we can," said Nina. "We try not to disturb anybody. We never go back to a place where we don't feel welcome."

"We never steal anything, although occasionally we might raid your fridge," said Sarah.

"You're homeless? Two women as beautiful as you, homeless?"

"Don't call us 'women,'" said Nina. "Do we look that old? We're *girls.*"

"Okay, it's 'girls.'" How long had it been, he wondered, since the word "girls" had escaped his lips? "So you two girls are homeless?" He shook his head in disbelief, then watched Nina inhale and hold her breath. When he declined the offered stick, she passed it to Sarah.

"We used to belong to a commune upstate, but that broke up," explained Nina, the smoke drifting slowly out through her nose. "Kevin and Josh are friends. We all kind of grocked as soon as we met."

"Grocked?" said Harris.

"Clicked, I mean. Kevin and Josh used to live in Spain and sell Moroccan beads and hash in order to study flamenco guitar with the gypsies."

"I'd like to live in Ibiza," said Sarah.

"I'd like Ibiza or the beach in Izmir, in Turkey," sighed Nina. "It's supposed to be cheap to live in those places, and the men are terrifically handsome."

Harris felt a twinge of jealousy. "Ibiza's not cheap anymore, so I don't know who you've been listening to," he snorted. He remembered wanting to go there himself, but he'd finished college instead, and then very sensibly got married—but the thought of Jennifer was the *last* thing he needed to dwell on at the moment.

"You're wrong," said Sarah, her lips against the back of his neck.

"We know," murmured Nina, tamping out the joint against the match cover and restoring both to her jacket pocket. Harris wasn't inclined to disagree, considering their talent for finding inexpensive lodgings.

"I feel so *great* now, like we're totally grocking," said Nina. "You won't stop our *friends* from crashing here, will you, Harry?"

"Kevin and Josh? Of course not."

"Because if you did, we wouldn't come back either."

"*Mi casa es tu casa.*" Harris reached out and cupped Nina's hard cool breasts in his palms. "When will you girls be back?"

"Same day next week," said Nina.

"Same day every week, if you're good," said Sarah, nibbling his ear.

Nina crawled over him and pushed him back upon Sarah, who wrapped her legs around him from behind. Hovering over him, her thighs grazing his, Nina kissed him long and warmly on the mouth. Then she worked slowly with hands and lips down his thumping, pounding chest.

Harris did not want to say it, but this being the nineties, there was no way in conscience he could avoid it. "Do you think we ought to use something? Aren't you afraid of… catching something?"

"Catch something from you?" said Sarah.

"Think of using what?" said Nina.

"Should we be thinking about AIDS?" he gasped.

Nina looked at him for a protracted poker-faced moment. "*I* don't need any sex toys," she said. She pursed her lips at him in mock reproof. "Sarah, how about you?"

"Don't own a single chain or whip. Don't think I ever will," said Sarah, rubbing her chest around Harris's back and emitting gasps of delight.

"You girls have a helluva sense of humor," said Harris. He thought of the condoms in the bureau in the back bedroom —only two doors down the hall—but his will had melted away. The tail wagged the dog.

6

The next encounter with the two was unalloyed bliss, and the week after that he was even happier—paradoxically, because only Nina showed up. With Billy's Beatles LPs playing in the background, Harris knew that he felt powerfully, drunkenly attached to this "girl" whose interest in him was totally and irresponsibly *pure*—uncomplicated, meaningless, and intensely superficial. She did not ask him what he did for a living or whether he was happy with his wife; she asked for no help and no money, just a sandwich (only once). She did not, in fact, want to "share" his life beyond their weekly intersection in a space of swirling blobs of light and the cadences of sixties music.

Once he asked her, "What's your last name, Nina?"

"I don't have one," she said.

"What do you mean, you don't have one? Everybody has a last name."

"Not if you don't want one," she said, and he left it there, not wishing to argue with Music.

For the first two weeks he lived in ecstasy. Even when he and his wife made love, Jennifer reported aftershocks of pleasure such as she hadn't known with him since the first year they went out together (up until that accidental pregnancy). At the office he worked extra hard to make up for the time he now regularly took off, and if his partner begrudged him anything, it was his continuous state of euphoria.

All would have been perfect except that now Nina's friends appeared to be *abusing* the hospitality he had implicitly extended them. "It's more than just Josh and Kevin who park here, isn't it?" he asked her just two weeks after their first encounter.

"I'm not in control of who comes here, sweet," she answered in that bell-voice that vibrated within him like a gong. They had just made love and he felt safe to broach the matter.

"Last week I found a piece of paper under the bed with scores written on it for some game or other—in three columns, marked Alice, Derek, and Jerry. Do you know them?"

"Could be," she said, kissing his shoulder. "I know people with those names, but I don't know if it's them."

"They're being very careless," said Harris. "Anywhere else they'd be found out and kicked out."

"If I find out who they are, dear, I'll tell them to be careful." Her voice in his ear was like an instant lobotomy, so thoroughly did it quell his agitation. A minute later, however, his annoyance bubbled over again:

"Josh and Kevin have been stubbing out their joints in that ashtray," he said, pointing to Billy's desk.

"You sure it was them?"

"I found the ash-marks Monday evening. You told me they use the place Mondays."

"I'm sorry it upsets you, Harry." She drew away from him, her back against the wall, and hugged her knees to her chest. "Does that mean you don't want them back?" she said, the hurt showing in her eyes.

"No, no, not at all! You don't understand.... Me, I don't give a damn, but if Jennifer..." Harris thrust his hand beneath the girdle of Nina's locked arms. After a few seconds, she relented. Smiling, parting her knees to his probing, she tumbled forward and jumped on top of him, rocking and bouncing upon him till the bed itself squealed with delight. He hadn't known such wildness since he was twenty. Running his hands down the V of her back, squeezing her love-slick buttocks, Harris wondered if he ought to tell her about Billy. But his body was already responding—once again, and so *soon!*—to her clownish bumping and grinding. No, the problem presented by Billy was Harris's own to solve, and not any business of Nina's. With the taste of her in his mouth, the smell of her filling his lungs, and her voice bathing his brain, why cast a shadow over this liquid body of light that, beamed down from the sky, had condensed into flesh in his arms?

7

Harris woke in the middle of the night to muted strains of Bob Dylan singing "Blowin' in the Wind." The music was pleasant enough—it conjured up memories of the day before, when he had twice made love with Nina—but there was one thing about that faint singing that disturbed him: it appeared to be coming from somewhere *within the apartment*. He dismissed the thought as absurd, then rolled over and stared into the wide-open eyes of his wife. The dim night-light from the hallway enabled him to see that Jennifer, too, was awake. Their faces were only a few inches apart. She did not look surprised to see him gazing at her.

"Been up a while?" he said.

"Yes, quite a while. I'm a light sleeper. You sleep like a rock. What got you up?"

"Where's that music coming from?" he asked.

"I guess from the apartment below us."

"I should get up and look," he said.

"Look for what?" She reached out and clasped his shoulder, gently drawing him to her till their knees touched. "Anyway, I looked already."

"I didn't hear you get out of bed."

"You never hear me get up," she smiled.

"How long have you been awake?" he asked.

"Hours."

"That music has been on for hours?"

"No," she said. "That's not what's been keeping me up."

"What then?"

"Billy."

"Funny you should say that. Billy's been on my mind, too," he said.

"He'll be back for spring break."

"Yes, that's something to look forward to, isn't it?" he said. "Ten whole days back home with a pair of bores."

"I feel bad about his not being able to go down to Florida with his friends," said Jennifer.

"Really?" said Harris. She had brought out exactly what had been weighing on his *own* mind for these past two-three weeks. He had been dropping hints to Jennifer about how guilty he felt to deny Billy his Florida romp. She hadn't wanted to talk about it—until now.

"But what can we do?" she sighed. "It's just too damned expensive, isn't it? I mean with the tuition, the room and board, the stipend..."

"Yes, it *is* kind of expensive," said Harris. "We shouldn't even be *thinking* of changing our minds."

"You're absolutely right," said Jennifer. "Why even talk about it? C'mon, let's try to sleep."

"So if we shouldn't be thinking about it, why are we thinking about it?" said Harris. "You sure it's just the money, Jennifer? Or is it just that you'd miss him too much if he went off to Florida?"

"Don't accuse me of smother love!" she said, kicking Harris lightly with her knee. "And *you're* the one who's telling me what we can and can't afford, Harris. You know I always listen to you in practical matters, dear."

"Well, I think we should think about it some more, then," said Harris, amazed at how smoothly it was going.

"You're always 'thinking about it.' Let's make up our minds right now, Harris."

"All right, damn it!" he said. "I'm going to e-mail Billy tomorrow and tell him he can make plans for Florida."

"Remember, Harris, that's *your* decision. I'm not the one who's going to feel guilty."

"I thought I was making *our* decision," he said.

"I'm just going along with it."

"All right, then. Don't give me a hard time about it." Harris was delighted. He thought she'd *never* agree to Billy not coming home for spring break. Somehow he had used reverse psychology and given even *that* an extra back-spin or two. He pulled Jennifer to him, and she didn't resist. Why did the two of them always wear *pajamas*? he wondered. When did they ever lose the habit of going to bed in the nude? He slid his hand under her jammie top and fondled her soft breasts. He thought of those other breasts, solid cones thrusting themselves imperiously into his mouth.

"Your fingers are cold," she said. She kept his hand pressed to her chest.

"Yours too." He felt her hand explore his thigh. What was it, he wondered, that had transformed him lately into so ardent a conjugal lover—to his own and to Jennifer's almost embarrassed surprise? Was it fantasizing about Nina while fondling his wife? Or was it the way Jennifer, in the dimness of the bedroom, *became* Nina in his arms?

8

Each time Billy called from Florida, Harris was tempted to ask him whether he'd ever given anyone a copy of their key, but how could he ask without jeopardizing those magical intervals of girl-flesh, those hours stolen from business, from rectitude, from the law of entropy, from the structure of the universe itself? To attack the growing problem of the "visitors" by hauling in Billy would be pointless. Could *Nina* be more effective, he wondered, at getting all those others to be more careful, to straighten up behind them after their rap-sessions or jam-sessions or pot-klatsches or love-ins, or whatever the hell it was they spent time doing in his apartment? If he were to dump all this on Nina again, he would have to choose just the right moment, when they were both mellowed out after melting in each other's arms.

There were other things, too, on Harris's mind on the one day he was able to be with Nina during the week they shunted Billy off to Florida. Harris looked at himself, at his soft, hairy, sybaritic body beside the slim, smooth-skinned, taut-muscled Nina and could finally not refrain from asking a long-festering question. "Nina, why do you… like me?" he said. "You could have switched on Wednesdays to another apartment, couldn't you?"

"If you wanted me out, sure."

"And there are so many nicer-looking, younger guys out there. All those friends of yours, for instance."

"I like them too. But I can only get real close to someone who has something special, not just looks."

"Something special?"

"Yes. Call it like *a space behind the eyes*, a space that opens into caverns or grottoes or storm-tossed oceans," she murmured, waving her hands in rhythm with the shifting yellow light. "Something *vulnerable* about a person, man or woman." She contemplated him for a moment, looking as thoughtful as he'd ever seen her. "You dig?"

"Sure," said Harris, not at all sure that he dug. He attributed her banalities to a lack of worldly sophistication and an unchallenging social environment of like-minded dropouts—sloppy in thought *and in certain aspects of behavior, too*—who exalted each other's clichés, especially when high.

Nina would make love only to sixties music, and she brought along her own transistor radio because Billy's collection of records, she said, was "deficient in acid rock." She found stations that played numbers he hadn't heard for many years. "Not exactly hi-fi," she said, propping the little radio on the fuzz below her belly, "but small as it is, it's got some pretty good stations, doesn't it?"

"What station's that?" he asked, pointing to the radio.

"It's the one you like to get off at," she said, her eyes twinkling like an elf's.

Harris grinned. He adored her kinky sense of humor and her understated, matter-of-fact way of making deliberately absurd remarks—like that one about Billy's "TV" that made Harris laugh out loud sometimes—even in Jennifer's presence once. He didn't try to explain, but fortunately Jennifer didn't ask.

"You ought to modernize Billy's room," said Nina.

"Really? How?"

"Well, first get him a waterbed."

"Real modern, sure! And how about a mirror on the ceiling?"

"Fine. Then get rid of that old TV and buy him a nineteen-inch diagonal." She pointed deadpan to Billy's computer and Harris cracked up.

"Damn thing doesn't work," she sniffed. Harris shrieked with amusement and began to cover her with kisses.

Overcome with tenderness, he blurted out something that had been on his mind for some time. "Nina, aren't you concerned about getting... pregnant?"

"Not really. I do sometimes forget to take a pill, but—"

"You must *never* forget to take a pill," he nearly shouted at her. "My wife got pregnant when we were dating."

"She get an abortion?"

"I felt awful about that. I'd never have let her go through with it if—"

"If you were sure that she was pregnant by *you*," she stated flatly, not as if she were posing it as a question.

Harris's ears burned him. How the hell could she *know*? She had put her unpolished fingernail right on the button of his pain. "Not even Jennifer knows that," he half-whispered, looking away.

"It still hurts you? Your selfishness?" she said, in that sublimely dusky voice of a muted bell that she had.

Harris nodded, heaving a broken sigh.

"I guess you're not totally hopeless then."

"What the hell did you major in, Psychology?" said Harris. He felt exposed. The louvered door swung open again before her, disclosing not simply a bulge in Harris's pants, but this time a lump in his chest.

"I'm a college dropout," she said.

To Harris, for this one moment, Nina seemed wiser than all the graduates he'd ever known—all those friends of his who'd become so serious within six months after getting their degrees. A few seconds later she managed to undermine that impression. Her favorite writer was Kerouac, she said, and she was "not a real hippie, just a worshiper of God through love."

When Sonny and Cher came on with "I Got *You*, Babe," she made a face and fiddled with the station selector. "Pseudo-hip crap to make the middle-class oppressor feel safe," she explained. When Simon and Garfunkel's "Mrs. Robinson" played, she asked him what he thought of *The Graduate*, and he told her he loved it. "Kevin and I have gone to see it *four times*," she said. Then she curled up to him and fiddled with his scrotum in hopes of exciting him all over again. She was insatiable and at the same time sensitively forgiving of all his middle-aged inadequacies.

"Do you regard *me* as one of those 'middle-class oppressors'?" said Harris, suddenly and for no clear reason annoyed.

"You haven't been oppressive to me," she replied.

"So why is it that your friends—or whoever they are—trample all over me with no regard for the… delicacy of our situation here?"

"What do you mean, 'trample all over' you?"

"Well," said Harris, "for starters, what do you call leaving a half-eaten sandwich on the dining-room table? What if my wife had come home before I did that day?"

"I'm sorry," said Nina. "I don't know who'd have done that. But wouldn't your wife have thought it was yours?"

"Is that really the point?" She seemed to be making light of the situation. "And tell me this, Nina. What kind of creature would strew Billy's bedcovers half over the floor and leak some sort of discharge right in the middle of the bedsheet?"

"It wasn't me. You're not accusing *me*, are you, Harry?"

"Of course not," he said. She gave him a cold look. It frightened him. "*We* always use this airline blanket," he said, "and I always put it back in Billy's closet." Amazing, thought Harris, that Jennifer hadn't discovered that mess first, since he himself hadn't entered Billy's room until *hours* after returning from work.

"You've got one foot stuck in the fifties, Harry."

"But my other foot's square in the sixties," he said, running his toes up her thigh. She sat up and brushed off his foot as if it were a fly. Harris felt that she was refusing to take him seriously. "And who was that slob," he persisted, raising his voice, "that barn-bred hippie slut, who dropped a tampon into her unflushed puddle of pee? Thank heaven she didn't flush the toilet. It might have backed up all over the bathroom floor!"

Nina had tuned him out. Janis Joplin was on. When the Rolling Stones or Jim Morrison or Janis Joplin came on, shouting and ranting at an adoring hysterical crowd, she'd light up a roach—the way she was doing now—and sit transfixed in a lotus pose, as if spiritually overcome.

"Nina, Billy's coming home in three weeks," Harris blurted. "Where and when can we see each other over the summer?"

He was annoying her, he could see it. "Can't I meet you at one of your other hangouts?"

For answer, Nina absentmindedly took Harris's hand and began to suck on his fingers, never once looking up at him until the Joplin number was over. From the trance-like look on her face, he knew she did not want to deal with the matter right now.

"I adore her," she said, as if awakening from a spell. "Joplin is the *end*."

"Awesome," said Harris.

She pondered the word for a moment. "That's a perfect way to put it." He couldn't tell if she was putting him on or not.

9

Harris tossed in his sleep. He kept running through alternate scenarios of what he *might* have said, and how Nina *might* have replied, if he had only been more forceful about arranging to link up with her over the summer. She made him feel, somehow without openly saying so, that they would be violating some unspecified condition of their relationship if they were to meet anywhere but within the sanctuary of Billy's bedroom. As if anywhere else would be the equivalent of "profane" ground. Awakening before dawn, he thought it was only in his dreams that he had been hearing the same rock music that had worked a spell upon Nina two days earlier.

But it wasn't in his dreams. Loud for a few seconds, the music trailed away down the hall, but did not disappear altogether. It persisted, even though faintly. Harris *had* to get up to investigate. By the dim night-light from the hall, he could see that Jennifer had already slipped out of bed. The implications came to him in a rush of anxiety. Why hadn't she screamed or alerted him in some way? Was she finally on to what was happening?... Was she *safe*? he wondered, shuddering as he rolled out of bed. Harris tightened his pajama strings and peeked around the doorjamb down the length of the narrow hallway. What if the slobs who'd been trashing the apartment were rapists and had knocked her unconscious—before she'd even had a *chance* to scream?

No one was in the hallway—except himself now. But at a distance up the hall he could see light leaking out from the bathroom door. The music he heard seemed to come from there as well. Barefoot, Harris proceeded slowly over the carpet, testing the floor with each step to avoid places that squeaked. Passing the first closed door, the door to his office, he hunched forward to the door to Billy's room, which poked out, as always, an inch or so into the hallway.

Even before he got his eye to the opening, he could see that the Lava Lite was on.

And he could smell the fragrance of grass.

Warily, Harris peered through the ample crack. The lamp cast medium-bright bubbles of light over the figures on Billy's bed. One of the threesome was a lanky-haired, gangly young buck who lay on his back at the far end and comically kicked at the air. He was engaged in pulling his pants on. The second figure he recognized immediately. From the near end of the bed, dark-haired Sarah leaned forward in profile, partially obscuring the person in the middle. He watched her breasts bobble as she lifted her sweater and pulled it down over her head.

The woman who lay sprawled in the middle was at first only a pair of naked legs. One of her knees was raised. Harris was sure it was Nina, and somehow he felt deeply betrayed—even though he knew she spent at least six days of the week (not to mention all her nights!) with people he didn't know. For some reason, though, what he didn't actually see didn't bother him, and he had long since ceased trying to picture Nina's life outside the door of his apartment. It had been none of his business. But now...

Sarah moved out of the way for a moment, and Harris caught sight of *Jennifer*—totally nude! Relaxed in a dreamy smile, her face glowed in the undulant light, her hand stroking the still-naked shoulder of the man beside her who was wriggling into his jeans.

Harris looked and looked at her, and his scalp prickled as if crawling with ants. He held his breath, expecting to be swamped with pangs of jealousy and anger. Inexplicably, they didn't come. Instead, transfixed by that dreamy look of hers, that contented-cat look of hers, he felt what *she* had to be feeling. He felt at one with her! Hadn't he too, time and again, sat naked in that same salvific spot just as she did?

This is not normal! thought Harris. What rose in him were feelings of both tenderness and lust. Glutted with the loves of both Nina *and* Jennifer, his veins were too full to admit anger. He did not need to picture to himself in graphic detail how the encounter in Billy's room—evidently just coming to an end now—had unfolded. Who did what to whom was irrelevant, as were the colloquial names that might be applied to their physical acts. It was as if he had stumbled upon the close of some secret ceremony, and that his intrusion could be forgiven, because he was a parallel initiate of these very same Cyprian rites....

10

There was a fourth participant, too! The one in the bathroom. Another man, or a woman? he wondered. He could not just stay out here in the hall. He tiptoed along the carpet to the bathroom.

The door was open wide enough for him to see her bare knees. She was seated on the toilet. Her jeans were crumpled down to mid-calf, no panties were evident inside them, and she held her little radio in her lap. Harris opened the door and stepped in. Showing no surprise, Nina acknowledged his presence by glancing at him, then looked back down at her radio. In spite of its tinny sound, the raucous vitality of Janis Joplin poured out of it.

"Excuse me," he said, "but the radio woke me up."

"I'm sorry." Her voice was heavy with sadness, and her face was ghostly pale. Her honey-blond hair was disheveled, and strands lay plastered to her cheeks.

"Is something the matter?" he asked.

She paid him no heed.

"You guys have an argument?" he asked.

She sighed deeply but still wouldn't talk to him. He started toward her but she put out her hand to stop him.

"Why are you treating me like this? What have I done wrong?" he asked, raising his voice. He saw tears roll down her face and teeter on the tips of her nose and chin before plunking down into her lap. He knew every inch of her body, but she would never really open her mind to him. "You don't treat me as if I'm *real*, damn it! Like I ask you how and when we can get together over the summer, and you act like you don't even hear me."

"First Jimi Hendrix, and now *this!*" she sighed.

"What the hell're you talking about, Nina?"

"You don't know. You don't know *anything*," she mumbled, her lips drenched with tears.

"Okay, if you want to dump me, just say so. But I deserve some kind of a freakin' answer, don't I?"

"Haven't you heard?" she whimpered. "They just announced it. It's Janis Joplin. She's *dead!*"

Her voice stabbed him with its grief, but her rocking and moaning and sobbing looked absolutely absurd to Harris. "Joplin? Of course she's dead. She O.D.'ed about *twenty-five years* ago! So why the hell are you..."

Nina clutched her radio and looked up at Harris with a growing, wide-eyed fright. Pee gushed out of her in a sudden squall that lasted about half a minute. She wrapped her arms around her body and her fright verged literally on terror.

"What's the matter?" he demanded to know.

"I'm seeing... *through* you!"

"You're on the potty, but you're also on *pot!*" He wanted to slap her, beat her. Tears blurred his eyes as he looked at her.

"You're not *real!*" Nina exclaimed, rubbing her eyes.

"What the hell's with you, Nina?"

"Fading away, right in front of me, like a... a *ghost!*" She clapped her hand over her mouth to suppress a bulging-eyed scream.

"Are you crazy?" said Harris. He touched himself, his solid puffy flesh, and watched as Nina wiped herself and hurriedly pulled up her pants.

"This is a ghost house!" she said, her voice cracking. She gazed in his general direction but no longer caught his eye. Flailing her hands defensively, as if brushing at cobwebs, she walked right at him as if he weren't even there. She cut right past him as he flattened against the wall. Her arm seemed to slice through him. Where she touched him he felt burned as if by a hot, stinging plasma. She lunged out of the bathroom and dashed back toward Billy's room.

Harris looked in the bathroom mirror.

He was there—balding, fleshy-lipped, hairy-chested. He opened his mouth wide. There was no hole in his head that revealed the wall behind him. "You're the one who's not *here!*" he wanted to shout after her, but the horror of the thought stopped his tongue. His hair bristled as if charged with an electric current.

Harris looked into the toilet. A pool of urine gave him back his face. He would have liked to leave the toilet unflushed. Reluctantly, however, he pressed down on the handle, and he immediately regretted having done so. Leaving the bathroom, he turned in the opposite direction from Nina—left, past the kitchen, into the large front half of the apartment that was lit only by streetlights from below and the vague blueing of dawn. Here in the comparative darkness he could disappear for the moment and try to organize the welter of his thoughts.

He pressed up against the living room wall next to a window that gave out upon the street. The curtains were pulled back and the shade, as always, was up, since Jennifer wanted her plants to get as much of daylight as possible. His head still pounding, Harris looked down at the lamplit street. Three stories below him a curious procession was in motion. He craned his neck to left and to right. Out of building after building, along both sides of the block, small groups of people issued quietly into the tree-lined street. They were not walking dogs, and they were not getting into cars to go to work. They sported jeans and casual jackets; and most of them, male and female, had long loose hair that shone richly when they passed under the lamplight. Young, brisk, and jaunty though they were, they proceeded in a manner both orderly and solemn. Each was somehow a part of one gigantic reptilian organism. Trickling out of apartments, collecting in the street, they all joined in a human stream that flowed in one direction, always uphill to the left, toward the still invisible sun. Where were they headed? Harris wouldn't even venture a guess. Was it always like this before dawn? he wondered. He had never been up to look out of the window this early.

Feet shuffled behind him also, and he saw the three of them, outlined in the night-light—the young man and Sarah supporting a sobbing and stumbling Nina. They emerged into the living room and silently hurried to the apartment door. Harris, diagonally across the room from them, huddled silent and motionless in the dark. In seconds they were out in the corridor. Soon they would be part of the procession in the street. Thoughtfully, they shut the door behind them, even took care to lock it. He was sure they must have been equally careful to leave Billy's room as they'd found it. Jennifer would see to that.

He gauged that it would now be safe for him to saunter back to bed. Jennifer lay under the covers, on her back. Her eyes caught a reflection from the night-light in the hall. Harris slipped under the covers beside her. He liked the warmth that flowed out of her when their hips and thighs came in contact during the night.

"I got up. I heard music," said Harris. He saw her staring at the ceiling.

"They're not coming back," said Jennifer.

Harris pondered a reply. "It's okay," he said at the ceiling.

That was the first and last time they ever talked to each other about the visitors.

With Arms Outstretched

Mort Fleisher did not wish to hurt his wife's feelings, but if she couldn't adjust to the deep-seated changes that had taken place between them, he would have no choice but to leave her.

"Mort, dear, I do mind!" said Maple. "It upsets me tremendously that when you come home, the first thing you do is hand me your briefcase— and then drape your coat over my arm."

"But I thought you've been trying to be *helpful*, holding your arm out like that! If you don't, I will have to step five yards from the door here to find the first convenient surface." He pointed to the doorway that opened left out of the foyer. Against the foyer wall, in the corner of the living room, stood a useless upholstered chair crouched on lion claws. When he got home from work, he would usually unload his gear on that chair, and his wife would then pick up after him. So why should he do in two steps what Maple collapsed into one?

"My outstretched arm is not a coatrack, dear. If I had extended only one arm, it might have been so construed. But I stretched out both—to embrace you. Knowing what a hard day you've had. Not that mine was much easier—trying to please a screaming throng on a sale day—but I get home before you do and try to make things pleasant for when you arrive." Maple looked at him with her usual stubborn willingness to give him the benefit of the doubt. To Mort her head seemed more bowed than usual, more sunken into the billows of her neck, as though physically in retreat, finally, after the thousand face-to-face staredowns they'd had with each other. Did she at last understand, he wondered, that she could no longer recover the Mort she used to know?

"I don't *want* your head-on embrace," said Mort. "But I do appreciate the Scotch-and-soda you put out for me on the coffee table." If he could puncture her Michelin bosom, he thought, and release about fifty pounds of pressure, he might again regard her armlock as a tolerable hurdle on the way to his drink.

Toward which he proceeded apace.

Hurrying behind him, Maple flung his coat and briefcase onto that same puffy, purple-striped chair anyway, wiping out the economy he had just effected. And just before he could align his rear end with his favorite easy chair, there she was, right up against his back, grabbing him around the waist with those bolster-like arms that used to be so shapely. It was already becoming a ritual. "If I can't have what's in front, I'll take the side you do present," she said, quite as he'd expected. "I love you, and I know you can't *always* be all there for me, so…"

Sinking rearward into her padded belly was not, in fact, that distasteful to Mort. On the contrary, the gyrations she performed against his hips proved relaxing, like an intense little back-massage—a pleasant thing after a day spent on your butt with your back bent over figures. He had loved that masseur-chair with adjustable height and speed of massage that he'd tried out once at a fancy shop on the mall. But a thousand bucks was highway robbery. So whenever Maple ground her fat into his coccyx, panting with excitement as she did so, Mort Fleisher stood there and let her have her way with him. It made them both feel better before cocktails and TV.

It was especially soothing on the nights he'd come home *very* late—after making it at a nearby seedy hotel with Darlene or another of the fun-loving girls from the bar down below called the Hip Flask. The soreness derived not so much from lumpy mattresses as from the physical wear and tear on his system. The younger girls who were workout freaks ("biceptuals," he liked to call them) could especially jerk him around. Pumped they were, with boobs like hammerheads, thighs of tanned steel, and pistons for behinds. Maximal exertions of the gluteal kind tied knots in his spinal column, and the perfect cool-down preceding his double Scotch was a close encounter with Maple's vibrating cushions.

Mort prided himself on drawing a sharp line between his fun life and his home life. After an evening with one of his playmates, he'd go over his clothing with packing tape to remove stray strands of hair. One night, however, his elaborate precautions failed to achieve their purpose. Not very long after he deposited his coat on Maple, that normally agreeable and placid woman confronted him with a fresh box of condoms she'd found in his pocket.

He could not very well say, "A surprise for *you*, dear!," as if caught with a bouquet of flowers intended for one of his sweeties—first, because the box was half empty; and second, because he and Maple had never used a condom in all their twenty-four years of marriage. Instead, he could express only moral indignation at the audacity she had shown in daring to rifle his pockets.

"But if I hadn't," said Maple, "I would not have known for sure what till now I could only surmise."

"And what do you propose to do about it, now that you've made yourself terribly unhappy?" asked Mort. He regarded with disgust the bloated flesh that had reached her ankles, outpacing her ever lower and lower hemlines.

"I expect you to be a gentleman and give up your secret life, which is draining us of a good deal of income," she said. "When your kids are away at college and you can barely send them enough money for their textbooks—"

"How can you blame *me* for squandering our income when *you* got yourself fired from your job?" Mort shot back.

"I was not fired. I quit. They were pushing me beyond physical endurance."

"Not true! You were simply unable to keep up with your normal responsibilities. Look at you!" A triple chin joined her face to her neck; her neck ran from her ears to her shoulders; and her middle was so stuffed with chocolates that her massive arms had almost nowhere to settle—so that nowadays she *always* looked as if waiting to be draped with his coat.

"It's all your fault," she said.

"Be grateful that I haven't yet talked of leaving you," he replied.

"Why don't you?" she challenged.

"Because," he said, "you're my home, my security. I've always believed in the sacredness of the marriage vows. But if you force me to choose, to give up my private life, which is very important to me… then I'll simply have to leave you. No two ways about it." He dropped his chin to his chest, dramatizing the sadness he would feel at parting. "I'll let *you* have the bed," he said, reaching down to the coffee table to pick up the Scotch she'd set out. "I m forced to sleep out at the edge anyway. When I don't, I roll down an incline into your belly. The television I think legitimately should be mine. The car, too, since you can't drive it anymore, and—"

"Don't leave! Please don't leave, Mort!" she pleaded, her puffy lids rising just high enough to reveal the sheer panic in her eyes. She came at him—gelatinously, it seemed—with arms outstretched (their natural position now, just about) and Mort, out of habit, turned his back on her, accepting the urgent massage by which she transformed her pent-up anxieties into useful work.

"Then we must reach a modus vivendi," he declared. "I accept *your* addiction to sweetmeats, you accept mine."

"If this is what I must do to keep you, dear. If you allow me to be close to you in *some* way… " He felt the vibrations of her voice blend with the oscillations of her paunch against his back.

Mort enjoyed untroubled bliss for several weeks thereafter. Maple did nothing to inhibit his freedom; his conscience was totally clear; and he prided himself on the way his two worlds, formerly at odds, had reached so perfect an accord. At whatever time he came home, his drink was always ready, and Maple didn't fuss and flutter about him after giving him the backrub he liked. Most of the evening she would simply sit nearby, and hardly utter a squeak, and hardly move a limb. The less he looked at her, the better off he felt, because she just kept getting rounder and squatter—at an accelerating pace, so it seemed.

The one thing that did start getting on his nerves was the dust that was accumulating around the house. He did not eat dinner at home very much, and he wasn't upset that Maple had ceased even *offering* to cook a hot meal for him. (He found plenty of excuses to spend time at the "office" even on weekend evenings.) But once, when preparing a snack for himself, he discovered that his once white shirtsleeves emerged filthy with grime from contact with the kitchen table. Hopping mad, he stomped off looking for Maple. There she was, seated or standing (lately he couldn't tell the difference) in front of the TV, in the place he'd last seen her. Clasped securely between her bosom and her ledge-like lap nested a freshly opened box of chocolates.

"Look at my sleeves! The house is becoming a pigsty!" he shouted at her.

It took her a long time to turn to him and reply. For Mort it was like watching a slow-motion film of a turtle peeking out from its shell. "I'm sorry, dear. I don't want to make you unhappy, believe me. But we just can't *afford* a cleaning woman at the rate at which our checking account keeps dwindling."

"Cleaning woman!" The very idea set his teeth on edge. "Since when have we ever needed a cleaning woman? Even when you were working, you found time to do the little tidying up that was necessary. And now that you have endless leisure, you're not doing a damned *thing* around the house!" He was not going to confront her about the rising cost of her chocolates. A pact was a pact, and he was committed to honoring it.

"I do feel bad about the housework, dear. I was afraid that someday you'd notice."

"Notice! You haven't even changed the bedsheets for a month!"

"I used to try to keep up, dear. But my joints are all so stiff. Arthritis makes it difficult for me to get around the way I used to. Even walking seems to hurt me these days." Maple's voice suddenly grew cheery, but if there was a smile on her face, it was stifled beneath the swells of her cheeks—which were themselves partly obscured by the high ruffled neck of her dress. "However, that doesn't mean that I can no longer give my darling his nightly restorative massage!"

"Don't be coy with me, Maple," he replied. "The idea of hiring a maid service is absolutely out of the question."

"Then the house will get dirtier and dirtier."

"Just let it… and see if I don't leave!" Mort threatened.

"Please, dear! I don't want you to leave." She moved her heavy arms out stiffly, as though to embrace him, but she didn't seem physically able to propel herself toward him from her squatting-place next to the sofa.

"What choice do you give me?" Mort muttered.

"There *is* a way," she said.

He refused to look at her, fixing his eyes on some inanity that filled the TV screen.

"You spend so much on hotel rooms, taking your girls out, dear."

He was about to flare up. Must he remind her of the bargain they'd made? But she didn't give him time to react.

"Why not take them home with you?" she offered. "Use one of the spare bedrooms. There'll be plenty to drink here, and you can order pizza from Domino's. Think of all the money we can save!"

"Take them *home*! Now come on, Maple. I don't wish to give up my pleasures, but I'm hardly going to impose them upon *you*!"

"Don't be silly, dear. There's no need to be puritanical. I see this as an entirely practical solution to a pressing problem."

Mort was not one to reject an idea out of hand, especially if it had enough good points about it to merit his closer examination. "But what about my… friends?" he challenged. "Look at it from their point of view. How would *they* like coming home with me—to a house where a *wife* is rattling around?"

"Oh, but no one will know I'm even here," Maple assured. "Not even you. I promise to make myself completely invisible. Tell them you live alone! I'll remove all signs of a wife's presence. Trust me!"

"It's not that I'm not *proud* of you in many ways, Maple. But just think how sensitive some women can be, and to bring them to a man's..."

"I *am* thinking of how sensitive they can be. As a woman, I know exactly what you're saying, dear. And that's why I can promise you that my presence will be entirely effaced.... Please just think of all the money we'll save! More than enough to afford a cleaning woman. Just think of how much cleaner and nicer it'll be for you here than in some overpriced, scuzzy hotel."

Mort gave it a minute's thought. Perhaps it was worth experimenting with. On a trial basis, sort of. First with Hildy, who would screw inside a coat closet, so that if *she* proved too sensitive—well, it was like bringing a canary into a mine-pit.

The first few experiments proved remarkably successful. Maple had removed all garments of hers from places that a guest might poke into. So too, she cleared knickknack shelves, bureaus and walls of family pictures and anything that looked suspicious. Thoughtful to a fault, she even set liquor and snacks on the coffee table for either "before" or "after"—going to all sorts of trouble for him in spite of the increasing difficulty she was having just in getting around. Mort could now indulge his passions with a mind free of petty financial concerns. It was only after inviting a girl to *sleep over* that Mort got flak the next day from Maple.

"That's absurd," said Mort. "It's assumed I'm here by myself. That means I have no excuse *not* to invite someone occasionally to stay for the night. If I refuse, what should I tell them, that at midnight I turn into a pumpkin? That I sleep in an iron lung?" He would not stand for any of her objections, which clearly had no basis in practicality, and once again Maple proved how wise he'd been to marry her by withdrawing her groundless scruples and capitulating to the very logic that she had herself set in motion.

Maple was so self-effacing that Mort, leaving a warm bower for a visit to the bathroom, would tiptoe through the house at times looking for her—and could not find her even in their conjugal bed! Perhaps she would leave home entirely during those nights. But where would she go?... No, he just had to take at face value her promise to keep herself entirely out of sight. After a while Mort ceased his foolish side-trips in search of her, nor would he ask her the next day where she'd been. Not out of pride. Simply out of a confident faith. "Better not look a gift-horse," etc., became his motto.

During the nights that he did sleep with Maple he made no objections to her grinding against his back, but after the second time she'd failed to put out snacks for his *soirées*, he grew testy and withdrew from her touch. She wept quietly next to him in bed, telling him that she could no longer get out as much as she used to, and how she would often, just to avoid the pain caused by moving her limbs, sit around immobile for hours. Mort quite easily forgave her and told her how truly he appreciated her efforts and that *he*, to relieve her of undue strain, would do all the household shopping from now on.

Darlene liked sipping Scotch in front of the big-screen TV *after*ward. On emerging from the bedroom that night, it was she who first noticed the slight change in the living room furniture. "Who in heaven's name would buy an armchair as ugly as that?" she exclaimed, pointing to a plump, squat easy chair with enormous bolsters for arms that hunkered just to the left of the sofa. It wore a ruffled doily for antimacassar and was covered in a pinkish purple splashed with big blue polka dots.

Mort was surprised to see it there but was hardly fazed by Darlene's little sarcasm. "One of my favorite chairs," he lied. "It's been around for years, but not always in this particular room."

"If I move in wit' choo, will you get rid of it?" she said.

"I don't see why I should."

"Yuk! C'mon, now, Morty boy. Show me you got taste in sumpm else beside women!"

Morty was growing piqued. "I assure you, it's an unusually comfortable piece. Look, I'll show you." He eased himself into its soft, solid grip. "Like a heated waterbed," he said.

Almost instantly its circular motions began soothing his lower back. "It's an auto-*masseuse*," he said, enjoying the stepped-up vibrations. "I've had it around for quite some time. It's excellent for all your aches and pains, believe me. Come, try it!"

Reluctantly, she took his place in the chair, which abruptly ceased its motion. "Where's the controls?" she said, trying to get comfortable against the squooshy feel of the cushions.

Mort picked up the VCR remote from the coffee table. He aimed it at the chair and pushed some buttons. "I guess you're right, Darlene. If it doesn't work as it should, I suppose I'll just have to get rid of it."

It didn't take but a moment. The gyrations started up again, increased in strength and frequency, and Darlene settled back with lids half closed into the luxurious rhythm of a backrub.

Refrigerator Blindness

For their first anniversary Ralph bought Amanda a fifty-inch HD TV so sharp and clear that he could track a bead of sweat down a pitcher's brow and even make out single blades of artificial grass in the outfield. Sucking on a third or fourth beer, he would ignore the drama of a three-two count and instead call her attention to the flight of a piece of trash cast adrift from the bleachers.

If Amanda wanted to go to sleep, he would urge her to stay up at least long enough to get him another cold one because, as he said, he didn't want to miss any HD action poking around the damn fridge for the rest of a six-pack that she had again managed to store in the back of some remote shelf completely out of sight.

Some months later, for her twenty-sixth birthday, Ralph surprised Amanda with a state-of-the-art ten-megapixel camera which he used to take pictures in such incredible detail that when he enlarged shots of some of the older highway overpasses (Ralph was a civil engineer) you could see cracks forming in places. Such fine-grained imaging disturbed Amanda, not out of fear of collapsing bridges, but out of her growing annoyance that when she pointed out an expanding network of cracks in the paint high up along the bathroom walls, Ralph claimed that he couldn't see a thing deserving his attention.

"Maybe you ought to get tested for glasses?" she suggested.

"Oh?" he retorted. "And you? I suppose you have X-ray vision?" That was just for starters. Such a volley of sarcasm rained down on her that she avoided ever mentioning glasses again and instead patched up the cracks herself with paint she bought at a local hardware store.

Not seeing cracks in the paint—well, that might have been understandable, but Amanda found it much harder to excuse Ralph's inability to "see" where the toilet paper was (on the shelf right behind him) as he sat on the toilet yelling for her to enter the stinking bathroom and end his hygienic perplexity. More frequently, however, Ralph had problems locating even larger things, like the vacuum cleaner, for instance. It was stored in a hallway closet with other cleaning supplies, but Ralph never remembered which of the four closets she had hidden it in, and if he did stumble upon the right closet, it was too damn dark for him to find the needed attachments.

"How do you expect me to find anything when nothing is ever where it should be?" he would shout.

"Oh, don't bother, dear, I'll find it myself," she would answer.

"I looked everywhere," he would insist.

"Except right under your nose," she would reply. But instead of pursuing a fruitless conversation, she usually found it much less wearing to do the vacuuming herself.

The good-looking couple in the apartment next door had their own troubles, as Amanda could see—opposite tastes in everything from books to movies to restaurants to where to go on vacation—but that didn't stop Amanda from socializing with curly-haired Jason and bottle-blonde Helena, inviting them for dinner at times, later for just coffee and dessert, gestures sometimes reciprocated, but Amanda did not keep count. She enjoyed their company, "their" referring mainly to the particularly attentive Jason who shared her taste in watching shows about nature and the environment. Normally, though, the two of them would not catch more than fifteen minutes of any such show, deferring to the action-drama-comedy preferences of Ralph and Helena.

One evening, just as they had all finished dinner, Amanda insisted on watching at least the beginning of a special about the Serengeti. Helena made a face and excused herself to go to the bathroom. Amanda, feeling vaguely guilty, reminded herself that she had not offered to make coffee yet, but coffee was definitely expected.

"Ralph," she said, "would you mind making coffee for everybody, dear?" For the best viewing angle, she sat down next to Jason on the couch directly opposite the TV. "I'd really hate to miss the beginning of this special."

"Sure," said Ralph, starting toward the kitchen after a sharp look at Amanda as if seeking confirmation of so incredible a request.

"More wine, Jason?" said Amanda, reaching for his glass on the coffee table.

"Enough playing the hostess," said Jason, extending his hand to stop her from picking up his glass. His hand, in blocking hers, slid warmly over her fingers—and Amanda felt something like an electric thrill at the touch. Exchanging darting looks, neither said a word, but the shock of Jason's touch spread warm waves through Amanda's body, as if she'd had a shot of some supercharged liqueur. They both stared ahead at the giant screen, but among the first segments shown was a violent attack of a lion upon some slender creature with beautifully curving horns, a scene that drew a gasp from Amanda, who involuntarily laid her hand on Jason's soft yet powerfully muscled thigh. She would have had just such a reaction if Ralph were sitting there. Ralph usually did sit there. Inappropriately, though, she allowed her hand to linger, as though it had a will of its own, and as she began to withdraw it, she felt Jason's hand close over it.

"Amanda!" Ralph shouted from the kitchen. "Where'd you stow the coffee? And I can't find the damn..."

Amanda shot up from the couch, not daring to glance back at Jason. "Don't bother, dear, I'll find it myself," she shouted back, for the first time half-grateful for Ralph's kitchen blindness.

"I searched in the closet, the top of the fridge, the—"

"Except..." she said, pointing below his nose.

Dismissing Ralph from the kitchen, she prepared the coffee and set out the dessert tray, conscious all the while of the trembling of her hands.

When the guests were about to leave, Amanda said, "A couple of nights from now there's going to be a National Geographic special on bats. I'm fascinated by bat echolocation. Would you two like to come over?"

"It's not my thing," said Helena, "but if Jason wants to..."

"Well," said Jason, turning slightly red, "watching it on your set would certainly beat watching it on ours, but I wouldn't want to..."

"Of course you should watch it on ours," blustered Ralph. "But you'll be so spoiled you won't want to look at your own box ever again!"

For Christmas Ralph bought Amanda a nineteen-inch laptop computer to replace the much smaller model she was used to. It would save her a good deal of eyestrain, he declared, offering to set it up in his own office first—to give it a "road test" and iron out any bugs, he explained—to which Amanda enthusiastically agreed.

Later that day Amanda stepped into Ralph's office and said, "I thought you were going to gather up all the gift wrappings before you took the garbage out back."

"And so I did," grunted Ralph, his eyes fixed on the giant computer screen.

"So what's all this?" she said, clutching an armful of crinkly paper and ribbons and boxtops. "I found this stuff in the kitchen and under the coffee table."

"What?" said Ralph, still not turning around.

"Don't bother," mumbled Amanda. "I'll dump it myself.… And what the hell are you looking at?"

It was a full-screen image of a woman's bare butt.

"Cheeky," said Amanda.

"Look close," said Ralph. "At this resolution you can make out every hair in the crack."

"Speaking of hairy cracks," said Amanda, "I'm smelling jocks and socks in the bedroom that haven't been scraped up for weeks."

"I'll get to it," said Ralph, now examining a different view.

"By the way," said Amanda, "at nine tonight they're showing a documentary about carnivorous plants. Do you want to join me and Jason in watching it?"

Ralph was busy scrutinizing another interesting image.

Amanda was concerned about what to do for Ralph come Valentine's Day. The more she enjoyed exploring the world of nature—from the hedonistic comfort of a sofa—with Jason there to multiply her pleasure, the more she felt a guilty need to affirm her conjugal commitment to Ralph. So, for V-Day, she got Ralph some chocolates and some specially sexy condoms. When she checked the coffee table later that afternoon, though, she noted that Ralph had eaten all the chocolates but had left undisturbed, without even reading the bliss-promising copy, the colorful condom box.

But the pièce de résistance—*that* she had reserved for Ralph for later that evening. She wore nothing but a milky, see-through robe, silky and seductive, the one she had worn quite often the first few months of marriage. Slinking down the hallway, she stopped and posed, hand on hip, at the threshold of Ralph's open office door. Suspicious sounds burbled from within.

"Ralphie," she cooed, "I've got a special Valentine's present I've been holding in reserve for you.… Ralph? What's *that* you're gawking at?"

"Incredible, the detail!" he said, his eyes glued to the monitor while he waved her on in with a behind-the-ear flap of the hand.

She leaned over him, hoping he would smell the cologne she wore, the first present he ever bought her, intoxicating even to the wearer. He was watching a pair of gorgeous lesbians convulsed in a writhing and moaning heap on a rug in front of an artificial fireplace. "Don't tell me," she said. "You can see every pore."

"The texture, Amanda—the texture of the flesh!"

Stroking his neck, as Amanda knew Ralph liked, she asked, "Don't you want me to call off Jason's coming over tonight? He's due in an hour, but I can simply—"

"Not at all. Enjoy!"

Drawing back, torn between arousal and anger, she slowly reduced the pressure of her breast on his shoulder. "And *please*," she shrilled, "will you pick up your dirty underwear that's been piling up in the bedroom, damn it?"

"I'll get to it right away."

"Now!"

"In a minute," he said, waving her off with the same hand-flap he'd used in inviting her in, except the fingers now flapped in the opposite direction.

Amanda hardly expected it when Ralph did finally stumble into the bedroom. A bedside lamp with a dark-green shade cast a warm, low glow over the bed. Jason tried to tumble off her, but Amanda held his sweating body firmly in place.

"*What* dirty underwear?" snarled Ralph. "What the hell are you talking about?" Amanda watched him drop to his knees and poke around the edges of the bed.

"Don't bother," sighed Amanda with a squeeze to Jason's shuddering buttocks. "I'll shovel it together myself."

"I don't see jack shit! I've looked everywhere," said Ralph, shaking his head as he made for the door.

"Except right under..."

He had lumbered out into the hall before she could finish the phrase.

Mariah My Soul-Mate

For the fourth time in two weeks of prowling the mall, Emily sat in the same bench gazing across the same beige-carpeted aisle at Mariah, who stared back through the plate-glass window with a look that said, "Stop kidding yourself, peanut, you can't even afford my boots."

The attitude of this decked-out display-case showoff—whom Emily somehow wound up naming Mariah—was molded deep in the plastic, wood, or whatever else she was made of, to get across the message to girls like Emily that no matter what they did, they'd never measure up. No matter the make-up, no matter the clothes, no matter what they could or could not afford to buy. Because attitude came from within.

And Emily was slowly catching on to the secret of how to develop attitude. Close observation, combined with a pinch of envy, would someday lead Emily to some sort of realization about her own inner potential—but for Mariah to suggest, in that silent-superior way, that her super-confident bearing had nothing to do with those cool outfits she wore... that was something Emily wasn't ready to believe. Mariah looked to be much older than Emily, say about seventeen, so maybe in three, three-and-a-half years, when Emily too would be completely mature, she would undergo an inner change to match the great changes that had already transformed her body. Feature for feature Emily felt she was a match for that big doll in every way. And as for that drop-dead gear on Mariah, every piece sporting some bitching hot label, what good were they hanging there frozen under glass when a living, breathing Emily could turn the whole ensemble into a sizzling lethal weapon?

So all it would take was money. And from a lost-in-the-crowd nobody out would spring this head-turning Somebody... Somebody just taking a ho-hum stroll through a scene full of nobodies, just glancing around, nostrils pinched, casting a subtle smile at all those punk-rock fake-Goth thrift-store indie wannabes that Christopher ("never call me Chris") always pointed out to her with an insider wink and a sneer. If not for a stroke of luck—her defending "Being John Malkevich," one of her fave films of all time, against a herd of sheep during lunch at school—Christopher, an undefinably vintage-hipster keep-'em-guessing dresser (and about to say bye-bye to stupid middle school), would never have leaned over from the next table to defend her defense, and they'd never have started having lunch together and finding out they liked so many albums and movies in common. Her former lunch-table bitches showed their jealousy, of course, with put-downs calling him a zit-faced clown—lies, especially nasty when labeling him a clown. Christopher did like a little in-your-face elegance, but if he wore the occasional bowtie, and sometimes sported an ascot, he managed to blend such touches into a highly personal style.

"Here come those same sheep that passed by an hour ago!" Mariah winked and Emily, too, registered their approach out of the corner of her eye. Emily's stomach twisted into a knot but there was no way to shrink out of sight.

"Still stuck to the bench here, emo-kid?" said Tanya, coming up tall and swaggering with hands on hips and a million fake-silver loops hanging from her wrists and ears and belly-button and probably from her ass-crack too, thought Emily.

"Don't know who you're talkin' about, Tanya. Emo's kinda passé, like the retro shit you three are into."

"That tee o' yours with that stupid skull is definitely emo," said shave-head Kaitlyn whose jeans sported tailored holes that crept right up to her crotch.

"It's not. It's a laughing skull. It makes fun of emo," Emily snapped back.

"She's mulched her Chris Carabba disks and now she's into what... My Chemical Romance?" jeered Meghan, whose black mascara was as over-applied as the peroxide to her head.

"Changed one Chris for another, looks like," Tanya laughed, rattling her loops.

"We hear that the Zit is into such cool rock that nobody's ever heard of it," said Kaitlyn, scratching through the holes in her jeans. "And poor Emo-ly hasn't even passed through her Goth stage yet!"

Emily sat with hand on hip, placed just like Mariah's, waiting for the storm to blow over.

"Where's he taking you, to a re-run of Batman?" said Meghan, whose mascara and matching vampire boots fittingly projected—in Emily's view—her evil personality.

Brushing back her non-existent hair, Kaitlyn faux-whispered to Tanya, "All the Zit wants is to get his finger wet."

The remark got Emily sizzling. Apart from seeing him at school, she'd spent two late afternoons at Christopher's gorgeously furnished house listening to really deep CDs and he hadn't thought of touching her even once. "You tools don't know shit about Christopher. Christopher is Straight-Edge. We leave that other stuff to all the dopers and sluts at school."

"Look who's lecturing us," Kaitlyn shot back, "the Virgin-fucking-Mary who's spilling out of her jeans."

"Is that what you wearing to the concert?" said Tanya, looking like an ad for hoola-hoops.

"What concert?" said Meghan.

"Sposta be a new blend of rock," said Tanya, "that's cooler than death in Siberia."

"A pet rock," Meghan quipped, launching her pals into a titter-fit.

"F.Y.I., buttheads," lashed Emily, "it's a joint performance by two new-movement groups from California, the Bled Herrings and Stoic Heroics—which I'm sure you've never heard of."

"That's right, and nobody else has either," said Meghan.

"Or will," said knob-headed Kaitlyn, still scratching.

Emily fixed on the ice-blue eyes of Mariah. Through the gimlet eyes of Mariah she surveyed her needling schoolmates.

"So what's little Em gonna wear?" challenged Tanya. "For sure she can't be slobbering over the rags on those dummies in the window."

"What am I gonna wear? Kick-ass threads to make you losers drool." That's what Emily heard herself say, but she'd swear that the words came straight to her head from Mariah, who was rapidly losing patience with this gang of troglodytes.

"Then you and the Zit better hurry over to Good Will, Em," said Tanya. "I hear they running an Abercrombie fire sale."

The girls left in a trail of laughter, continuing their totally self-consciously nonchalant mall-rat stroll.

"Still shopping for a leash for your nose-ring, Tanya?" Emily shrilled as they receded, swinging her elbow out in disdain—a wasted gesture, since no one looked back. What did they know about clothes or music or anything, those lemmings? she thought. If Christopher bought a tux at a thrift-shop to go with his pricey new rock boots shipped direct from the UK, it was out of individual stylistic mix-and-match choice. He could afford to buy anything he wanted, unlike that troupe of knock-off brats.

"And you, Em, can you afford to keep up with Christopher?" Mariah's faint smile sent shudders of despair through Emily—but Emily was in love with Big Doll's current outfit, this week's especially, which she'd just had to come back to gaze at, this crazily eclectic mating of rhinestone jacket, silky shirt, glitter belt, studded gaucho pants and tawny leather knee-high boots soft as a baby's behind. So totally me! she thought. In a get-up like that, which fit into no little pigeonhole, she was sure that Christopher would be proud to be with her anywhere. And the only problem was that it cost so much that she couldn't even scrape together enough to buy the damn shirt! Christopher had his own credit card. Emily's mom had taken away her cell-phone because she'd run up a bill only thirty bucks more than per usual. They really charged too much for text-messaging! Stranded is how she felt! But maybe, she wondered, if she offered to give up her cell for a couple months her 'rents would plunk for the cash she needed right now. But shit, could she really live cell-deprived for as much as even a week?

Pondering other impossible solutions, she paid no attention for several minutes to the person who had sat down at the other end of her bench. Glancing to her right, she saw a neatly dressed guy in a yellow shirt and brown pants—kinda old, at least twenty-five, anything but cute with his flaring nostrils and puffy lips, and he flashed a say-cheese saw-toothed smile right back at her.

"If I'm disturbing you, I can find another place to sit," he said very politely.

"It's not my bench," said Emily, shrugging her shoulders and gazing again back at Mariah.

"Pretty cool outfit she's got on, isn't it?" the guy interrupted again.

"Not bad."

"Not bad?"

"I've seen better."

"I'm sure you have. You wouldn't be admiring it if you didn't have good taste."

"Champagne taste on a beer budget," Emily snickered, proud of her comeback—a phrase her mother often used to put her in her place. ("At least you don't *sound* like a peanut."—Mariah's thin-lipped comeback, that.)

"I think that outfit would look absolutely terrific on *you*," said the guy, looking her up and down from where he sat a little closer now, sliding up from the corner of the bench.

"Fat chance," sniffed Emily.

"You've got the perfect figure for it."

She wanted to snap back "How would you know?" but she knew that in her year-old jeans she didn't exactly, as her mother would say, hide her light under a bushel. But instead she replied, cowering under the ironic gaze of Mariah, "A lot of good it does me."

"I'd love to see you decked out like that. You remind me of my sister. Since I hit it big in the market, I buy her anything she wants."

"Lucky girl," pouted Emily, feeling a pang of envy.

"And she can't look half as good as you whatever she puts on."

"Sounds like a waste of money then."

"Money doesn't mean anything to me. I'd really like to see *you* in that outfit, you know."

"I'll bet you would," Emily sniffed, and at the same time a male store employee climbed into the window, right behind Mariah, and began stripping off her top. Emily felt uncomfortable. It was like watching a dirty movie, or like stuff you could see on the Internet, in the company of a stranger. But Mariah didn't blink.

"Changing of the garb!" punned the fellow who'd now slithered up a bit more along the bench.

"What?" said Emily.

"If you remember what's she's wearing, I'll get it for you," he said.

"What! Just like that?"

"Just like that."

"Sure. And I can imagine what you'll want in return." She did not like looking at Puffy Lips' jagged front teeth.

"Not much."

"How much?" Emily stared at the naked nippleless cream-smooth breasts of Mariah now shorn of her top.

"Just to see yours, like that, uncovered," he said, pointing at the stripped-down torso in the window, "while you're trying on what they're taking off her."

"You're a perv!" snipped Emily. She wasn't wearing a bra and felt half uncovered just by his crude suggestion.

"But I'm a generous perv. And it isn't to just anyone I'd make such an offer."

Emily fixed her glance straight ahead at Mariah, who seemed totally unperturbed at having her breasts—and soon her whole body, it was clear—exposed to everyone's view. "It's nothing, peanut. I don't feel a thing. You won't either. Be proud of what you have. Let them drool is what I think. I'm getting stares from everybody, but for you it's only one guy, in private… And he's offering you a deal you may never see again." (Did he really pick me out specially? wondered Emily.) "Of course he did, you dumb-ass! If you've got it, flaunt it, stupid!"

"Getting near closing time," sighed the perv on the bench, shaking his head.

Rudely uncovered now, Mariah's buttonless belly thrust its bareness out at the world for everyone to see, as defiant as her cold, hard, insolent breasts. Nothing could touch Mariah. Unflappable, she gazed upward as the stranger in the window manhandled her, leaning her back to remove her boots. Gripping Mariah's naked calf, the man in the window suddenly looked out and winked suggestively at Emily. Emily stared back unruffled as if watching some bozo on TV. She knew, of course, that Mariah would emerge victorious again in some dazzling new display that would render insignificant the mishandling she had to endure. The man in the window had no more reality for Emily than a screen composed of pixels.

Emily narrowed her eyes at the other pixel-man, the one who had now sidled up to within two feet of her. His cologne was so strong it almost made her sneeze. "It's only to look?" she said.

⚞⚟

Inside the store, which was as familiar to her as her own house, Emily got right to where she needed to get, picked out the items in the sizes she needed, worrying all the while that someone might have grabbed the last one since she'd checked a couple days before—and all the while trying not even to look at the weirdo alongside her who existed, for her, reduced to little more than a credit card and a disagreeable smell. When it came to trying on the boots, which she just had to do before trying on anything else, Emily reluctantly acceded to pixel-man's help in pulling them on, but she did not think it was necessary for him to grab her so high up the leg. By the time she leaned forward to push at his hand, the boot was on. A terrific fit! Rejecting his help, she managed to pull on the other by herself, sucking in the heady fresh-leather smell, then pranced around in delight, looking at her legs repeatedly in the angled mirror.

"Incredible boots for incredible legs!" marveled puff-lips.

"Not bad, I guess," shrugged Emily.

"Wouldn't you like some fabulous panties too?"

"Don't need any," Emily snapped. Now she was really getting annoyed with him.

As they approached the dressing-room area to the left and at the back of the enormous floor, Emily slowed up. The clothes caressing her arm seemed suddenly to weigh a ton.

"Forget anything?" asked her companion.

"You can't come in."

"Of course I can. C'mon, it's getting late."

Just then Emily caught sight of Mariah, whose stiff, unbending body moved in the same direction, to the storage room adjacent to the women's try-on area, swaying under the arm of the man who had stripped her down. She looked so vulnerable, Emily thought, then thought how stupid it was to even have such a thought. Emily had heard of what some men do to female bodies in morgues, and she'd also heard of dentists putting women under and taking full advantage. Lucky for those women that at least they didn't feel anything. What did those pervs get out of it? she wondered.

"Removing that manikin's outfit," said credit-card man, "means you won't find these items on the rack anymore. Tomorrow they'll all be in mothballs."

Emily locked eyes with a defiantly hand-on-hip Mariah. "I can't have it, but you damn well can, peanut! Never mind his smell."

Emily at last remembered the word she was trying to think of: voyeur. The guy was just some weirdo voyeur.

No one was on guard in the dressing-area. The place was deserted. Not a squeak from any of the six or eight cubicles. Emily chose the first one to the left, adjacent to the storage room. Through the wall she could hear the steps of the man who was lugging in Mariah. Emily could envision the stripped-down, stiff-lipped Mariah as clearly as if there were no wall between them. Inside the cubicle a mirror filled the separating wall. A bench stretched opposite the mirror, and hooks protruded above it out of the false pine-wood paneling.

Sliding back the thick beige curtain, Emily turned to her companion and said, "I'll push this back and show you what you want, when I'm ready."

"Don't be silly," said her companion, slipping in behind her. "I expect to help you. That way we'll get out faster."

Emily's ears prickled, her cheeks burned, and her heart pounded so loud she was sure that *he* could hear it too. She laid down all her new clothes on the bench. Their smell of newness obliterated his, and their rhinestones sparkled under the warm light from above. She stood up facing the mirror, and the man positioned himself behind her, pushing her slightly forward. "See, I'll only be looking at the mirror," he said.

Emily sidestepped and sank down on the bench. "I'm taking off my sneaks first," she mumbled, fumbling and delaying as much as she could. When they were off, she stood up and faced the mirror, and Puffy Lips slipped in behind her again.

Her skin tingled from her neck to her ears as he gripped the bottom of her T-shirt, doing what she was too numb to do, and gently pulled it up over her breasts. She felt stuck like a fly in resin from a tree. Molasses-like, it filled the entire chamber.

"It's only like he's watching you on television, peanut," a voice drawled in her head. And as he pulled her shirt up higher, up over her face, her leaden arms following till she could see the mirror again, Emily seemed to be gazing at the shiny torso of Mariah, braless and proud of it, jutting out of the resin-bathed glass.

"You look terrific, don't you think?" His hot breath spilled over her neck, launching cold ripples up from the base of her spine to her scalp. "That shirt and jacket are going to look great on that chest," he said, and as she pondered a snippy reply, he was already undoing the top button of her fly.

"What are you doing?" she said, pushing at his encircling hands.

"You agreed you'd let me look at you, didn't you?"

"Wasn't it only the top?"

"You wanna break the deal? Okay!" he said, hands still working at her jeans.

"Think ahead, peanut!" the unmoving lips in the mirror advised. "They'll be goggle-eyed when they see you at the concert." Emily resisted as if fighting a growing paralysis, pushing back more and more weakly at his hands. "They strip me out there in public, and do you think I give a damn? Who cares who's peeking through a window?" observed the rigid figure in the glass. Pixel hands peeled the figure's jeans to the floor, and a mirror-man removed them, lifting its stiffening legs one after another against the increasing viscosity of an all-engulfing, transparent gel that had rapidly begun to harden.

Ice-cold hands circling in from behind suddenly cupped the breasts in the mirror. The figure shuddered. An arm half rose to intervene, then dropped, the elbow lacking full articulation. Hot breath steamed on an unfeeling neck, a trembling, hairy hand squeezed a carved, unyielding breast, while the other hand snaked through from behind, forcing stiff, wooden knees to spread apart.

"Christopher will be so proud," thought Emily, glancing back at the pile of shining clothes. Soon she'd be warmly wrapped in them, just like in a cocoon. But now she could no longer smell them. The smell of Puffy Lips, that alone, pervaded the entire chamber, stealing into her throat, making her gag, forcing a burning path right down to the pit of her stomach.

"It doesn't hurt. Doesn't even make a dent, peanut. The men who drag us back here do it all the time. Pointless. And someone always comes and cleans up afterward," the bobbing figure in the mirror behind the window reassured. "Think boots. Boots. You're going to look fantastic in those boots!"

The man mirrored in the plate-glass wall finally bent the splintering manikin's knees and set her down on the bench. "Try everything on," he said. "I'll wait outside. When you're satisfied, put your clothes back on and I'll pay for all your new duds over at the register."

Alone now, motionless, she sat a long while on the fiery, sticky bench. Mechanically, stiff joints resisting, Emily managed finally to pull on skirt, blouse, drop-dead jacket and soft-as-baby's-ass boots. She watched as the figure in the mirror, shining through a blur, came totally to resemble Mariah, right down to that faint, ironic smile on tight, unmoving lips. She examined that haughty figure in those drop-dead rags from this angle and that, up and down, until she was entirely satisfied. But Emily didn't waste time jumping back into her own shabby clothes before stumbling out of the cubicle.

Pushing back the curtain, she glanced around, but her patron was not in the try-on area. Her stomach tightened into a horrible, iron knot. Exiting the try-on room, she stood in the doorway frozen, scanned acres of floor, searched from left to right. Why hadn't she asked him his name? she thought. Right now she could be shouting out his name.

A few straggling shoppers still wandered the aisles and no one was at the nearby check-out. Hand placed saucily on her hip, bling-bling sparkling from belt to breast, Emily stood stock-still, leaning against the door-jamb, not a thought in her head, staring intensely at nothing in particular, oblivious to the passing of time.

At last a pair of store-clerks scurried by. "Sorry to hurry you, Miss," said one. "We're closing in five." Advancing a step, he peered at Emily closely, carefully tapping his glasses back up on the bridge of his nose. "Why ain't this dummy in the window?" he grumbled to his partner.

Great White Hope

1

"They lost our luggage," said Angie, applying dark-red lipstick while looking into the mirror of the compact she dug out of her alligator bag. "Fuckin' Aeronaves is totally full of shit and you believe 'em."

Jason slumped against the back of the stone bench and resisted the urge to disagree. Angie's bag was the same shade as her Acapulco tan. The shellacked head of the alligator fixed him with its red-beaded eyes. It reminded him of the snake-heads at the base of the serpent columns flanking the portal of the Temple of the Jaguars. Stony eyes glaring, still guarding sacred mysteries. That was at—where? Uxmal? No. Chichén Itzá. Two weeks ago in Yucatán. He'd like to have stayed longer, but ruins bored Angie, and besides it almost never stopped raining.

"Just a simple, ordinary flight from Acapulco to Mexico City, and those morons—I bet they stole them," she said, switching from lipstick to hairbrush as she spoke. It was warm and sunny and dry, and the late afternoon breeze whipped her hair against her lips. "I'm a mess. Why we ever took that bus full of chickens to get here instead of the plane—"

"We wanted to see Morelia."

"A total bust!" said Angie.

If Jason were to name Angie's one outstanding feature—leaving aside her slinky hips and melon-breasted torso—it would be those glistening waves of hair that flowed like black gold down to the middle of her back. The raggedy kids and the neatly dressed adults who occupied separate stone benches in the square were united at least in their stares, which

Jason had learned to ignore in the States but seemed triply intrusive in Mexico. After three weeks of travel, he still felt the mosquito-like buzz of those eyes, whereas gawkers never bothered Angie.

"You're supposed to know Spanish?" said Angie. "Well how come you couldn't *demand* that we get our stuff back—*before* we left Mexico City? Three days' delay so far! How we going to enjoy Guadalajara now without our fucking luggage?"

"Fortunately," said Jason, patting a red leather bag on the bench beside him, "our carry-on has basics for three or four days."

"One dress! Only one dress, just what I'm wearing."

"And they promised to notify American Express as soon it arrives by bus."

"You should've yelled at them in English, Jay. As soon as they heard you fumfering in Spanish, they knew they had you over a barrel." Angie put away her toiletries and snapped her handbag shut. "If my father'd been there—"

"I don't want to hear about your father."

"If my father'd been there, that clerk would have shit his pants so hard he'd have catapulted off to Acapulco—and back the same day—with our bags, and with shit to spare."

"Gee," said Jason, "maybe we should've invited your father to come with us. I guess it's not enough being in each other's faces, the three of us, all day long, five days a week, all year long. And that's not to *mention* the weekends I've spent running rush-jobs off for him."

"What's your problem, Jay? He gave you all the overtime you wanted. In the two years we've been married—"

"He piled on the overtime because he thought I couldn't handle it."

"What?"

"Do you think he really gave a crap about my wanting to save up money so I could go back to school?"

"Of course! He's even given us this vacation—so you can practice your freakin' Spanish and be a better teacher for it."

"You're about as eager for me to quit working for him as he is."

"You're a good worker. You know all the offset presses as well as he does. In another year you'd make manager."

"In another year we'd all be in jail if he carried out his plan to print *money*."

"That's a lot of crap, his way of joking," she said, turning around, feigning interest in the market behind the square. They hadn't explored that sprawling market yet. They first had to find lodgings they could agree on. After a cab dropped them off in the city center, near the Cathedral, they had wandered around on foot, looking for an acceptable, medium-priced hotel, then stopped for a rest where they now sat and argued, in the Plaza San Juan de Diós.

"You never acted positive about my wanting to go back to school. All it'll take me is three semesters to finish my Ed degree. One more lousy year and a half."

"I'm positive, I'm positive! But meanwhile, what's in it for me, Jay? Another couple of years as Dad's bookkeeper, that's what in it for me."

"Instead of?"

"What do you mean, 'instead of'?"

"I mean, instead of what he and your mother want you to do, stay home and pump out a baby."

"Have I ever told you I wanted to have a baby?"

"I don't know, Anj. It's like they're always hinting, putting pressure on us, on *me*, to sacrifice my career goals so that—"

"If it happens, it happens."

"What's that supposed to mean? You're on the Pill."

"It's not one hundred percent effective."

Jason grew suddenly anxious. "You do have them on you, right? You didn't leave them in the luggage?"

Frowning, Angie unsnapped her bag, poked around, and drew forth the compact-like container of her month's supply. Jason felt both embarrassed and relieved. One slip could ruin his greatest hope.

"Seen enough?" She thrust the pale-green disc back into her purse. "There are rumors that they're not even safe," she muttered, looking off at the wind-ruffled trees of the plaza. "They only came out a couple years ago, you know."

2

"Got the time, fella?"

The gruff American voice descended from Jason's left. He looked up into a weathered face, into iron-gray eyes beneath a stormy, bushy brow. As they sized each other up, the old guy stood there tall and ramrod straight. His pinstripe suit and yellow tie showed hardly a wrinkle. It took Jason a few seconds to switch gears and glance at his watch.

"Six-fifteen," he said.

"Thanks. Americans?"

"Yes. From New York."

"Pittsburgh for me. Mind if I sit down?"

"There's plenty of room," said Jason, pointing to the space beside him. The elderly stranger patted his tie and tugged at the lapels of his suit. As far as Jason could judge, the intruder was in his seventies and looked pretty hale for his age.

"Do I have the lady's permission?" he asked with a courtly-comical bow. His abundant white hair, streaked with yellow and combed straight back, was not covered with a hat, but if he'd worn one, Jason thought, he'd have doffed it.

"Feel free," said Angie.

As he eased down next to Jason, the oldster thrust out a big, knobby hand and pulled back the sleeve. "Frank Moran wore a gold Rolex, right on that wrist," he said, "up till last week, when some jackass where I go dancing decided to insult me. So I gave him the old one-two—"

"And you lost your watch in the scuffle?" Angie offered.

"No, ma'am. My watch paid the cops to let me go. A very undignified scene, let me tell you, for a man with an M.D.—not to mention four other degrees."

"That's very impressive," said Jason, imagining two old farts flailing at each other over a sixty-something babe in some geriatric Mexican version of Roseland. "I'm working toward a college degree myself."

"Education's what matters," the old man said. "Not that I regret those interests in oil that I have in California."

"Nice to have some back up," Jason agreed.

"Well, if I hadn't been a broker on the New York Stock Exchange I'd have easily been burnt. Can't trust those oil stocks, you know."

"I'll take your word for it."

"California's crazy. Did a lot of acting out there in the old days—for the movies. *That* was the gold rush!"

"I'm Angie," said Angie, "and this is my husband Jason. So you were an actor, Mister…?"

"Frank Walter Moran," he said, crushing Jason's hand in a boa-constrictor grip. "You've heard of Frank Moran?" Lighting no spark of recognition, the old guy tried to hide his disappointment. "Long before your time," he mumbled.

"Wait," said Angie. "The boxer?"

"You knew? I'll be damned!"

"My older brother fought in the Golden Gloves. He used to talk boxing all the time. Taught *me* how to box, too. Used to beat the shit out of me. I loved it."

"Well Frank Moran would have loved to have a sparring partner like you, young lady." The old man smiled, and the tip of his rugged nose turned pink. "Might have helped him flatten out Johnson."

"Jack Johnson?" said Angie.

"Exacto!" Moran gazed at Angie in silent admiration. "Ever hear of the Great White Hope?... No? Well Frank was the Great White Hope who fought Jackie Johnson to a standstill. Stayed the course, a full twenty rounds on his feet."

"Jackie Johnson?" said Jason, looking at Angie, who frowned as if he should know.

"Never heard of Jack Johnson, fella? He was the Negro heavyweight champion of the world. No white man ever went the limit with him—except for Frank Walter Moran."

"As far as boxing goes," said Jason, "my knowledge doesn't go back before Joe Lewis."

"The Negro heavyweights who came after Johnson were pussies by comparison. Pardon, Miss. No offense meant."

"None taken," said Angie, leaning over Jason as if drawn by a magnet. "My brother told me all about boxing in the old days. No gloves, endless rounds."

"Who goes twenty with anybody these days?" Frank asked rhetorically.

"I bet you still could," said Angie.

A faint blush colored Moran's leathery cheeks. "Thank you kindly—Angie, is it?... Well, Angie, I didn't settle in Guadalajara to look for a fight, but to court the beautiful women for which this town is famed."

Jason smirked.

"You doubt I'm still virile?"

"Of course not," said Jason, his eye on that meat-hook that Moran waved palm-up right under his nose.

"Don't make any mistake. I'm searching for *love*. I'm gonna marry a young señorita. I've been fooled, I've been used, but I'm still trying."

"Great fighters never give up," said Angie.

This is getting bizarre, thought Jason.

"I want a family. I want children. I still got a nice few rounds to go—if you know what I mean." The old man winked and clenched his fists. Feinting with his left, he grazed Jason's midriff with a rack of stony knuckles.

"Older sperm makes smarter babies," said Angie.

Where the fuck did she ever hear that? thought Jason, his stomach in a knot.

"In the meantime, till Frank Moran and his true love are united, a man's got to settle for whatever entertainment he can get."

"Yes, we noticed there are plenty of movie houses," said Jason, hoping to change the subject.

Ignoring the remark, Moran looked right past Jason. "Some of the cantinas are taxi-dance joints," he said. "A dance costs less than one American nickel."

"Is that how you meet girls?" asked Angie.

"Not the nice ones. These are the ones for sale. You dance to arrange a quickie, or an all-night shack job... Excuse me if I'm being too 'frank.'" He smiled at his own pun. Angie laughed appreciatively. Jason did not smile. He thought that Angie *should* have looked offended. "There are other places to meet women, though. Have you been to the Woolworth's lunch counter?"

"We've just got into town," said Jason.

"The girls that work there are beautiful, really exotic. Do either of you read Spanish?"

"Jason does."

Moran whipped out a letter from his inside jacket pocket. "Can you do me a favor and tell me what this says? I got it today from my favorite waitress at Woolworth's. She's very interested in me, you know." He searched Jason's eyes for the least flicker of doubt. "I asked her to be my bride."

"That's so romantic," said Angie.

"Be glad to translate if I had the time, but it's getting late," said Jason, " and we still haven't found a hotel."

"Hotel? Your worries are over. An American friend of mine runs a great place—cheap and clean—only a few blocks down past the Mercado here. Harry Baker. Used to spar in his prime. Do you mind?" he said, shoving the letter at Jason.

Between the opening "Atento Señor" and the closing "Su servidora," the page-and-a-half letter was riddled with errors in spelling and punctuation. But the message was clear. The girl's parents would not hear of it and would not allow her to have anything more to do with that very kind and generous norteamericano. Jason looked up at Frank Moran, wondering how a man with five degrees couldn't read simple Spanish. Moran eyed him with mounting suspicion while grinding his fist into his palm.

"I can't really make this out," said Jason, watching Moran's hands. "The handwriting isn't too clear, and it's full of bad spelling."

"I can't much follow her conversation either. I just kinda look into her eyes and guess." Moran grabbed the letter and tucked it back into his pocket. He even seemed relieved not to know.

"If she accepted your offer, she'd tell you in person," said Angie.

"Angie, keep your opinions to—"

"She's right," said Moran. "It's a TKO. They flatten you while you're still on your feet."

"There's plenty of fish in the sea," said Angie.

"You're absolutely right. Hey, I like that wife of yours. She don't pull any punches!"

"We really have to go," said Jason.

"I know. I'll introduce you to Harry Baker."

"Don't trouble yourself," said Jason. "We have a list of recommended hotels."

"You don't think I get a commission, do you?"

"Of course not," said Angie. "Lead the way, Frank. It's late, Jay, and we're tired."

Shrugging his shoulders, Jason went along. Moran walked between him and Angie, occasionally draping his hands around their backs. Jason thought the old guy's arm slipped down once or twice and strafed Angie's buttocks, but he couldn't be sure. She'll be pissed, thought Jason, when she sees this dump he's taking us to. Then she'll take it out on me because we won't have the guts to turn it down.

3

Only two blocks past the Mercado Libertad and a block to the left of Mina, the Hotel La Coronada, "The Crowned Lady," nestled short and squat between two gray apartment buildings. Jason noticed that the second "o" of the glued-on letters that made up the word "Coronada" was missing, resulting in "Cor nada," meaning "a wound inflicted by the horn of a bull." He thought this worth mentioning, so he mentioned it.

"Is that supposed to be funny?" said Angie.

"Not particularly." She was probably already sorry, he thought, that she hadn't resisted Moran's offer to help. "You lodge here too, Mr. Moran?" he asked, still hesitant about going in.

"Me? No, I board by the month in a house a few blocks away."

The small lobby consisted of a registration desk, a frayed brown sofa, armchairs, and a TV. The stained beige wallpaper was covered with little gold crowns. A heavy-set man about fifty lurched up from his seat behind the counter and stared at them. "Well, if it isn't Frank Moran! Where you been these past few weeks?"

"Been out knockin' 'em down."

"The bottles or the ladies?"

"None of the above. Just those bastards who keep lookin' at me cross-eyed. Harry, meet a couple American friends of mine. Angie and—and—"

"Jason," said Jason.

"Angie and Jason, from New York," said Moran. "Told 'em you had great rooms at rock-bottom prices."

"And that's no lie," said Harry, reaching a beefy hand to Jason that a lifetime of sparring must have pounded into jelly—the way Mexican chefs treated steaks. "How long you folks staying?" His heavy-lidded eyes locked on Angie, reverted to Jason, then swiveled back to Angie.

"Two-three days, I guess," said Jason.

"Possibly as much as a week," said Angie. "We have a reservation to fly home from Mexico City."

"Hey, you might like it here enough to change your flight, maybe stay even longer," said Harry.

"Could be," said Angie. "Depends."

Jason looked at her, eyed the dreary lobby, and wondered whether she had lost her judgment or was cannily lying about a possibly extended stay to snare the guy's best room.

"Well, we're a pretty popular establishment, but…"

Jason scanned the grid of pigeonholes on the wall behind the desk. Every little box had a key dangling beneath it.

"…but just happens you're in luck. Big tour group just moved out. One of my best rooms is yours. Shower and *cama matrimonial*. Number 3 down the hall, second door on your left." He pointed to his right, at the entrance to the dim hallway beside the desk. "Does twenty pesos a night sound agreeable?"

Jason was stunned. Only a buck-sixty a night? What was wrong with this picture? He glanced at Angie, to catch the wince he fully expected.

"Fine, we'll take it," was all she said.

"Angie, shouldn't we first take a look—"

"I'm sure it'll be adequate," she said, cutting him off.

Plucking a key wired to a clumsy wooden block, Harry handed it to Jason. "You can sign in later. That all your luggage?"

"American Express said they'll notify us when it arrives at the bus station," said Angie. "We'll call them from our room and tell them where we are."

"You can call them from out here. No charge."

"No, that's okay," said Angie.

"No phones in the rooms. Keeps costs down," said Harry.

"Look," said Jason, prepared to beat a retreat and only waiting for a sign from Angie, "I think we'd better—"

"No problem; thanks," said Angie.

"You'll like it here," said Moran, sidling up between them and draping his big hands over their shoulders. "Would you two like to join me for lunch tomorrow at the Mercado?"

While Jason searched for a polite way out, Angie said, "Sure, we've got shopping to do anyway."

Jason watched the tall ex-boxer leave the hotel. He could not help admiring that sturdy frame; he took note of his stride, oddly rigid, almost wooden. Determined. As he and Angie headed for the hallway, he glanced at the sagging sofa against the lobby wall to the left. It was book-ended by tables decked with oval-leafed rubber plants (probably *made* of rubber), and on the wall above the sofa hung a framed poster of the *Cenote de Sacrificio* that they'd actually seen in Yucatán—the "Well of Sacrifice," an enormous circular limestone pit carved out naturally by water over the eons, a hole down which the ancient Mayans threw the occasional sacred virgin and respected enemy warrior and anyone else they decided to honor to death.

Their room came furnished with a double bed, a seedy armchair, a tall wardrobe that tilted forward on the uneven floor, and a writing desk with chair opposite the bed. Except for the light-green flower-pattern wallpaper, everything seemed brown, including the stained old carpeting that made Jason yearn for the slippers still to come in their luggage.

"Well," said Angie, with a shrug of the shoulders, "what do you think?"

Jason watched her toss her handbag onto the desk, then pull out the empty drawers and snap them back in place as if expecting to find abandoned underwear or a shriveled condom or two. "It's okay. It'll do," he said. He knew that if he were to voice any obvious displeasure—which meant criticizing her judgment—she would accuse him of failing to take a forceful stand earlier, when they still had a chance to back out.

"You're sure?" she said, testing him.

"The basics are all here," he said, trying to sound cheerful. He dropped their red leather bag next to the bed, then strode up to the window against the far wall, parted the thick beige curtains, bent back the dusty venetian-blind slats, and peered out at the cement-block wall of the adjoining building. "Not much of a view," he said. "Let me check out the bathroom."

The bathroom door was a step away from the window, between window and bed. He flicked on the light. The toilet yawned open. Soundlessly, he lowered the seat. A green plastic curtain hung over a lion-clawed bathtub. He parted the curtain, heard a whirr, saw something shoot past his head, looked at the tile floor and spotted a giant roach skittering for shelter in the direction of the toilet. Abdominals stiffening, he stepped on it, squashing it, and kicked the carcass behind the toilet, out of sight. There was no sense telling Angie. She'd never forgive him for failing to object to her impulsive decision to stay here. He shook the white towels folded over a bar on the door, making sure that nothing else lay in ambush.

"Anything wrong, Jay?"

"No. Just testing the shower." Behind the bathtub curtain there were the usual two knobs, American-made because labeled H and C. Gingerly, he reached and turned the knob with the "C" on it, the one that should signify "cold" but here in Mexico usually stood for *caliente*, hot. Good, there was plenty of hot water, hot enough to fry a roach. Fortunately, he could see no others.

"That's what I could use right now, a shower," said Angie.

"Don't you want to eat first? We haven't had dinner. On the way here we passed that Hotel Gerente that looked like it had a nice restaurant."

"The Gerente can wait, don't you think?" She smiled at him and unbuttoned her blouse. He sat at the desk across from the bed and watched her undress. When she was down to bra and panties, she sauntered over, took his hands, and slipped his arms around her. After he unhooked her bra and peeled her breasts out of the stretched cups, she stared into his eyes and placed his thumbs under the edge of her peach-colored panties. "You take them off so much better than I do," she said in that throaty way that never failed to arouse. The sweaty-sweet smell of her breasts made his scalp crawl. He felt as if his hair were on fire. "You need a shower too, don't you think?"

He nodded. But he was tired and hungry.

"You'll just have to get back into practice, Jay."

"For what?"

Her eyelids fluttered. "For how to spend your spare time once you start school again."

"You really don't mind that I'm going back to...?"

With her underthings strewn at his feet, she ground herself into him, then turned away as soon as she felt him swell. She'd known exactly what to say to dispel his lingering inertia. His was a knee-jerk resistance—born of habit, of anticipating her countless turnings away, of remembering their innumerable late-night quarrels back home—often over their plans for the future, over the hopes he had to finish his degree.

She picked up her purse and wended her way to the bathroom with a pronounced lurch of the hips. They were both so tired, he thought. Where did she find the energy? Back home she was never so constantly seductive, so sexually imperious, as she'd been so far for all three weeks of this month-long trip of theirs. At home, in fact, she was often so indifferent to him that they didn't make love for two weeks at a time, and when she did want him to accommodate her, in the middle of the night sometimes, her approach was passionless, crude, mechanical, as if scratching an itch that wouldn't let her sleep. Often, when he did want her, overcome by the warmth and fragrance of the smooth, soft body beside him, she would push him away, even punch him with her elbow, so that negotiating for sex had become a nerve-racking issue and he had progressively shied away from being the initiator. Now, however, all vacation long, it was almost like in the early days before they got married—almost, not quite. Her sexual hunger was genuine all right, but she seemed to feel she had to be theatrical in order to excite him. Her advances sometimes turned him off, but more often than not they succeeded. He guessed that her job, and the boring routine of their lives at home, had done much to dampen her libido. And the effect on both of them of constant exposure to her father couldn't be discounted either. Did she expect to make up in one single month for all she'd held back for two years? Jason wondered.

The heady aroma of Maja soap wafted out of the bathroom in a cloud of steam. The name of the soap, not its black-and-red, sexless, Flamenco-dancer wrapper, conjured up for Jason Goya's *Maja desnuda* posed bare-assed on a couch, and the *Maja* in turn took the shape and odor of Angie. Unbuttoning his shirt, Jason looked up at the wall above the desk and noticed, for the first time, the framed print hanging there. It was a large photo of the *chacmool* they'd encountered at Chichén Itzá, among carved columns at the top of the Temple of the Warriors. The reclining stone figure with cylindrical head gazed blankly off to the left as it rested on its elbows and extended a flat stomach, shaped like a plate, that had served the Mayans as an altar of human sacrifice. He remembered how he had clowned around, posing on the *chacmool* like a victim waiting for slaughter. Angie had laughed, but the memory of his mockery, even now, sent a mild *frisson* coursing through him.

As he contemplated the image, he was distracted by what appeared to be a defect in the wall near the top of the frame, on the right. Jason planted himself on his knees on top of the desk. In that position he was at eye-level with what turned out to be a hole in the wall—in a section of the wall thin enough that, with one eye pressed up against it, he could see a large portion of the room behind it. For there *was* a room behind it, room Number 1, thought Jason. A room very similar to their own. The mirror image of their own, in fact, judging from what he could see, which included the entire bed and a few feet to either side. There appeared to be no one in the room just then, but it was furnished with the same bed, the same light-green wallpaper, the same ugly wardrobe to the left of the bed (corresponding to Jason's right if he were to turn and look back at their own room), and on the floor to the right of the bed… *a piece of red luggage.*

A volley of darts stung Jason's neck. He spun his head around. Their own red bag still lay where he had dropped it, in exactly the same position—between bed and bathroom—as in the room behind the wall. Surely, he thought, it couldn't be precisely the same type of luggage. But before he could look through the hole again, Angie had turned off the shower. She'd be out in a minute. If she saw him up there and figured out why, she'd place all the blame—for an ugly situation he could no longer keep under wraps—on *him*. He looked frantically around for something to serve as a plug. He tried tipping the *chacmool* picture, but that wouldn't work. Then he dug around in his pants pocket and came up with a crumpled Kleenex. Measuring off a piece, he stuffed it into the hole. It would do for the time being.

He had just slid down off the dresser when Angie called out to him. "I thought you were getting ready to shower, dear." Her voice was as sweet as her incipient anger would allow.

"I thought I should go out front first—and sign us in, and call American Express."

"Can't that wait?"

"I suppose it can," he said, relenting. He gauged that her lust was greater than her anger, and that as soon as he'd washed off the grime of their long day, he'd be ready to snuffle the *Maja*-smell of her flesh, magical flesh which, night after night, managed to slough off the stale dry skin of their marriage.

4

In the morning Jason got up early to pee. Angie still slept soundly, her covers kicked aside, her naked ass facing him in rosy contentment. Remembering the peephole, hoping he'd only dreamt it, he slipped out of bed and blinked repeatedly, focusing on the wall opposite the bed. There it still flickered, like an irregularity in the wallpaper alongside the *chacmool*. The Kleenex plug was gone. It had fallen out—or been *pushed* out—and lay on top of the desk. A cold vise gripped Jason's testicles. They had made love with his bedside lamp on. Angie could not sleep without a light on.

Jason picked up the plug again, moistening it this time with saliva. Climbing up and planting his knees on the desktop veneer—as he imagined the *other* must have done during the night—he placed his right eye up against the hole. He saw motion, bodies in violent motion in the light of a familiar-looking bedside lamp. The room looked just as it had last night, a replica of their own. The red bag had been moved, though. It lay at the foot of the bed. He focused on the arching bodies of the woman and the man on top of her. He did not recognize the woman, but the man, even from the back, he identified as Frank Moran. Moran had said he boarded elsewhere, but he must have had a landlady with a restrictive visiting policy. There was no doubt that it was Moran—the same shock of gray-white hair, the big bony shoulders and hands. The skin of his ass was wrinkled and gray, Jason noted with disgust. He looked like a fornicating lizard. But why did they make so little noise? Either the bed did not squeak much, or the sounds they made were baffled by the wall, a thick enough partition except, probably, only in the vicinity of the peephole.

So the peeping Tom was either Moran or Harry Baker! But what could they have seen through a plugged up hole? *But*, thought Jason, how could he know when the plug had been dislodged?

Jason shuddered at a sound from behind him. He turned around, fearing the worst. But all Angie had done was roll over onto her right side. She was still sound asleep.

Their red bag too, he noted, had migrated to the foot of the bed!

He wanted to peer through the wall again, distrusting his memory, but Angie might spring up any moment. He re-plugged the hole, unable to come up with any better idea, and quietly descended from the desk. One thing he knew: for the time being, not to tell Angie. And that meant keeping what he knew to himself.

5

"Where you guys off to?" asked Harry. "I've got coffee and brioches in the breakfast room."

"Thanks, but we're in kind of a hurry," said Jason. By way of tacit agreement, they both felt the need to start the day in a more cheerful setting, perhaps with a touch of class.

The nearby Gerente served Continental breakfast on a spotless linen tablecloth with napkins shaped like hats. They slathered their rolls with imported preserves as if to balance the energy budget raided by last night's love-making.

At what seemed an appropriate moment, Jason tried to dissuade Angie from keeping their date with Moran. "We don't have much time left in Mexico, and there's so much we want to see here on our own. He'll understand."

"But Frank is part of the *fun* of being here. He's what makes our trip out of the ordinary. We actually met someone famous!"

"A has-been."

"What's your problem, Jason?"

"Wouldn't you rather have lunch right here? Look, they've got *pozole* on the menu. It's a local Jalisco specialty."

"They'll have it at the market too," said Angie.

She was beginning to show displeasure, so Jason decided to drop it. After walking around the city center, from the Plaza de Armas to the Parque de la Revolución, they returned to La Cor(o)nada about eleven. Harry Baker greeted them. In a talkative mood, he asked them how they'd happened to hook up with Moran. "He and I have a special relationship," he said.

I'll bet you do, Jason thought.

"Have a seat," said Baker, pointing to the sofa. Exiting from behind the *Recepción*, he settled into an armchair opposite them where he could still keep his eye on the lobby.

"He tells us he was the 'Great White Hope,'" said Jason, balancing on the edge of the lumpy couch. No less uncomfortable, Angie perched to his left.

Baker waved his hand dismissively. "There were dozens of Great White Hopes. Jack Johnson beat 'em all."

"But he says he was the only one who fought him to a draw."

"A standstill," Angie corrected.

"That's right. He went a full twenty with smilin' Jack and fought him to a *standstill*. He's not telling you that he *lost*."

"He's accentuating the positive," said Angie.

"At the cost of a great deal of truth," said Baker.

"Like what?" Jason asked.

"Is it any of our business?" said Angie.

"I'm curious. What's wrong with that?"

Baker smiled and shook his head and patted his stubby fingers together. "Frank'll never tell you, but that fight was fixed. It's a part of boxing history, but Frank hasn't read the books."

"Hasn't read the books? A man with five degrees?"

"He told you that?"

"Among other things," said Jason.

Baker clucked his tongue.

"Even if the fight was fixed," said Angie, "it still doesn't mean it was Frank who fixed it."

"They fought in Paris in the summer of 1914. It was the biggest sporting event on the eve of World War One. It was such a big attraction, in fact, that their managers arranged to have it filmed—so they all agreed to make it go at least ten rounds. It was all a question of money."

"So it was as corrupt back then as it is now?" said Jason.

"Frank played the game just like everyone else," sniffed Angie.

Why, Jason wondered, was Baker bad-mouthing Moran? To appear not so chummy with the Great Lost Hope? To avoid being eventually suspected of collaborative voyeurism? He imagined the two at the peephole, leering, switching off with each other, sometimes lucky, sometimes not. "I thought you two were good friends," he said.

"We are, but I wouldn't want him to mislead you."

"He says he doesn't board here, but I was just wondering," said Jason, looking pointedly to his left down the hallway, "does he sometimes happen to sleep here?"

"On rare occasions. Why?"

Jason stared right at him, but Baker didn't blink. "Just curious."

"Few months ago he got blind drunk. Landlady threw him out, so I put him up."

"It must be very frustrating for him to live alone with just memories," said Angie.

"Very selective memories," Jason added. "Speaking of which, how recently did you say Frank slept here, Mr. Baker?"

"How recently? How the hell would I—"

"Jay, who the fuck cares?"

"Speaking of the devil," Baker whispered.

Jason glanced first down the hallway, but Frank Moran entered from the street, dapper in gray suit and solid red tie.

6

At the open-sided, two-tiered Mercado Libertad—the biggest, newest market in Guadalajara, said Moran—Jason and Angie were overwhelmed by the scope and variety of goods displayed for sale. Handicrafts shouted bright colors at them, and foodstuffs whispered alien scents from teeming wicker baskets and groaning wooden tables that stretched for acres in row after twisting row of individual concessions. Pyramids of beans mingled with cages full of squawking birds in a dizzying panorama of sights and sounds as the three of them sashayed through bustling aisles barely wide enough to navigate. Vendors of food and embroidered garments, furniture and paper flowers, clamored for their attention. Guitars, leather purses, hats and huaraches called out, flirting, whirling around them, as Jason tagged behind Angie with Moran holding up the rear.

"Here's what I need," said Angie, stopping at a table loaded with underwear—bras, panties, stockings. As she picked up pairs of skimpy panties, stretching them across her waist—and thereby causing a traffic jam—Moran didn't hesitate to offer his opinion as Angie dangled them in front of him. Jason thought she was being a bit crude.

"Try the black ones," Moran urged. "Black drives *me* wild, I'll tell ya."

Who gives a shit what drives you wild? thought Jason, nudging Angie toward a section of sensible white cotton undies. But Angie twisted away. "You don't think black's too daring?" she said.

"For a girl like you?" said Moran, raising his brows.

"Well, if there's matching bras my size..." Self-absorbed, Angie stretched pair after pair over her blouse.

"There, that's a fit," said Moran.

"Think so?"

Jason couldn't believe that her decisions about underwear could be influenced by the opinions of a drooling old lecher like Moran—who undoubtedly fantasized seeing her wearing them, especially seeing her take them off. She wound up buying five pairs of panties and an equal number of bras. "Damn luggage may never arrive," she said. Jason bought a couple of tee-shirts, some socks, and two pairs of briefs.

"How about a couple dried hummingbirds?" Moran said with a wink. "Mexican ladies stick 'em in their bras for good luck."

Jason spun around to the table behind him and picked up one of the bowie knives he'd been eying off and on. Slipping it in and out of its sheath of tooled Mexican leather, he admired the heft of the blade, sniffed the fresh, earthy scent of the scabbard, then raised the bared blade above his head in both hands the way those Mayan or Aztec priests must have done, he thought, when performing a sacrifice. "Popocatépetl Teotihuacán Quetzalcoatl," he intoned.

"You nuts?" said Angie, flinching. Moran watched him without even blinking.

"I'm getting it for your father. We haven't gotten a present for him the whole trip, remember?" Not waiting for a reply, Jason haggled for a while then bought the knife for the equivalent of about twelve U.S. dollars.

"I'm hungry," said Angie.

"Where do we eat?" asked Jason, tired of watching neck after neck craning in her direction.

"Upper deck." Moran pointed to a wide central staircase.

The open floor was sectioned into a series of competing restaurants, each a rectangle bordered all around by long counters crowded with patrons who seemed to talk more than they ate. Moran found them three seats together, and they studied the blackboard menu on the post behind the counter.

"I like the *cuerdo con pipián*," said Moran.

The prices, Jason noted, were ridiculously low. "Look, Angie, they've got *pozole*."

"Great. I'll taste yours," said Angie. "Order me the—what'd you call it, peepee, Frank?" Moran broke into counter-slapping laughter.

The *cuerdo* was a sorry-looking pork dish, a slab of fatty meat sunk under a thin brown sauce. Jason offered Angie some of his *pozole*—an aromatic stew of shredded pork and chicken steeped in an oniony tomato broth thick with beans. Angie wound up eating more of Jason's lunch than her own.

"Excuse me," said Moran, sauntering off to the right, to the end of the counter. Jason watched him chitchat with a pair of señoritas whose butts and bosoms strained against their dresses.

"He seems to know everybody," said Angie.

"He's probably offering to marry them," said Jason.

"What's your gripe, Jay?"

"You seem to think he knows everything, but he sure as hell doesn't know food."

"So? What's wrong with trying new things?"

"*Pozole* is new. We said we wanted to try it, didn't we?"

"Oh, we could get that anywhere. If not for Frank, I'd never have heard of peepee."

"The only Spanish he can read is from a menu."

"For a guy who doesn't know the language, he seems to be making out pretty well," she said with a nod to the right.

Jason managed to pay the small bill just before Moran came back.

"Gotta ask you guys a favor," said Moran. "It's kind of embarrassing. You still going to the picture show?"

"As soon as we drop off our purchases at the hotel—and go peepee," Angie said, laughing.

"We're going to see *Spartacus*, with Kirk Douglas," said Jason. "We missed it back in the States."

Well... I wonder if you'd mind lending me your room while you're gone."

"For what?" said Jason.

"See the cutie in the red dress I was talking to?"

"Don't *tell* me!" said Angie, clapping her hand to her mouth.

Jason peered again down the counter. He saw her in profile. It was *she*! He'd swear it was the same "hot tamale" he'd seen Moran thumping in the morning.

"My landlady's the strict kind, you know," said Moran. "If my sainted mother were to drop down from heaven, she wouldn't get past that old witch."

There had to be a rational explanation, thought Jason. He couldn't have seen an event that had *not yet happened*. Anyway, could he swear she was *exactly the same one*? These sexy young pepitas looked so much alike. For sure, though, the old goat *had* been bopping someone. But twice in one day? And at his age? And why couldn't he just use the same room again? (Unless, of course, it was booked.)

"Walk back with us and we'll give you the key," said Angie, the Good Samaritan.

"But," Jason feebly protested, "we really don't know when we'll get—"

"It'll take us at least two hours," said Angie.

"You'll come back to clean sheets. Scout's honor," said Moran. He hurried back to his red chili pepper to let her know where to find him.

"See? To survive in Mexico," said Angie, "you really don't need any Spanish."

"This is unbelievable!" said Jason.

"What? That we'd do an old warhorse a favor?"

"No, I meant..." His scalp felt creepy. He ran his hands through his hair as if chasing after ants.

"You meant?" she said as if gearing up for a fight.

"Nothing. I mean... it's all so weird. That's all."

"It makes things that much more exciting, doesn't it?" she said.

7

The paper plug had dropped out—or so it seemed—once again. Chastened by the afternoon's uncanniness, Jason resisted the temptation to peek. This time, while Angie showered, he plugged up the hole with a wad of gum he'd been chewing. But there was no closing his eyes to the temptation posed by Angie when she emerged from the bathroom in slinky black panties and tight-fitting bra and danced a là go-go while unbuttoning his shirt and unbuckling his belt. Arousing him, she continued to disrobe him while Jason removed her bra and sunk his face in the slick groove between her breasts. Drawing him back toward the bed, she suddenly yanked him down on top of her. "Take me," she commanded.

"I... I want to, but the Pill! You haven't taken your—"

"One fuckin' pill won't matter, Jay."

"Maybe not, Angie, but to put in jeopardy everything we've been planning for..."

"All right, no problem. I'll show you I'm taking my pill." She dashed into the bathroom for water from the plastic container of *agua purificada* they always carried with them. Last thing they needed was a case of Montezuma's Revenge. Emerging with water-glass in hand, she deposited it on the desk, rummaged in her handbag, and extracted a little white tablet. Waving it grandly in the air, she flicked it onto her tongue and downed it with a swig from the glass. Alligator eyes glared fiercely at Jason in reproach for his boorish caution.

"Wanna peek into your parlor?" she said, opening her mouth and vibrating her tongue. She got him to laugh. And then it all became silly and unendurably sweet again.

8

Jason awoke from a horrifying dream. On putting his eye to the hole, he met another eye gazing back. He sprang up in bed, but Angie, unperturbed, kept right on sleeping. The light of early morning filtered in through the blinds. Edging out of bed, he tiptoed to the writing desk and examined the wall. The plug had once again "fallen" from where he had squeezed it the night before. *When* had it fallen? he wondered. When they were making love?... What if the gum had just dried up, and then dropped out on its own?

Climbing up on the desk, careful to minimize noise, Jason placed his eye at the peephole. No other eye met his, but he'd rather one had—as opposed to what he did see. He was peering into the same room, no doubt about that, and again there were two actors naked in bed... but this time the couple at foreplay—Jason bit down on his lower lip—were *Angie and himself!* The insuck of his breath was enough to rattle the desk. But he couldn't keep his eyes off what unfolded.

While Angie fondled his genitals, stroking and kissing them, this other Jason looked away—even gazed up at the peephole, as though aware that he was watching himself—and the only thing to harden was his unsmiling face despite all his wife's efforts to excite him. Was this still the dream, and he hadn't really awakened? he wondered.

Fascinated, he followed Angie's every industrious move.

"What am I doing wrong, Jay?" she said, peering up from his belly. He watched himself, thin-lipped, refusing to respond. Then Angie sat up, folded her arms, and said, "I fuckin' give up. I've tried everything I know to stiffen that 'Jack Johnson' of yours, but—"

Then he heard himself reply, "I can't believe you'd do this to me. All this time, using me as if... as if..."

And then he saw Angie jump out of bed, pull off her ring and toss it at him.

At this point, his head pounding, Jason had to back away from the peephole. Glancing back at the "real" Angie, he let out a troubled sigh.

Still sound asleep! And was he, in fact, right there beside her, dreaming all he was "seeing"?

Jason had had enough peeping. He descended from the desk, knees aching in a very real way from pressing against wood. Physically, nothing felt dreamlike at all. He needed to use the bathroom. Peeing felt absolutely life-like, and he was not inclined to test its reality by spraying the floor and the shower curtains and trying to fly through the wall. Maybe it was only when he peered through the hole that his mind entered a dream-like state, he reasoned. A prophetic state? Ridiculous! It was a warning. His unconscious was showing him a *possible* future if he—if he *what?* he wondered. He never got into snits like that, spurning Angie at a time like that. That was not him. He vowed to be affectionate to her all day. He mustn't allow anything to come between them that could sour their intimacy at bedtime. When he crept back beside her again, he leaned against the headboard, his whole body throbbing. The vibrations woke her.

"Up already?" she said, rubbing swirls of black hair from her eyes. "What time is it?"

His watch lay next to his bedside lamp. "Seven-fifteen." He heard her stomach grumbling.

"I'm hungry," she said. "But first..."

Jason felt a warm hand cup his testicles. His body's instant response was proof enough of the absurdity of the scene he had just seemed to witness.

9

This time their hôtelier insisted. They must stay for a Continental breakfast on the house. "The coffee's fresh-brewed, and the rolls are just in from the bakery."

Jason wanted an absolute minimum of Harry's hospitality. The sooner he left the Cor(o)nada, the better he would feel. "Thanks, Harry, but it's a bit too early for breakfast."

"C'mon, Jason, we're both out of energy," Angie said with a broad wink. Jason cringed on seeing Harry grin back—at both of them, like some sort of privileged insider. It was almost as if she *knew* about the peephole—as if she knew *Harry* knew, and as if she knew that Harry knew *she* knew, and that she didn't give a damn. "A little breakfast before breakfast?" she persisted.

"I don't see any breakfast nook," said Jason.

"Follow me," said Harry, taking them into the hallway. He stopped in front of the first door on the left.

Room Number 1! Jason stiffened. "I thought this was a guest room, Harry."

"It's been used for various things."

"I'll bet," said Jason, staring straight at Baker, who played oblivious.

The door opened upon a bright, clean space furnished with several sets of cheap wooden tables and chairs. An aluminum coffee pot and a wicker tray of rolls occupied a cart to the left. No bed, no desk, no wardrobe. All that seemed unchanged was the light-green, pink-flowered wallpaper. Jason felt dizzy. Angie pushed him forward, giving him a pissed-off look as Harry guided them to a table. While Harry did the honors, pouring them their coffee, Jason stared at the wall—the wall behind which lay their own room. Over the peephole—over the spot where the peephole *had to be*—there hung a framed poster.

"What are you looking at, Jay?"

"That poster. Looks like a festival."

"That's the big fiesta at Tlaquepaque," said Harry. "It lasts for days. In fact, it's going on now."

"Why don't we go see it?" said Jason.

"I'm festivaled out," said Angie. "Dad always drags us to the San Giovanni feast on Mott Street. Calzones there, tacos here, what's the difference?"

"One of you should go," said Harry. "Didn't your wife say she needed to do more shopping?"

"If I go, she goes," said Jason.

"Of course, I only meant..."

"What the hell, so we'll go," said Angie.

"Good plan," said Harry. "By the way, I have a message from Frank. He wants to take you to dinner tonight at a favorite restaurant of his."

"Really?" said Jason. "Tell him thanks, but we doubt if we can make it."

"He says you took him out for lunch, and he insists on treating you to dinner."

"We'll be delighted," said Angie. "Tell Frank we look forward to his company."

"Says he'll pick you up at eight sharp."

"We'll be back in plenty of time."

"Good. I'll tell him that. May I join you two for coffee?"

"Of course," said Angie.

To Jason's extreme annoyance, Harry stuck with them till they finished. Business must be booming at La Cornada, thought Jason. They all walked out together. He did not get the chance he was hoping for to peek under the picture frame. Nor could he understand how, in the brief time it took them to fool around, shower and dress, Harry could have switched all the furniture—and without lots of noise, at that! Why make such an effort? To cause him to doubt his sanity? But maybe the furniture had *never* been switched, and this was the décor he *should* have been seeing with every peek he had taken. What, then, would account for the visions he had been having? The only explanation he could fall back on was some peculiar state between waking and dreaming wherein his mind projected, as onto a movie screen, his own deepest fears and anxieties. That peephole triggered it all, acting on his brain like a lens. Even that earlier vision—of Frank getting laid—was it "prophetic," was he seeing the actual future, or was it, as seemed more likely, an extrapolative reaction by his unconscious mind to the old goat's primitive vitality?

10

He and Angie bussed out to nearby Tlaquepaque, only to discover that the fiesta had been over for weeks. Angie was pissed and blamed Jason for not double-checking. Jason now had twice as much reason to be highly suspicious of Harry. "Did you notice he was angling for you to stay while I came out here alone?" he said.

"What's that supposed to mean?"

"I don't know. Nothing, I guess." He was determined, in light of what he'd "seen" through the peephole, not to do or say a thing that might further dampen their spirits. Since Angie looked forward to dinner with Moran, he avoided grousing about the coming evening either. They saved the day by having lunch at a little place serving Bírria, a tasty dish of goat meat in tomato sauce that they'd never tried before. Later, back at the Mercado Libertad, Jason insisted on Angie's buying a new dress. Still no word from American Express, and he knew how much a change of clothes would please her. Especially now that they were going out.

Moran appeared exactly on time, in a neat blue suit with a handkerchief in the jacket pocket. In a show of gallantry, he extended a fresh red rose to Angie, which she pinned to her new black dress. The cotton dress showed plenty of cleavage and fit her ass like a glove. Since Angie was unconcerned, Jason decided not to let it bother him either.

11

Frank had made reservations at the not-very-fancy La Roca, where they were seated at an upstairs table for four, Jason across from Angie, Frank to Jason's right. A handsome waiter of about thirty paid them close, even finicky, attention. When Frank proposed shrimp cocktails for starters, the waiter leaned over Angie's shoulder, studied her menu with his head close to hers, and whispered a counter-suggestion directly in her ear. Angie paid no attention and went along with Frank. Jason was undecided whether to attribute the waiter's behavior to discourtesy or to the Hispanic proclivity for close conversational distance. Returning with the cocktails, the waiter set them down with a disapproving smirk and then, gratuitously, reached for Angie's napkin. Draping his arms over her shoulders with a caressing familiarity that left Jason speechless, he placed his cheek against her hair and proceeded, with a fussy ceremoniousness, to arrange the cloth napkin across her lap. Normally unflappable, Angie flinched.

"I would suggest the steaks," said Frank, narrowing his eyes at the waiter. Still bent over Angie, the waiter whispered again. This time Angie jerked away, as if pestered by a mosquito.

"This man is making me uncomfortable," said Angie, looking straight at Jason.

Glaring at the waiter, Jason searched for the Spanish equivalent of "Stop making an ass of yourself," but his brain froze. The words wouldn't come.

"What's your problem, *muchacho*?" said Frank.

Ignoring Frank's comment, the waiter brought his face within an inch of Angie's cleavage and pretended to be smelling her rose. Angry and humiliated, Jason strained for just the right phrase to put the slimy bastard in his place. "*Oye, camarero,*" "Listen, waiter," was all he managed to shout before Frank rose to his feet—shot up, rather, knocking his chair behind him to the floor. A pink flush overspread his stony gray cheeks. He took a step forward, grabbed the waiter's left arm, and yanked him away from Angie. What Jason next saw occurred in a flash, a blur. Moran's left fist flew forward. The waiter tumbled to the floor. A hush descended over tables all around. Forks hung suspended in mid-air.

"Lucky you didn't meet the famous Mary Ann," said Frank, this time holding up his clenched right fist. "But if you want an introduction, I'll oblige you."

The waiter, leaning on an elbow, rubbed his chin and scuttled backward, retreating over the tiles with his eyes fixed on Frank. As co-workers inched near and asked him what had happened, he muttered a little and shrugged his shoulders. Picking himself up, he retreated like a peacock minus a tail. Moran, meanwhile, crooked his finger at one of the newly arrived waiters.

"Hey, you!" he said.

"*Sí, sí, Señor, momentito!*"

"Maybe we should go," said Jason.

"Why?" said Frank. "I told you the steaks are good here. They hammer the hell out of them, true, but they're tasty and tender. Waiter, three steaks, *por favor.*"...

No one mentioned the incident all through dinner, but Frank did regale them with stories of fights in which his famous *right*-hand punch, which used to be known as Mary Ann, brought him victory. Each tale of conquest affected Jason like another kick in the scrotum.

12

"I think you should take your clothes off in the bathroom," said Jason, watching Angie, in the middle of the floor, wriggle out of her dress. Standing in front of the chest of drawers, he turned and stole a glance at the naked peephole at his back. He hadn't had the chance to plug it up again, and not being eight feet tall, he couldn't block the line of sight between Angie and that hole.

"Why the bathroom? Don't you like what you see?" She curved her hands over her bra cups and down around her thighs.

"It's just that... we shouldn't be stepping barefoot on this rug."

"Whatever disease is there, we've caught it already," said Angie, unhooking her bra and tossing it onto the bed.

In spite of his suspicions about the extent of Angie's audience, he couldn't keep his eyes off her as she enacted her nightly ritual. All that was missing was the music.

"I would've whacked that fucking waiter myself, you know," said Jason.

"What for?" said Angie, slipping out of her panties. "It was no big deal."

"I wasn't close enough. Frank was right next to him."

"I'll never forget the look on the guy's face," Angie said with a distant smile.

"It also crossed my mind that I could've wound up in jail."

"It's a thought that didn't seem to occur to Frank."

"It damn well should have!"

"I'm glad *you* didn't do anything stupid, dear."

"I think Frank is crazy, don't you?"

"It *was* kind of exciting when you think about it, wasn't it?"

"To me?" said Jason. "I wouldn't call it exciting."

"It was stupid, of course. But also exciting."

"Exciting?"

Angie backed into him, smiling at him over her shoulder, grinding her bare cheeks into his pelvis. "What's the matter?" she said. "I'm knocking and I don't hear a hello."

"Your friend is speechless with admiration."

"Oh, he'll be talking soon. I'll have him singing like Frankie."

"Like Frank?"

"Sinatra," she said, sauntering off to the bathroom.

As soon as he heard her taking a shower, he balled up a wad of tissue, moistened it with saliva, and stuck it in the hole. Wishing he had a strip of tape to hold it in place, he wondered if Angie had Band-aids in her purse. He didn't like rummaging in a woman's purse. It was like violating some unspoken taboo. He flinched at the alligator's beady red stare, but the purse lay on the desktop in front of him and he looked inside and began to poke around. There was too much junk for him to see what was there, so he spilled out the contents. Among hairbrushes, lipsticks, makeup and tampons, her plastic folder of traveler's checks fell out. Jason had recently counted his own—those that could be countersigned only by him, and he now thumbed through Angie's, satisfying himself that together they had enough left to last the rest of the trip.

Strewn among the spilled objects were a bottle of aspirins and her contraceptive compact. For no particular reason, Jason opened the little green clam.

Not a pill missing!

With shaking hands, he stuffed everything back into the beast's dark belly. He wanted to run in and scream at her, right in the middle of her shower. Not now, though, he cautioned himself. Not tonight. Perhaps there was an explanation. She didn't like the way the pills made her feel? So fucking what! He thought of the consequences of her having a baby—

Angie quitting her job, the ruination of his career hopes and dreams, his return to the prison of working for her father. They had planned to trick him, the three of them together, Angie, her mother and her father!

Sick to his stomach, he undressed for a shower. A shower might dampen his anger, he thought. Angie came out, sweet-smelling and warm, toweling herself down. He brushed swiftly by her. But she grabbed him by the elbow and pulled him to the bed.

"Fuck the shower," she said, thrusting him down and kneeling beside him. "I want it to taste like Mexico—sweaty, with all the local flavors intact." Lying on top of him, she slithered along his chest, kissing him as she descended, her breasts sweeping a warm path down his body, tickling as they rode his thighs. Part of him wanted to forget that little green clamshell as she took him in her mouth, but the other part flowed like ice through his veins, and he wondered if she could literally taste the coldness that he felt coming over him. His blood refused to flow where she directed it. He felt his face stiffening. Nothing but his face.

After a while she looked up at him. "Jay, is something the matter?"

"I don't know, Angie." He tried to stay calm. "Maybe… if you hadn't stopped taking your pills…"

"Am I doing something wrong? I've tried every trick on that Johnson of yours—"

"Didn't you hear me?" he said, raising his voice. "You haven't been taking your pills."

"Once in a while it's okay to skip one. I told you they make me feel ill."

"One? Who's talking about one? You haven't taken any the whole fucking month!"

"How the hell do you know?" Her face turning red, she pushed herself up into a kneeling position, straddling him.

"I checked. I can't believe you'd do this to me. All this time, using me, making a damn fool out of me, you and your parents, planning to fuck me over!"

"You checked? You went through my purse, you son of a bitch? I fuckin' give up." Backing off the bed, she stood up and, to Jason's horror, proceeded to twist off her wedding ring.

"Wait!" said Jason, hoping even now to change the scenario he had vowed all day to prevent. "I'm sorry. You don't have to do that."

She tossed h er ring at him. It hit him in the thigh and he picked it up. *No!* he said to himself. *This is not happening!*

"All you do is worry about your own fucking self. You never gave a shit about me," she said.

"You said you would help me. You promised!" said Jason, his tone more hurt now than angry.

Angie stood with her back toward him, saying nothing, rubbing her forehead. Suddenly, spinning around, she placed her hands on her hips. "You checked my purse? Okay, and what did you find?"

"You know what I found," Jason whispered, avoiding her angry stare. "Look, Angie, I'm not against having children. It's all a matter of timing."

"I'll tell you what you found. You found a completely unused pill pack, that's what you found."

"Isn't that enough?"

"Isn't it possible that I only just recently used up the old pack?"

Jason looked her in the eye. He knew she was lying. What if he asked her directly, *Did you?*—and she admitted she was lying? Would he have the courage to follow through and announce, there and then, that they were through? Did Angie want it to be over? Surely not. If she was lying, she was lying for his sake, for both their sakes, for the sake of their marriage. She'd been playing the forgot-to-take-the-pill game for at least six months now, but he had allowed himself to overlook those little "mistakes" of hers because they'd hardly got it on all those months anyway. But these past few weeks of nightly and sometimes daily copulation, all this time with nothing to guard against pregnancy, amounted to an all-out assault on his hopes for a meaningful future—a campaign of sabotage to which he'd been utterly blind. What if she was already pregnant? What if she had promised her mother, her father, her Golden-Gloved brother, that she would come back pregnant no matter what, and that they'd better scout for a good sale on a crib and accessories in the interim?

"Isn't it possible?" she repeated.

"It's possible. Sure, sure it's possible."

"Asshole!" she said. "Give me that fucking ring." She snatched it away from him and slipped it back on her finger.

For a long time Jason was unable to sleep. He tried to persuade himself that the morning's vision had not come true. They had not split up after all—in spite of that hole-in-the-wall's apparent prediction! Even better: now fully alert, he was not likely to fall for any new tricks of hers in that department any time soon. As the night wore on and he thought more about all that had happened, a further notion obtruded itself: if he had watched through the peephole long enough, he would have *seen* that their quarrel would resolve itself as peacefully as it did. But that would be to accept that a mere hole in the wall *could* be a window onto the future! He finally fell asleep, awakening at the end of a troubling dream in which Frank Moran hammered him with his trusty Mary Ann, knocking him over the ropes into—his erstwhile bedroom in his parents' house in Brooklyn.

13

Disoriented, Jason was startled to see a tangled cascade of ink-black hair sprawled over the pillow beside him, almost touching his nose, exuding an earthy perfume. It took a couple of seconds before reality kicked back in. The indirect light of another bright morning in Guadalajara seeped through the heavily curtained window to his right. Rolling away from Angie, he stared at the photo of the *chacmool* and focused on the peephole beside it. It just then occurred to him that now, having seen through Angie's game of deception, he might very possibly have simultaneously cured himself of the tendency to "see" beyond that wall only his own darkest thoughts. The paper plug had "dropped" out again. Still and all, he knew quite well that the room behind that wall was a breakfast nook. The hole was probably covered by that picture of Tlaquepaque.

Slipping out of bed, he tiptoed to the desk, slid the alligator bag aside, and supported himself on his knees while putting his eye to the hole. What he saw brought hot, blurring tears to his eyes. He could barely contain the cry that filled his lungs.

Again, their own bed faced him. On it lay a naked Angie, her legs spread wide, her sun-tanned skin aglow in the light of her bedside lamp. Between her legs she cradled the bobbing head of a man, whose white hair she stroked in rhythm with the gurgling that spilled from her lips. Eyes half closed, lips pouting, she rocked back and forth, in time with the motion of the head between her legs. The crack between the cheeks of her partner's wizened ass moved back and forth also, looking up at Jason like a lizard blowing kisses.

Jason turned away, blood pounding in his ears, his throat closing to strangle a shriek that threatened to burst through his chest. Descending from the desk, he stole a glance at Angie—his sleepyhead wife still sunk in blissful slumber. Squeezing his head between his hands, he closed his eyes and reproached himself. How could he be so paranoid? he asked himself.

Why did he persist in torturing himself? Why didn't his nightmares cease to pursue him the instant he awoke? Was it possible that what he was perceiving was a projection, not of his own mind, but of *Angie's* dreaming brain—that Angie had been transmitting *her* fears and desires into his own highly susceptible unconscious? There he was, doing it again, looking for some sort of "rational" explanation for nothing but his own sick fancies.

How stupid he was to dwell on all this! There was no way in hell that the scene he had just witnessed could ever achieve real-world embodiment. He was going to be with Angie all day—and all night. Apart from a trip to the bathroom, there'd be no reason for either of them to leave the other's side.

14

"Coffee and a roll?" Baker offered, addressing Angie.

"What kind of 'roll'?" said Angie, arching her brow.

"Any kind you like, dear."

"Not this morning. Thanks," said Jason, facing the lobby door as he tugged at Angie's arm. She shrugged her shoulders but didn't resist. He didn't want to step foot again in that room that was—and then wasn't—there. He didn't want to spend another unnecessary second in the hotel. "By the way, Harry, any word from American Express?" asked Jason, fully resolved that they would sign out of The Crowned Lady as soon as they'd recovered their bags.

"Called 'em half an hour ago. Still no word, but don't worry, I'm keeping on top of it."

"Thanks. Shit!" said Angie.

"Double shit," said Jason.

They toured a couple of churches recommended in the brochures, had lunch at the Gerente, and then returned to their hotel, expecting to go out again to take in another afternoon movie. What Jason didn't expect was that old scaly-ass would be lying in wait. Dapper in blue pinstripe and solid red tie, Moran sat on the sofa playing cards with Harry Baker. Harry occupied an armchair across from Moran. On the coffee table between them stood a liqueur bottle and shot glasses.

"Top o' the day to you," said Moran, rising and making a theatrical bow. "Join us for some seven-card stud?"

"I don't think so," said Jason.

"Oh, c'mon. We can for a little while," coaxed Angie.

"We have to freshen up."

"You go freshen up, Jay." She sat down next to Moran although she could—as Jason noted—even more easily have taken the armchair next to Baker. "A little stud is just what Momma needs," she said, making the two men smile.

Jason wanted to take a leak, but instead he parked himself in the vacant chair. They were playing for loose change. Angie dumped a bunch out of her purse. The various denominations of centavo coins felt weightless to Jason; unreal, as though made of air; phantom money not worth bothering about, like the recent coinages of his mind. Harry got up and was back in seconds with another pair of shot glasses. The brown bottle with yellow label said "Kahlua." It was a Mexican coffee liqueur that Jason remembered enjoying. Harry filled their glasses, refilled his and Frank's, and offered a toast: "May the best man win!"

"Or woman," Angie corrected.

"Absolutely," said Frank, clicking Angie's glass. When the round of clicks was over, Moran dealt the cards, two buried and one open for each. Jason liked the Kahlua more than he liked playing cards. He wondered if this was how Frank and Harry spent much of their time with each other. It was relaxing, seductive, like dozing under a mental sombrero. Meanwhile, he and Angie—especially Angie—were winning most of the hands. Jason felt certain that Moran was throwing games—for Angie's sake, of course. Baker had to attend to the front desk only once. That was when Jason found it convenient to go to the bathroom. Baker kept topping off everyone's glass, and Jason didn't even remember seeing him leave and return with a whole new bottle of the same.

"You're not so tough if I can beat you in one round," said Angie, playfully jabbing Moran with a soft right to the ribs.

Moran bent over and winced as if hurt. "So you think you can land one on Frank Moran and survive, young lady?" he said.

"I can beat you with one hand tied around this glass," said Angie, taking a quick swig and handing the glass to Harry for a refill.

"Tell you what, missie. I'll double that pile of winnings of yours if you can land one legitimate punch on old Frank Walter Moran." So saying, he lurched off the couch, barely steadying himself, and stepped out past the armchairs. "I'm not hitting back, you unnerstand, but I'll block anything you can throw."

"You're fooling with the Girl with the Golden Gloves," said Angie, rising with fists circling in front of her and stepping around the table.

"A woman can throw a fit, but never a punch," said Moran.

"Oh yeah? You'll wish you were facing Jackie Johnson."

"Angie," said Jason, "will you please sit down? This is kind of stupid." In spite of himself, though, he started laughing, joining Harry Baker in a fit of snorts and sputters as Moran waved her on and Angie squared off, her right fist thwacking the cushion of an open palm.

Angie grew red in the face. Jason knew that mood change, recognized the stubbornness that gripped her when she felt she was being bested. She lashed out with a left, followed that with a quick right, but Moran's magic landing pods proved quicker—in spite of the fact that he seemed a little shaky on his feet. Face flushed pink, eyes bright with cunning, he quaked with soundless mirth, grinning as he kept on blocking Angie's flailing fists.

"Enough, Angie!" Jason managed to shout between hiccups of laughter. But Angie wouldn't listen. Finally, she landed a one-two punch to Moran's oaken chest, withdrawing in pain while the old man pretended to slump. Following up on her apparent advantage, Angie pounded Moran's chest another couple of times—until the old codger caught her in a clinch. Jason watched them stagger back and forth, whispering, neither seeming to want to let go. When Angie started giggling against the old man's neck, Jason grew uncomfortable.

"I'll bet you didn't clinch as much with Johnson," said Angie.

"Got that right, baby."

"Angie, will you sit down!"

"The winner is—Angie!" declared Harry, lifting his glass. Angie finally released Moran, and they both sank red-faced back on the couch.

Moran whipped a ten-peso note out of his pocket. "Here! I never welsh on a bet," he said laughing. "Someday, Angie, tell this to your grandchildren: you're the only woman who ever spanked the stuffing out of Frank Walter Moran."

Everyone laughed again, and Baker dealt the cards for another round of poker. "Shit!" said Baker, slapping himself. "I forgot to tell you. American Express called. You can now pick up your luggage at the bus station."

"Great!" said Angie. "Be a sweetheart, Jay, and go get it."

"Come with me," said Jason.

"Can't you see I'm a little tired?" she said, rubbing her fists and grinning at Moran.

"We can go together later, then."

"The *consigna* may not stay open for more than another hour or so," said Harry.

"If we're going out tonight, I need another dress, Jay."

He knew his resistance to leaving had to sound petty and unreasonable, so he quickly came to his senses. What in the world could happen, he reasoned, in the hour or two he'd be absent? Old reptile-butt had got as close to Angie as he ever was going to get. It was Baker who bothered him. How come Baker "suddenly" remembered the call about the luggage? All along, Harry had been extremely conscientious, letting them know whenever he made a call to American Express, reassuring them he was on top of things. It was the Kahlua, Jason figured. Enough of that stuff could drill a hole in anyone's memory. As woozy as he himself felt at this point, Baker and Moran had started tippling much earlier.

15

"You must be mistaken," said Jason.

"I make no mistake, Señor."

"It has to be here! They called me from American Express to tell me it had arrived." Jason leaned over the narrow counter and checked out the snaky line of tagged bags and parcels that wound over the floor behind it. "You have more in your office," he said, seeing other pieces of luggage through the open door of the *oficina* to the left.

"I know what's in there. Your luggage is not in there."

"Let me in. I'll look for myself."

"I'm sorry, Señor. Unauthorized personnel are not allowed in my office."

Officious little prick! Thought Jason. He stood back, scratched his head, and stared blankly at the rot-green wall of the *consigna*. What was wrong with those idiots at American Express? he wondered. How could they make such a stupid mistake?

"Do you know who you spoke to at American Express, Señor?"

Jason shook his head. Only Baker had been dealing with them. Baker couldn't have misunderstood them. The agents there all spoke English.

"I will call them for you," said the official, retreating into his inviolable little cubicle.

"Thank you."

"*De na*."

While Jason waited for some explanation, a slyly smiling Harry Baker popped into his head. As Jason left the hotel lobby to try to grab a taxi, he had turned around and looked at Baker, catching that sneaky grin—then instantly dismissing it from his mind.

Jason now already knew what the clerk would come back and tell him. Blood rushed to his head like a surge of electricity. His face and neck prickled as if breaking into hives.

"I'm sorry, Señor. The agent I spoke to—"

"I know, I know," said Jason.

"The agent I spoke to was there all day and he is sure that no one could have called you because your—"

"Those fucking bastards!" Jason shouted, breaking into English. "They set me up, the three of them!"

"Señor?"

Jason could see them: Harry the pimp looking the other way as Frank and Angie disappeared into the hallway. He could see Angie stripping, Frank's pants molting to the floor, Angie stretching back on the bed…

Jason checked his watch. He hadn't been away very long. Yet how long would it take her, them? If he hurried…

The shortest path to the exit found him leaping from side to side to slip through lines of human traffic that interwove and eddied like a clutch of mating snakes. A dozen taxis lay in wait, lined up like a yellow cobra lusting to strike. He hopped into the first in line.

"You are in a hurry, Señor?"

"In a hurry?" Jason sat back against the wrinkled leather seat. He stared into space and took several deep breaths.

"Where to, Señor?"

"*Adonde?*" Jason repeated. It seemed quite clear where he wanted to go—where he *had* to go. "Are there planes still flying to Mexico City today?"

"Sí, Señor. You have plenty of time."

Jason had no doubt that, once in Mexico City, he could quickly connect with a flight to New York.

"Very well. *Al aeropuerto, por favor.*"

As the taxi entered the outskirts of the city, Jason began to feel queasy. His palms grew sweaty, and his breathing grew erratic. The sight of those green expanses outside the cab window afflicted him with a kind of agoraphobia. He wished the windows had blinds, wished he could shut out the suffocating light of the sky.

"Driver," he said, "I changed my mind. Turn around and go back, please."

"To the bus station?"

"No, not to the bus station."

"*Adonde*, Señor?"

"Do you know what they use to fill up holes in… in wood?"

"*Masilla*?"

"Yes, putty, exactly. Could you take me to a store where I can buy a little can of putty?"

"Sure…. And if you will excuse me for asking, for what do you need this putty?"

"I live in an apartment that has a hole in the wall, and terrible smells keep coming in from the apartment next door. I want something to plug it up."

"I see. May I make an observation, Señor?"

"Of course."

"You will not keep the smells from coming in by plugging up one little hole."

"Why not?"

"Because it is likely that there are many other holes that you can't even see, all around the moldings and where the wall joins the ceiling, and that the smells are coming in from all those cracks at once."

"Makes no difference," said Jason. "In a couple of days we're moving out of that damned place anyway."

"If I may say so, Señor, you are a martyr. As for me, I wouldn't have lived in such a place even for a day."

Jason caught the grin in the rear-view mirror. The man seemed to be mocking him. The cabbie made a couple of turns and drove back into the city. As the taxi pulled up beside some nondescript store, Jason spoke up again. "Driver, I've changed my mind."

16

Jason pushed open the lobby door expecting to see Baker, but a young Mexican with a trim mustache stood behind the counter in his place. "Where's the boss?" asked Jason.

"He left, Señor. I will be here all night. Do you need your key?"

"Yes, number three." Son of a bitch! thought Jason, frustrated at being denied the pleasure of calling Harry a liar to his fat pasty face.

The clerk cast him an ironical stare as Jason swiped the key from his hand and rushed on into the hallway. Tiptoeing up to his room, he put his ear against the door, inserted the key as quietly as he could, then kicked the door open.

No one was there. The bed was made. Jason was not surprised. But the air smelled sweaty, salty-sweet. It smelled of Angie. He wondered if maybe it always smelled of Angie, always smelled of sex, and he normally didn't notice. He paced around the room, clenching his fists, pressing them to his forehead, shaking his head. He examined the bathroom, found nothing amiss, then stopped in front of the bed, where he stood like a statue for several minutes, unable to take another pointless step.

Collapsing face-forward onto the bed, he began to sigh heavily, then found himself sniffing at Angie's pillow. When he looked at where he sniffed, he froze, as if he had nuzzled the beard of a dragon.

There were hairs on the pillow. Several black ones—and a couple that were iron-gray.

Jason seized the pillow and flung it with all his might against the framed *chacmool*, which clattered to the desktop. Springing forward, he grabbed the print by its sides, but he could not follow through on the impulse to smash it to pieces. Theatrics were just not his style. Breaking things and punching walls would not cure the ache in his chest. His hands shook uncontrollably as he climbed up onto the desk. It took him several tries to get the picture wire to finally snag the hook.

Jason now stared at that winking, unpluggable peephole again. It drew his eye and easily conquered his will.

The sight of Angie stopped his breath. Emerging from the bathroom, she sauntered across the floor, toasty-warm and glowing from her shower, as though coming straight at *him*—but not looking up as high as she'd have to if she suspected he was there. As she approached, her hands made love to her breasts and slipped down over her glistening thighs. Her familiar smile and heavy-lidded gaze were directed to someone just below Jason's field of view, someone standing in front of that chest that was just like the one on which he knelt. As she approached him (for it had to be a "him," Jason knew), she exaggerated the sway of her hips and stroked her wet bush with lacquered fingertips.

"Hiding something?" she said with a grin, tongue-tip cruising her upper lip, staring down at the lower half of the man who remained out of sight. "Oh, you want *me* to find the Easter egg?" she said.

No sound came from the invisible man. Instead, a pair of arms swung up, visible down to the elbows. The hands, joined like the head of a bird, cupped a beak of steel.

"Jay!" she shouted in disbelief. (How could she know he was up there, behind the wall, observing? But what could he do, Jason asked himself, perched like a parrot, high off the ground, to stop those arms from descending?)

The movement was swift, allowing her no time to counter with a forearm block. The blade swooped down between her breasts and Jason heard the crunch of metal on bone. Cheek to the wall, he could not stop watching. Absurd! he thought. Absolutely impossible! he said to himself as the hands, raised again, plunged down for a second time in a smear of red the color of Angie's nail polish.

"What the hell are you doing?"

Angie's voice, coming from right behind him, ripped through his spine like a saw. Jason lowered himself carefully to the floor, leaning on the dresser to support his buckling knees.

"The *chacmool*," he said, pretending to straighten the picture-frame.

"What about it?" Angie's face sported a deep rosy flush as if she'd just stepped out victorious from the ring.

"We're leaving the hotel right now," he said, picking up the sheathed knife from the dresser-top and stuffing it into their red leather bag.

"The hell we are."

"We're leaving *Mexico* right now!" he said.

"Are you nuts? It just so happens that we have a date with Frank tonight."

"We are *not* going to see Frank tonight—nor ever again." His voice was shrill. He would not back down.

"Okay," Angie pouted, her eyes liquid-bright. "Then *I* have a date with Frank tonight. If you don't want to keep us company... well, you do what *you* have to do, dear."

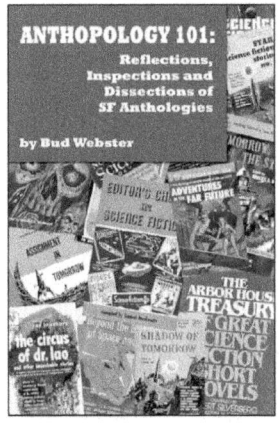

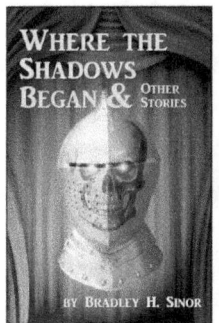

www.ingramcontent.com/pod-product-compliance
Lightning Source LLC
Chambersburg PA
CBHW060930180626
46817CB00004B/1476